Shut Up and Drive

Shut Up and Drive

Ted Darling crime series

'a serial sex attacker on the loose'

L M Krier

Contents

About the Author

L M Krier is the pen name of former journalist (court reporter) and freelance copywriter, Lesley Tither, who also writes travel memoirs under the name Tottie Limejuice. Lesley also worked as a case tracker for the Crown Prosecution Service.

The Ted Darling series of crime novels comprises: *The First Time Ever, Baby's Got Blue Eyes, Two Little Boys, When I'm Old and Grey, Shut Up and Drive, Only the Lonely, Wild Thing, Walk on By, Preacher Man.*

All books in the series are available in Kindle and paperback format and are also available to read free with Kindle Unlimited.

Contact Details

If you would like to get in touch, please do so at:

tottielimejuice@gmail.com

facebook.com/LMKrier

facebook.com/groups/1450797141836111/

https://twitter.com/tottielimejuice

For a light-hearted look at Ted and the other characters, please consider joining the We Love Ted Darling group on Facebook.

Discover the DI Ted Darling series

If you've enjoyed meeting Ted Darling, you may like to discover the other books in the series:

The First Time Ever
Baby's Got Blue Eyes
Two Little Boys
When I'm Old and Grey
Shut Up and Drive
Only the Lonely
Wild Thing
Walk on By
Preacher Man

Acknowledgements

Thanks to all those who helped with this fourth book in the DI Ted Darling series, beta readers Jill Pennington, Emma Heath, Kate Pill, additional editing Alex Potter, Alison Sabedoria.

Special thanks to Chris Gillies for expert advice on the martial arts scenes.

To Domi

Ted's No 1 fan in France

Chapter One

An early Monday morning summons to the Ice Queen's office was always low on the wish-list of both DI Ted Darling and his opposite number in uniform, Inspector Kevin Turner.

The formidable Superintendent Debra Caldwell, who was also Assistant Divisional Commander, brought out the inner schoolboy in both men. For moral support, they made a point of meeting up in Kevin's office first. It was a chance to spruce up their appearances before facing their boss, with her impeccable turnout and stiff, formal manner.

'It's about the latest case, I imagine?' Kevin speculated, as he adjusted his uniform and smoothed down his hair.

Ted would have laughed at his preening, except that he was too busy checking to make sure his own top button was fastened and his tie was up high enough to cover it. He only just stopped himself from rubbing the toes of his shoes on the backs of his trouser legs.

'She'll be wanting a progress report, I suppose. I haven't made any progress to report on, so I'm hoping you have and I can hide behind you,' he replied.

Their humour was a way of dealing with the harder aspects of their job. They were working together on a serious case which had somewhat stalled and neither of them had anything new to report, despite all their joint efforts.

'Come in, gentlemen, and please take a seat,' the Ice Queen told them, after Kevin had pushed Ted to go in first. He always reckoned that Ted's four black belts in martial arts would give them some degree of protection from her wrath.

At least there was the smell of the freshly-brewed excellent coffee she favoured. She placed bone china mugs and the steaming glass pot in front of them, inviting them to help themselves. She knew Ted's sweet tooth by now so there was already milk and sugar left at their disposal.

'So,' she began. 'Three serious sexual assaults, combined with three car hijacks, and not a single lead to show for it so far. Does that about sum up the situation? As you can imagine, I am coming under a lot of pressure from high up to make some sort of progress with this case. So what can you offer me?'

Ted took a quick gulp of his coffee before replying.

'Ma'am, we have fingerprints and DNA for the attacker, and it's the same person in all three cases. There's just no match on record anywhere so far. Anywhere in the UK, that is. We're going to have to start looking further afield. Unless, of course, he's not a previous offender, in which case we really are looking at needles in haystacks.'

'It's the same from the car theft point of view, ma'am,' Kevin Turner told her. 'We're not finding any matches there either. And it's an unusual case, the combination of taking a vehicle and sexually assaulting the driver.'

'Right, so you've both told me what you haven't achieved. Now what I need is some positive action to offer up,' she told them briskly. 'I want to arrange a press conference, to ask for the public's help, and I want you both to attend.'

She saw Ted's grimace and said firmly, 'Yes, even you, Inspector Darling. I know you don't enjoy such occasions, but it's vital that we show the public a united front. They need to have confidence that we are doing our utmost to arrest this attacker.

'These are serious crimes, especially happening on busy supermarket car parks. Young women being kidnapped at knife point, then raped and left while the attacker goes off joy-riding in their cars. It's the stuff of nightmares. We don't want to spread panic, but we do need to appeal for help.

'So far we've escaped much of a savaging in the press for our lack of success. I can only assume your efforts at building bridges with the local reporter are paying dividends, Inspector Darling.'

Ted wisely said nothing. Although his boss had told him to make more of an effort, he still avoided the local news-hound, universally known as Pocket Billiards because of his undesirable habit, like the plague.

'I'd also like to use the opportunity to give some sensible and practical advice in the hopes of preventing any further such terrible attacks,' the Ice Queen continued.

'It will be a tricky line to tread, between giving a warning and causing alarm,' Ted replied.

'You are quite right, of course, Inspector, but I am aware of that risk,' she replied dryly. 'Now, we need to see what can be done by us to reduce the potential for further attacks. We all know that these offences seem to be escalating in violence. We need to find this person, before they go on to kill, which is a strong possibility.

'Inspector Turner, can you get your officers to drive round the car parks of the big supermarkets whenever possible, to show a visible presence?'

'With respect, ma'am,' Kevin replied, ignoring her expression when he used a phrase he knew she particularly disliked, 'with the latest round of cuts, I don't have enough officers to handle crimes which have already been committed, let alone putting the few I do have out there to try to prevent future ones.'

'I am well aware of the issues regarding staffing levels, Inspector.' Her tone was now frosty. 'I assure you that I raise the matter whenever I get the opportunity. All I'm saying is that the public need to feel protected from a crime such as this. Whenever you have a car near to a supermarket, surely a five-minute drive around the car park is neither here nor there in the greater scheme of things and can only be helpful?'

Kevin Turner maintained a mutinous silence. The Ice Queen turned to Ted.

'Clearly, your officers will not present the same high-profile reassurance, in plain clothes and unmarked cars, but ask them please to do the same, just to see if they notice anything. It does at least give me something to tell the powers that be, to show them that we are making a serious pre-emptive effort.

'In the meantime, I will arrange the press conference for tomorrow. I would like you both to let me have your thoughts in writing by the end of today on what content should be included. That will be all, gentlemen.'

Both men drained their coffee before leaving her office, then headed back once more to Kevin's, to discuss what she had said.

'It's all for bloody show, Ted,' Kevin grumbled. 'It's all fur coat and no knickers. I don't have enough officers to go round as it is. If they're spending time driving round the car parks, the public are just going to think they're skiving or doing their Christmas shopping in work time. Plus if the local scrotes get wind of the fact that it's how we're spending our time, instead of chasing them, they'll have a field day. Crime rates will rocket and that will be our bloody fault, as usual.'

Ted nodded.

'I know, Kev, but we really don't have anything much else to suggest at the moment. Whoever this attacker is, we need to stop him, and soon. Like the Ice Queen said, he's been getting handier with that knife each time, and I don't like that.

'There's another thing that worries me. He's picking cars with a bit of something about them to go joy-riding in. With young Jezza driving that limited edition Golf of hers, I hope she's not going to be a target for him.'

'Don't worry, I'll sort her out a spray to keep in the car, just in case the bastard does go after her. Though knowing your

Jezza, she'll think her kickboxing will be enough defence.'

Kevin had heard about Ted's first encounter with his new Detective Constable, Jessica 'Jezza' Vine. It had been on an occasion when she had been drunk enough to try out her kickboxing skills on a stranger in the street, not knowing that the stranger was actually her future boss, a martial arts expert.

Ted snorted in disdain.

'Kickboxing will be no use to her at all in the confines of a car. I'm just off to brief the team now, so I'll tell her to come and see you. I'll also warn her off from any ideas of heroics or going looking for trouble.

'Let me know when you've got your notes ready for the Ice Queen. Perhaps we can go over them together before we submit them? You know, copy each other's homework, so we don't get kept in after school,' he added with a grin, as he headed for the door.

Ted's team were all in on time, as usual, sitting expectantly at their desks, when he went upstairs to start the morning briefing. He told them of the Superintendent's plans to hold a press conference and asked for their input, before firing off a few suggestions. He stood in front of the white board which already had on it the names and details of the three victims of the attacks – Kathy Finn, Helen Lawrence, Jayne Wright.

'How is our attacker getting to the supermarkets? Does he use public transport or take his own car? If so, how does he get back there, once he's done his joy-riding and dumped the stolen vehicle?'

'Sir, I could check bus timetables against the times of the attacks,' their young Trainee Detective Constable, Steve Ellis, suggested. 'If I look at buses for, say, an hour before each attack, I might be able to get some idea of where he comes from, if he is using buses.'

'Good idea, Steve, it's worth a shot, at least,' Ted told him encouragingly.

He turned to his Detective Sergeant, Mike Hallam.

'We need to keep trying to find similar crimes in other parts of the country, in case our man is only an occasional visitor to Stockport. Get someone onto that, please.

'Inspector Turner is going to try to get some of his officers to swing by the supermarkets whenever they have five minutes, but you all know that resources are tight and it won't amount to much. Likewise, when any of you are doing your shopping, please keep your eyes and ears peeled for anything, anything at all, that looks suspicious.'

DC Dennis 'Virgil' Tibbs spoke up.

'I'll find out if that former homeless witness from the Sorrento case still works at the supermarket. He may have seen something, possibly without realising it. And I'm in and out of supermarkets at all hours of the day and night, now the wife has started the food cravings.'

Ted turned to DC Vine.

'Jezza, I don't know what your shopping habits are, but I'd strongly suggest you consider when and where you shop, for your own safety, at least for the time being. I don't have to spell out for you that your car is just the sort of thing that seems to take the fancy of our attacker. Don't put yourself at risk, please.'

'Maybe I could draw him out of cover, if I start shopping more often?' she suggested. 'I can take care of myself ...'

Ted interrupted her firmly.

'Kickboxing would be no use against a man with a knife inside a car. He's used the knife before, he'll do it again. Go and see Inspector Turner, he has something for you. And I repeat, don't put yourself at any risk. That is not a suggestion. Take it as a direct order, DC Vine.'

Jezza was his newest team member. When she had first joined, she would certainly have argued with him. This time she simply nodded, though still looking defiant, and muttered, 'Yes, boss.'

'This is a very unusual case. Our man doesn't fit the

normally perceived image for the joy-riding part of it. We all know that anyone can be a rapist, but joy-riding sporty cars is usually a younger person's crime. All three victims say our man is in his forties, ordinary-looking. They say you would take him for an average family man, if you passed him in the street. So we need to keep an entirely open mind towards suspects.

'We have his fingerprints, his DNA, but nothing on record. And he doesn't try to hide his appearance from his victims. What does that tell us about him?'

'Maybe he wants to get caught, boss,' DC Rob O'Connell put in. 'Maybe he knows he's seriously sick and in need of help, so he's actually hoping he gets identified and brought in, before things get any worse.'

'That's another possibility,' Ted conceded. 'No doubt after the press conference we'll get the usual run of phone calls, people reporting neighbours they've always thought looked strange. So let's just hope that someone out there recognises the behaviour, if not the e-fit of the attacker, and gives us a lead we can run with.

'Right, you all know what you have to do, let's get on with it. Let's try and stop this attacker before it gets any worse than it already is. And don't forget to let me have your thoughts about what we need to raise at tomorrow's press conference.'

Ted's hours were never regular or predictable. His long-term partner, Trevor, knew the score of living with a copper and never made a fuss. It was getting late by the time Ted and Kevin had presented their ideas to the Ice Queen at the end of the day and Ted had driven home to park his elderly Renault in the garage, where Trev's Triumph Bonneville motorbike was already safely locked away.

Trev was in the sitting room, sharing the sofa with their six cats, when Ted walked in. There were inviting smells wafting from the kitchen. Ted suddenly realised he was starving hungry and couldn't remember if he had actually eaten anything at lunchtime. He leaned over the back of the sofa to plant a kiss on Trev's cheek and stroke the head of each cat in turn.

'You look tired,' Trev said, pushing cats aside so he could stand up and give Ted a warm hug of welcome. 'Supper's ready when you are. Hard day?'

'Hard day, hard case and no further forward than we were last week. Can we eat now? If I sit down on the sofa I'll probably just fall asleep, and my belly thinks my throat's cut.'

'Have you not eaten today?' Trev asked, his face concerned, as they went into the kitchen where the table was laid ready.

'I think I forgot,' Ted said ruefully, as he washed his hands at the kitchen sink, then sat down while Trev took their supper out of the oven and dished up. Ted fell on his meal like someone ravenous, but after not many mouthfuls he put down his knife and fork and pushed his plate aside.

'This is really delicious, thank you, but I think I'm so tired I've gone beyond the point of eating. Would you mind if I just went up to bed?'

Trev stood up and started to clear the table. 'I'll just put the dishes in to soak, then I'll come and join you.'

Ted shook his head.

'No, really, don't let me spoil your evening. I just want to go to sleep. Stay and enjoy your supper, watch a film or something. I need to get some sleep if I'm going to be functioning at all for the press conference.'

He kissed Trev lightly on the cheek and headed for the stairs. Trev sat back down with a sigh. It was never easy, living with a copper in the middle of a difficult case.

Chapter Two

Unusually, Ted didn't even stir when Trev and the cats came up to bed later. He appeared to be out for the count, so Trev simply slid quietly under the duvet next to him and left him to sleep.

Not at all unusually, neither Trev nor the cats opened so much as an eye between them when Ted got up early the next morning to shower and dress, ready for work. As he munched wholemeal toast and drank green tea, Ted scribbled a brief note for Trev, telling him he would be late home and not to wait to eat with him.

He headed for the hall to pick up his car keys, then turned back and added a brief apology and a kiss to the note. He knew he was lucky that his relationship with Trev was strong enough to withstand the demands of his job when so many other coppers' marriages didn't. He promised himself he would make it up to his partner as soon as he had made some headway with the current case.

The day's press conference was scheduled for mid-morning so that it would hopefully catch both the lunchtime and early evening local news slots. The Ice Queen wanted Ted to say a few words, as the officer in charge of the case, so had called a briefing with him and Kevin Turner. She was keen to go over what they would each say and which questions Ted would answer or which he would pass on to her to deal with.

There was not a large press presence and Ted felt a moment of disgust in knowing that the lack of a body to date meant the case was not yet of great interest to the nationals. The local TV and radio stations were represented, which might help them, although he knew that as ever, it ran the risk of inviting time-wasting callers.

Although he disliked and distrusted the man intensely, under the watchful eye of the Ice Queen, Ted made a point of going over to the local reporter and shaking his hand.

'Nice to see you, Alastair, glad you could come,' Ted told him, trying hard to sound as if he meant it.

'Have you got anything exclusive for me, Ted?' the reporter asked, his familiarity grating on Ted's already frayed nerves. 'It would be nice if I could have something no one else has got.'

'As soon as I have something, Alastair, you know I'll send it your way. For now, it's as much about asking you and the public for help as giving you any information,' Ted replied, as smoothly as he could manage.

The ordeal passed off as well as it could for Ted. It was in the hands of the media now to see if they could bring the breakthrough they so desperately needed in the case.

Ted and three of his team would be staying later that evening, hoping there would be a flood of calls after the early evening news. Inevitably, most of them would be of no help, just the usual random collection of disgruntled ex-wives out for vengeance, which any serious sexual assault tended to throw up.

'Tenner says the first call is Honest John,' DC Maurice Brown said to the rest of the team, naming their local regular confessor. The man always rang up to confess to a crime as soon as there was anything in the local papers or on television.

'No one's going to take that bet. It's a racing certainty, surely?' DS Mike Hallam laughed.

'I'll take your money, Maurice,' Rob O'Connell told him. 'I think he'll be second after an ex-wife shopping her late and not lamented other half.'

It was good-humoured enough and Ted let it go. It was the

team's way of dealing with stress, much the same as his own schoolboy exchanges with Kevin.

'I want two people available to answer the phones all day today, so make sure you stagger your breaks. And it could be a late one tonight, for some of you, so make sure your other halves know that,' Ted warned them.

They didn't have long to wait for the first of the calls to start, after the lunchtime news. Maurice lost his bet, as in fact the first few calls were people reporting neighbours who they claimed behaved strangely or looked odd.

Then Ted got a call from Bill, the duty sergeant on the front desk.

'Got someone here asking for you by name, Ted, after seeing the news. Thing is, I know her, I know what she wants to talk about and I can tell you now it's a waste of your time. But she's insistent, won't leave without seeing you. Can you come down and give her five minutes, then I'll fill you in on the history, once you've got rid of her?'

Ted sighed as he stood up and headed downstairs. Listening to time-wasters was par for the course on a case after a public appeal for information, but he could do without it. He went first to the desk to talk to Bill who nodded to a woman, seemingly in her mid to late thirties, who was waiting.

'Seriously, don't give her more than ten minutes, Ted, then come and talk to me,' he told him in a low voice. 'I tried to send her packing, but she wasn't having any of it. She's called Jenny Holden. She prefers Ms. Interview Room 2 is free at the moment.'

Ted nodded and walked across to where the woman was sitting.

'Ms Holden? You wanted to speak to me? I'm Detective Inspector Darling. Would you like to come through and we'll find an empty room, so we can talk.'

Once they were sitting opposite one another, Ted took his notebook out and said encouragingly, 'What was it you wanted to tell me, Ms Holden?'

'I was raped,' she began, looking him frankly in the eyes. 'It was a historic case, it happened about twenty years ago, but I didn't know about it until ten years ago.'

She saw Ted's puzzled expression and explained.

'I'd been having a few problems, ten years or so ago. Not sleeping, sleepwalking when I did, very stressed, difficulty concentrating. I was working as an accounts clerk, training to be an accountant. I initially put it down to that, working a bit too hard.

'It got so bad that a friend suggested I went to see someone; a psychotherapist. She used a type of hypnotism technique to help me recover memories, things I'd buried away in the back of my sub-conscious. That's when I learned that I'd been sexually assaulted, by a man I had known and trusted for years. It happened when I was fifteen.

'As soon as I found out what had happened to me, I went to the police, of course. I came to this station. They were kind and helpful at first, as if they believed me. Then after they'd started their investigations, their attitude towards me changed completely, as if they thought I was just making things up, deliberately wasting their time.

'Not long after, they came to see me. They said they had investigated at length and were convinced there was no evidence of any crime, so they weren't going to take any action. I was furious, because I knew what had happened to me. I … I'm afraid I tried to take the law into my own hands. I finished up going to prison myself, while that man walked free.'

Ted was scribbling notes as she spoke. He looked up at her and asked levelly, 'And why do you think this might have any relevance to our present case, Ms Holden?'

'Because the man who raped me, Kenny Norman, had a thing about sports cars. He had a little vintage MG that he'd spent hours restoring. He used to love roaring round in that. He took me out for drives in it many times. And you said this rapist targets sporty cars to go for a joy-ride.'

'And is the man still in this area? Have you had any contact with him, or have you seen him at all since this happened?'

'He disappeared off the radar after the police told me they weren't going to pursue any charges against him. And it was one of the conditions, when I left prison, that I was not to try to make contact with the family again, in any way.'

'Ms Holden, as we disclosed at the press conference, our current attacker is armed with a knife and has used it. Did this man,' he looked back at his notes, pushing the notebook away a short distance so he could read his own writing, 'this Kenny Norman, ever threaten you with a weapon of any kind, or show any violence towards you?'

'Not that I can remember. But my therapist told me there will probably be aspects of the attack which I've buried so deeply, because they're too painful, that I may never recover them. I do remember, though, that he always carried a knife.'

Again, seeing Ted's querying look, she went on to explain.

'He had ponies. He used to rescue them from the sales at Beeston, to stop them going for slaughter. He had a little place outside town, in the countryside, sort of, a bit of a smallholding. I used to go up there after school and in the holidays to help with the ponies. He always carried a folding pocket knife for taking the baler twine off hay bales, opening feed sacks, that sort of thing.'

Ted sat back in his chair and looked at her. If he'd not had Bill's warning, he would have taken her seriously. Whether or not what she was telling him was true, it was clear that she believed it to be. He took more detail, thanked her for coming in, then went to find Bill to hear his version of the story.

Bill had been at the station for years and knew everything which went on inside it and in the town. He was always putting in for extra shifts since he had lost his wife young to an aggressive cancer. There were no children and he seemed glad of the company the workplace brought him.

'So, let's go and get a cuppa and I'll tell you the full story behind our Ms Holden,' Bill said, calling out to a colleague in an office behind the desk to watch the counter while he went on a break.

He and Ted headed to the rest room, where two young constables in uniform were sitting with their tea. They made to rise when they saw Ted but he waved the gesture away. He wasn't much for formality, although he hated to be called 'guv', always preferring sir or boss. But at the sight of the look Bill threw their way, both young men got up with their mugs and left the office with just a brief, 'Sir, Sarge,' before they left.

Ted laughed in admiration.

'I wish I could master that withering look of yours, Bill. It's hard to get taken seriously when you're knee-high to a grasshopper, like me.'

'Oh, I think everyone in the station knows well enough about your martial arts, Ted. So, what did you think of Ms Holden?'

They made drinks for themselves and sat down at the table.

'If you hadn't warned me, I'd have taken her seriously and sent some of the team round to have a word with this Kenny Norman, at least to see if he had an alibi.'

'Even better than an alibi,' Bill told him, taking a deliberately long slurp of his coffee, milking the moment for all it was worth. 'The reason there was never any further action on her allegations was that Kenny Norman was born a woman. He, or she, I'm not sure which is politically correct these days, didn't have the wherewithal to commit a rape. No meat and two veg.'

Ted put his mug down and gaped at him.

'Kenny Norman was transgender?'

'Is that what we're meant to call it? She was born female, went to school as a girl, then later on, decided she should have been a he. As I understand it, she took pills to deepen her voice and grow facial hair, that sort of stuff, but never had any form of surgery to change her bits, from what I remember.'

'He,' Ted corrected him. 'If he was living as a man, then he.'

'Of course, we could never tell Ms Holden the cast-iron alibi for why her rape allegation just didn't stand up, pardon the expression. She thought we'd just dropped the case on a whim, so she set about taking her own revenge.

'Kenny Norman loved those little ponies of his, he spent all his spare time, and his money, on them. He worked as a book-keeper, I think that's how the two first met. Jenny went up there one time, after the case was dropped, when he wasn't there. She at least made sure all the ponies were safely in the fields, then she torched the buildings, the hay barn and the stables.

'The whole lot was destroyed. I think in the end the RSPCA came and took the ponies away as there was no food or shelter for them. Kenny was devastated. He disappeared off the scene. He didn't even appear at her trial. She went down for six months for criminal damage. She was lucky not to get charged with arson.'

'But she seemed so convinced that it was true. Is this the false memory thing I've heard about? Did anyone talk to the psychotherapist at the time? Are there still records of the investigation around somewhere?'

'It's ten years ago, Ted. I only remember it as it was so unusual. I'm not even sure there would be much in the way of a record, as it never went any further than the initial investigation. If it ever got transferred to computer somewhere, your lad Steve will sniff it out, for sure. If not, send him to see me and I'll point him at the old hard copies in the archives. Though that might be quite a job.

'But is it worth your while to go ferreting around in an old case that went nowhere? Haven't you got enough on your hands looking for a rapist who has got the tackle to do the job? What would the Ice Queen think?'

'It's just got me intrigued,' Ted confessed. 'How could someone who's been to a professional therapist come away with completely the wrong end of the stick like this? Is she still around, still on our patch this ...' he took his notebook out to check the name, holding it at arm's length as he read, 'Dr Heather Cooper? I wouldn't mind ten minutes talking to her at some point, just out of interest.'

'You need reading glasses, Ted, your arms aren't long enough,' Bill laughed.

'Really? Glasses?'

He hadn't realised quite how far away he was holding his notebook until Bill mentioned it.

'Comes to us all in time,' the sergeant was still chuckling.

'Well, now you have depressed me. You've made me feel old, as well as incapable of solving this case,' Ted smiled. 'Thanks for the heads-up, Bill, I could have wasted valuable time following this up if you hadn't warned me off. I appreciate it. Erm, I suppose it was considered at the time, but there are things someone could use, if they didn't have the wherewithal themselves ...'

He left the sentence hanging in the air.

'Oh, believe me, we certainly thought about things like that,' Bill laughed. 'Ten years ago we didn't all have to mind our Ps and Qs quite as much as we do now. There were some right old suggestions put forward, I can tell you. Our Kenny was interviewed at length, and in quite graphic detail, I believe, and her house, his, if you prefer, was searched for anything like that. But in the end, it was just ruled out as a non-starter.'

Ted, Mike Hallam and DCs Rob O'Connell and Sal Ahmed stayed late into the evening, answering the spate of calls which followed the early evening news. None of them was any more promising than Ted's interview with Jenny Holden. They all took copious notes, to be followed up with some phone calls and house to house the next day, but eventually Ted called a halt and sent everyone home, himself included.

Trev put a plate of hot food on the table for him as soon as he walked through the door and into the kitchen.

'I don't care how tired you are tonight, you need to eat something,' he told him, giving him a hug and a kiss. 'Any progress?'

'Lots of progress. All of it backwards,' Ted told him as he sank wearily down onto a kitchen chair. 'I think I'm losing my touch on this one. I seem to be getting nowhere fast.'

Chapter Three

'Got one match so far, boss,' Rob O'Connell said, to start the morning briefing. 'In Folkestone. Same MO, DNA match, the same attacker.'

'He's a long-distance lorry driver,' Jezza Vine said confidently.

'How d'you work that one out, bonny lass? Women's intuition?' Maurice Brown asked her.

Not long ago, Jezza would have been immediately on the defensive, seeing the remark as sexist and patronising, at best. It was a mark of how much she had become a member of the team that she didn't fly off the handle.

'Folkestone for the Eurotunnel Shuttle. He gets bored driving a lumbering big juggernaut round all day, so he likes something sporty for his jollies in between.'

'Where do the rapes fit in?'

Mike Hallam was genuinely interested in her theory. Jezza often had a way of seeing something the others didn't.

'We all know sporty cars are penis extensions,' she said mockingly, waggling a limp little finger at the rest of the team.

Ted suppressed a smile but stepped in before it crossed the line into disrespect, which he wouldn't tolerate.

'All right, settle down. Let's not forget that three young women have been subjected to violent sex attacks in this case. Did he use the knife this time, Rob?'

'He used it, but the wound wasn't serious. Clearly more of a warning than anything else.'

'Let's not get fixated on the lorry driver idea, although it's a possibility, certainly,' Ted told them. 'Don't forget, when you're following up all the calls after the press conferences, we need to know occupations, just in case Jezza is on the right lines.

'So, what do we know about the knife?'

Blank looks greeted him. Ted tried to keep a note of irritation out of his voice.

'Come on, everyone. Basic police work. It's all we've got for now. The type of knife might be important; it might give us a direction to go in. Mike, get someone onto the statements and medical reports, checking that. If we need more information about a likely weapon, we can always ask Professor Nelson if she has any input. He could be ex-military, a fisherman, a butcher, anything.

'Let's get a bit more flesh on the bones of the white board, too. Similarities, differences. Days of the week, times of day, makes of car. It's a lot of work, on top of chasing up the calls, but it's what will get us the results. Rob, let's have every detail of this Folkestone case. Do it as a print-out we can all look at.

'And we also need to collate every bit of information we have on the attacker, from the victim statements. I'll try and go through them for that today some time. What have we got so far? Ordinary looking, average height, English accent with a hint of something else, but not a strong regional accent. It's not a lot to go on. We need to think about interviewing the victims further at some point, when they've had a little time to recover from the ordeal, just in case they remember anything else.

'Thanks, everyone, let's get to it. Steve, there's something I need you to chase up for me. Come into my office, will you,' Ted said then, seeing the TDC going red right to the tips of his ears, added, 'Don't worry, it's nothing you've done wrong or not done. I just need your help with something.'

Still looking ill at ease, Steve followed Ted into his small office. Ted was universally known as one of the easiest bosses to work for in the division, if not the force. He was always scrupulously fair and took the welfare of each of his team members seriously. Even so, Steve remained more than a little on edge around him, for reasons Ted didn't fully understand.

'Take a pew, Steve,' Ted told him, nodding to the spare chair as he sat down behind his desk. 'This is just something which came up as a result of calls after the press conference. Something and nothing, probably, just a loose end I'd like to tie up. It may not even have anything to do with our current case.

'By the way, how's the dental work going? It's looking good. Is there much more to do?'

Steve grinned self-consciously, revealing impressive new crowns to replace the teeth he'd had broken in an assault whilst working on a recent case, centred on the Hotel Sorrento.

'Nearly all finished now, sir, and I think they look better than the real ones did.'

Even in a relatively informal setting, Steve still found it difficult to drop the 'sir'.

'Good, glad to hear it. Now, I need you to find out everything you can for me about an old enquiry, ten years ago, which didn't lead to any action. A man called Kenny Norman, a rape allegation. Go and see the sergeant on the front desk and he'll point you in the right direction.'

Seeing Steve looking anxious again, Ted reassured him. 'Don't worry, he doesn't bite. And he knows more than anyone about what happens in this division. I want a current address for Mr Norman, and if it's remotely possible, I'd like it by end of play today. Like I said, it's just something unfinished I'd like to be able to put to bed.'

Once Steve had gone off on his mission, Ted spent some time going over the victim statements and anything else they had to go on so far. Ted was not one to delegate unnecessarily. He always worked as part of the team, probably harder than any of them. It was another reason he had their respect.

Reading through the ordeals the young women had suffered, he realised it was going to take careful and sensitive questioning if they were to get any further useful information from them. He scribbled himself a note to ask the Ice Queen about some victim support training. It might possibly be something which Jezza would be interested in.

Once again, he found himself holding paperwork a distance away, and had to rub his eyes once or twice while he was working. They seemed a bit blurred at times. Maybe Bill was right and the time had come to think about reading glasses.

Steve had come up with the goods quickly, as Ted hoped he would. Although he could now discount any involvement by Kenny Norman in their current case, he still felt he needed to know the end of the story. He wanted to find out what had become of the man. He could barely begin to imagine what he and his family must have gone through. It was little wonder he had kept a low profile ever since the affair.

Steve handed him a computer print-out with a local address on it. Ted wondered fleetingly if the young TDC ever wrote anything by hand or if it was a totally alien concept to him. He almost pulled him up on the waste of a sheet of paper but decided against it, thanking him instead for the information. He looked at the details on the paper, again having to move it further away in order to read it clearly.

Ted took out his mobile phone and called Trevor at work.

'Hi. I might be held up a bit this evening but I'm still hoping to get to the club at some point. If I am running late, could you take my kitbag for me when you go, and I'll come straight there in the car?'

As well as their own judo training session, it was also the night Ted and Trev ran the self-defence club for children. Ted hated to miss it, but he wanted to follow up on Kenny Norman. The idea of what the man must have gone through was troubling him.

Martial arts training was how Ted and Trev had first met. It was also their main leisure-time pursuit, something they both enjoyed and were good at. It kept both men in good physical shape and for Ted, it provided an essential release from the tensions of his job.

'No worries,' Trev told him, 'but don't be too late. I've got something exciting to talk to you about.'

Ted could tell from his voice that his partner was bursting to tell him whatever it was, but he didn't really have the time to listen. He added it to the long mental list of things he needed to make up to Trev, if and when time allowed.

The address Steve had given him, the last known one for Kenny Norman, was not far from where Ted lived, in Offerton. It was a quiet side road of solidly built post-war houses, which probably now commanded a hefty price tag.

Ted parked his Renault outside the address he had been given, then walked up to the front door and rang the bell. There was a light on inside but it seemed to take some time for anyone to come to the door. It was opened only as far as the safety chain would allow, then a woman's face peered out at him through the crack.

'Miss Norman?' Ted asked, as the information on record had shown that Kenny Norman's last known address was at this house, living with his unmarried sister. 'I'm sorry to disturb you. I'm Detective Inspector Darling. I wondered if I might have a word with you about your brother, Kenny? Here's my warrant card.'

He held it up towards the gap. She leaned closer and peered at it, then put out a hand to take hold of it.

'I don't see very well these days, I'm afraid. May I look at it a bit more closely, please?'

Ted relinquished it and waited patiently while she held it close to her face to scrutinise. She looked back towards him and said, 'It looks quite genuine, but then I wouldn't know. Should I phone the police station to check you are who you say you are?'

Ted smiled as he said, 'Please feel free to do that if you like, Miss Norman. But if I was an imposter, I would probably have turned tail and run at this point, and not given you the chance to check.'

She handed back the card, then pushed the door to so she could release the chain and allow Ted to come in. The hallway was dim and as soon as Ted stepped inside, he could smell the familiar scent of a tom-cat who had been laying claim to his territory.

The woman, who looked to be in her seventies, invited him to follow her. Ted noticed that she let a hand trail along the wall to guide her as she walked. She led the way into the front room, where the light was on and the television was talking away to itself in a corner, tuned to a news channel. She fumbled for the remote and turned it off, inviting Ted to take a seat, before sitting in what was clearly her customary place.

'What can I do for you, Inspector?' she asked, folding her hands in her lap.

Ted hesitated. He wasn't even sure he knew himself. He just felt he needed to know how the story had ended.

'I came across your brother's name, quite by chance,' he began, rather awkwardly. 'I wasn't working in Stockport at the time of the case. I just wondered what had happened to him. Does he still live here?'

'Well, I must say you are more courteous than some of your colleagues with whom we had to deal at the time. You at least afford Kenny the consideration of referring to him as a man.'

She paused for a moment, and there was a catch in her voice as she continued, 'My brother is dead, Inspector. Nearly ten years now.'

'I'm very sorry to hear that,' Ted said, his voice sincere, then, sensing her need, he asked, 'Would you like to talk about it?'

She looked at him for a long moment, although how much she could actually see, he wasn't sure. Then she took a deep breath and began.

'My brother was born a girl. Caroline. He went through his

school years as a girl. He felt all his life that he was trapped in the wrong body, as he put it. Our mother was very old-fashioned, very religious. She wouldn't hear of it. She kept telling him they were wicked thoughts, a sin. Sometimes she would even try to thrash the idea out of him.

'Our mother died when Kenny was nineteen. We were living in Macclesfield, so he and I moved here and he began to live the way he felt he should, as a man. He took tablets to help him to change his voice and his appearance, but he always refused anything surgical. He had a complete phobia of hospitals and any kind of procedure. He'd had a bad time having his tonsils out when he was small.

'He was very happy, with his work, and his ponies. Children used to come to see the ponies. He loved having them around. In some respects, he was more at ease with children than grown-ups. He was highly intelligent, very articulate, just not socially very adept. Everything was fine.

'Then, just over ten years ago, the police came calling for him. That young woman, that Jenny Holden, suddenly made all those totally ridiculous allegations. We both remembered her, from the time she used to help Kenny with the ponies. Then we lost touch, when she left school. We heard she'd got into trouble, hanging around with the wrong crowd, drinking, taking drugs, that sort of thing.

'The police came for Kenny and took him away for questioning. Kenny was always a very private person. It was excruciatingly difficult for him, talking about himself. Of course, when he told them the truth, your colleagues insisted he was examined by a police surgeon, which Kenny found mortifying.

'Things were said and done to him which should never have been. He was traumatised. And when your colleagues had finished with him, they just let him go. No word of apology, no explanation, nothing. I still have no idea why Jenny said such dreadful things about him, nor why she went on to do what she did to the ponies. That's what finally broke Kenny. Those ponies were like his children.'

She paused in her narrative and looked at Ted, tears in her eyes, trying to regain her composure.

'I'm so sorry, please excuse my lack of manners. I haven't even offered you a drink of any kind, Inspector. A cup of tea? A small sherry, perhaps?'

'No, thank you, it's very kind, but no,' Ted assured her, then waited for her to continue.

'When Kenny was at school, still living as a girl, he had a pen-friend, Marie-Anna, in Luxembourg. They visited one another, and after he became Kenny, they stayed good friends and continued to visit. Marie-Anna was a wonderful, compassionate friend to him, very supportive.

'Kenny suffered a serious depression when it all happened. He was on strong medication and for a time he couldn't even get out of bed. As soon as he felt able, he decided to go and stay with Marie-Anna in Luxembourg, just to get away from it all. Not long after he arrived there, he went for a walk in the city. He jumped off the high bridge, the Pont Adolphe. Because he died out of the country, I kept it quiet. I just let people believe he had moved away.'

There was a catch in her voice as she finished her story. They sat in silence for a moment, and Ted realised for the first time that there was a softly ticking clock on the mantelpiece. It broke the sombre quiet of the moment by striking the half-hour.

'Miss Norman, I am very sorry to hear that, and so sorry for the way in which you and your brother were treated by the police. When I heard of your brother's case, I just felt I needed to know what had become of him. Please accept my condolences.'

'You're very kind, Inspector,' she replied. 'I wish you could have been there at the time. I'm sure you would have seen to it that Kenny was at least treated with dignity and respect. I can show you the death certificate, I have it here in the bureau.'

'Please don't trouble yourself, there's really no need …' but she stood up and made her way over to an antique writing desk in a corner of the room.

'I don't wish to sound discourteous, Inspector, since you have shown me nothing but consideration and compassion. But my brother and I learned the hard way that police officers accept nothing at face value and want physical proof of everything they are told. Everything. So here you are.'

She handed him an official document. It was in French, but even Ted, who was not a language scholar, could make out the essentials.

Ted felt he really needed his martial arts session that evening after the distressing talk with Kenny Norman's sister. He was pleased to finish in time for it. His mood was sombre, after hearing the story, but he put on his professional face for the children, then used his own training session to burn off some of the day's frustrations, sparring fast and furiously with Trev.

In the car on the short drive home, he smiled at Trev and said, 'I've had a pretty rough day, so let's hear this good news you're bursting to tell me.'

Trev turned to him, grinning from ear to ear.

'Geoff's offered me the chance to buy into the business, as an equal partner. He's told me before he's leaving me his share when he dies, as they have no children. But he's offering me a chance to join the business as an equal partner now.'

Ted put a hand on his arm and patted it fondly. Trev adored his work in a motorcycle dealership. Despite being fluent in several languages and scarily intelligent, all he wanted to do was to be with his beloved bikes.

'Fantastic. If that's what you want, bring the accounts home for me to look at, let me know the costs involved and I'll talk to the bank. Let's do it!'

Chapter Four

'An update on the knife, boss,' Rob O'Connell told Ted and the team the following morning. 'All four victims describe it as a stiletto, about six inches long, and two of them say the blade was black.'

Ted felt his blood run cold.

'Sounds like a Fairbairn-Sykes commando knife.'

'So you're saying our man is military, or ex-military?' Mike Hallam asked him.

'I'm not jumping to any conclusions. It's an easy enough weapon to get hold of on the Internet. Alarmingly so. I'm just hoping our man isn't fully trained in how to use it. All four injuries to date have been slash wounds, rather than stabbings, haven't they?'

Rob checked his notes for the Folkestone case and nodded his head in confirmation.

'If that's what it is, it's a close combat fighting knife, designed to deliver a quick and lethal stab wound. It will go through the rib cage like the proverbial knife through butter. Which makes it even more imperative that we find this man, and soon,' Ted told them.

When he'd been a Specialist Firearms Officer, Ted had trained with an ex-SAS man, so he knew all about knives and how they could be used, as well as how to defend himself against them.

'How are we getting on with following up the phone calls? Any likely suspects yet?'

'Not so far, boss,' Mike told him. 'We can certainly eliminate a few though; completely the wrong size and build to match any of the witness statements. Also some have a record and their prints and DNA don't match our attacker's. Plus, one of them is away, so we can't check him out yet, and he's a long-distance lorry driver.'

'Told you he was a trucker!' Jezza said triumphantly.

'All right, let's not get carried away with that idea, it may be purely coincidence,' Ted said good-naturedly. 'While you're going door to door, though, be very careful. Don't go alone and above all, no heroics. Anything else to report, anyone? If not, let's get on and see if we can make a bit of progress.'

Ted reached for his phone when he returned to his own office. Although not connected to the current case, the Kenny Norman affair was still troubling him, particularly the absolute certainty Jenny Holden had shown that she had been raped by the man. Ted felt the need to find out more, and he knew someone who could hopefully help him.

'Carol? It's Ted Darling,' he said, when his call was answered.

'Ted! Nice to hear your voice. How are you?'

'I'm fine, it's not for another appointment for me,' he hastened to reassure the therapist who had counselled him through a difficult time. 'I just thought you might possibly be able to help me with something which has come up in the course of a current case.'

'I don't do psychological profiling or anything like that, if that's what you're looking for,' she said guardedly.

Ted laughed.

'I'm glad to hear it. I have yet to be convinced of its value. I think what I'm interested in is possibly something called False Memory Syndrome. Would you have any time to spare to help me with a few questions about it? Any time soon?'

'Well, I have just half an hour between appointments today so I was going to eat at my desk. If you were to come bearing edible gifts, I could supply drinkable coffee and see what I could do to help you?'

'You have a deal. What do you like to eat?'

'I probably shouldn't use the expression to a police officer, but I would kill for a smoked salmon and cream cheese bagel, after the morning I have lined up.'

'Consider it done,' Ted said, thankful she had chosen something he knew where to buy locally. It was something he sometimes bought for himself as a treat, from a nearby deli. 'What time?'

'One o'clock. See you then.'

Ted was punctual, as always. Carol had not quite finished her last consultation of the morning so he waited patiently, relieved that for once he was not going to have to talk about himself.

Once Carol had ushered her client out, she turned to Ted with a warm smile and shook his outstretched hand.

'Come in, Ted, come and take a seat. I'll get the coffee on.'

Ted waggled a paper bag in front of her and said, 'I come bearing bagels, as promised.'

She nodded to him to sit down, while she prepared the coffee. Ted looked around at the familiar muted tones of sage and cream. He sat down in the comfortable leather chair, where he'd spent many an hour trying to talk through his difficulties.

Carol put coffee, mugs, sugar and milk in front of them and helped herself to a bagel.

'So, tell me what I can help you with,' she said, then took a bite of her lunch. 'Oh my, this is good. I've been day-dreaming about it ever since you called. I wouldn't have had time to go out and get myself one, so this is bliss.'

Ted quickly outlined his visit from Jenny Holden and her evident belief that she really had experienced the rape, which she had only found out about under hypnosis. He told her all the details of the affair, knowing she was bound by confidentiality.

Carol interrupted him.

'Ted, I really can't comment on a fellow professional or an individual case of which I have no knowledge. If you're asking me in broad terms if False Memory Syndrome exists, then yes, it does, it can happen. Or,' she looked at him searchingly, 'are you actually asking me if your own memories of past events could be false?'

Ted shifted his weight awkwardly in his seat. She was uncomfortably close to what had been preying on his mind.

'Are you getting a bit too personally involved in this line of enquiry?' she asked him gently.

'I'm trying not to,' he told her. 'It's just that I've not come across this type of thing before and it's rather unsettled me. Is it common, false memory?'

'Not common, no, but well documented. I can email you a few links of things to look at for reference. There's a British society for it, with a website, which publishes a lot of interesting information. It's not my field of expertise, but it is something I've looked into from time to time.'

She paused for another bite of the bagel and some coffee, then went on, 'As for your own memories, that's a different thing entirely. You were never hypnotised by me and I assume it's unlikely that you ever were by anyone else. It is my professional opinion that what you discussed with me is what actually happened to you.

'As I said, I cannot comment on this other case, nor on the person carrying out the therapy. That would be improper and unprofessional of me. But you have told me that the young woman concerned had problems with alcohol and drug abuse in her past. It is therefore a possibility that those things may have been a contributory factor in what happened in her case. That can sometimes happen, from what I do know of the condition.'

'But is it theoretically possible for someone using hypnosis or other techniques to plant an idea in a person's mind, which then becomes a certainty?'

'To what end? What do you see as their motivation?' she asked.

'I have no idea,' Ted admitted frankly. 'I'm just trying to get my head round it.'

'Are you sure this is not becoming something of an obsession? Are you letting what happened to you in the past cloud your judgement of the relevance of this to your current enquiry?'

Ted swallowed his mouthful of bagel before replying. He knew she was probably right. He was getting fixated on a historic case which, although tragic, had nothing to do with the current crime he needed to be working on.

'Let's just say, for some reason which I don't yet profess to understand, this person had done just that, planted the germ of an idea, which led to tragic consequences ...'

'I think this is about the nicest bagel I've had in Stockport. You must tell me where you got them. The ones I've been buying aren't a patch on these.'

Ted realised it was her way of telling him that the discussion was closed. And he knew she was right. He needed to let it drop. He promised himself that he would read the links which Carol sent him and then let it go at that.

It had inevitably crossed his mind that his own disturbing flashbacks might in some way have been distorted or manipulated in his mind by the passage of time. But he trusted Carol completely, both professionally and as a person.

He decided to take a turn round each supermarket car park he passed close to on his way back to the station. It was unlikely to produce any result, but it was worth a shot and wouldn't take up much of his time. The attacks had so far been early evening, often when there were still a lot of shoppers about, though always after dark.

Their attacker was certainly bold because, approaching the end of the year, the shopping frenzy was already starting to be evident. Last Christmas had been a horrendous time for Ted and he was not looking forward to the one to come, with the memories it would inevitably bring. It seemed to him that the build-up was starting earlier every year. He wondered how long it would be before the shelves were full of cards and tinsel in September.

He cruised slowly round the first supermarket he came to, not really sure what he was looking for. As he drove back down between the parked cars, heading for the exit, he saw an attractive young woman, pushing a fully-laden trolley, get her keys out and activate the remote central locking of a smart, sporty BMW hatch, parked a good few yards away.

There was a space on the left of the silver car and Ted swung his Renault into it, pulling out his warrant card. As the woman reached her car and went to open the tailgate, Ted approached her in the silent stealth mode his team knew to their cost, warrant card in hand.

'Excuse me,' Ted began quietly.

The young woman was just leaning into the back of the car to load her shopping. She nearly jumped out of her skin. Her head shot up, hit the underside of the car's roof and she dropped a shopping bag, scattering apples and oranges all over the floor.

'I'm sorry, please don't be alarmed, I'm a police officer,' Ted said hastily as the woman swore loudly and rubbed her head.

Now feeling a complete idiot, Ted started to scramble round trying to pick up her dropped shopping.

'What the fuck are you doing, sneaking up on people in a car park? Are you some sort of pervert?' the woman demanded, her tone aggrieved.

Ted had managed to retrieve some of the fruit and stuff it back in her bag. He held his warrant card out again so she could see it more clearly.

'No, I really am a police officer. I'm very sorry I startled you, I was just trying to warn you. I wondered if you'd heard about the recent sex attacks in Stockport and realised the danger you just put yourself in?'

She was still rubbing her head and looking at him with undisguised suspicion, clearly not convinced he was genuine. She was taller than Ted, which was not unusual. His short stature often posed difficulty for him in getting people to believe that he really was a copper.

'Of course I've heard about it; it's been all over the papers and the telly. But it's broad daylight. I've stopped shopping after dark. Where's the danger?'

'You have just the sort of car the attacker targets, and you unlocked it from quite a distance away. I was in the next parking space. I could easily have got into your car.'

She gave him a withering look and snapped, 'Have you ever been smacked in the face with a Jimmy Choo?' looking down at the short boots in which she was teetering on impossibly high heels. 'Now why don't you do one, officer?'

Still apologising profusely, Ted slunk back into his car, feeling he had just made a complete prat of himself, and drove off. What had just happened had given him an idea though, something he needed to discuss with the Ice Queen as soon as he got back to the nick.

But first he had an errand to run. He was starting to realise that Bill was right. He either needed longer arms, or it was time to bite the bullet and get a pair of reading glasses. He was dreading it. It seemed to be a further indication that he was turning middle-aged, which might explain why he wasn't making the progress with the current case that he would have liked to.

Even the formal and strictly professional Ice Queen appeared to have difficulty keeping a straight face as Ted described his encounter on the car park when he got back to the station. But he was in deadly earnest.

'Ma'am, I know nothing about fashions, men's or women's,

but I do know there's not a shoe been designed that's a match for a Fairbairn-Sykes knife, especially if it's in the hands of someone trained in its use.

'The public may not be taking this seriously enough. Can we get the press office to put out more advice on self-protection? Things like not using the remote from too far away, and being careful who's next to your vehicle before you get into it?'

'I can certainly sort out something on those lines. It can only help us if we attempt to make things more difficult for this attacker,' she said, then added, still struggling to hide a smile, 'Meanwhile, I do hope I am not going to get calls from members of the public reporting one of my officers as a sex pest?'

Carol had been true to her word and found time to send Ted some links to further information on False Memory Syndrome. Ted printed them out to take home. The paperwork on his desk had been breeding again and he needed to spend some time making a concerted effort to clear it. He'd look at the information when he got home, as it was not strictly related to his current enquiry.

He was home before Trev for once, as his partner had gone to karate club. Ted would have liked to have joined him but couldn't justify the time to himself. It also gave him chance to try out the reading glasses while he was on his own. He was feeling self-conscious about the need for them and wanted time to get used to the idea.

Trev had been in the house to collect his karate kit on his way home from work and had also left Ted the accounts he had asked to see, with a note of Geoff's proposals for Trev's half share. The figure was slightly higher than Ted had expected, but it should still be feasible. They had a reasonable joint income, never spent lavishly and had a bit put by. Ted was in steady employment, with an excellent credit rating. Even in the current risk-averse times, he thought his bank would probably advance him what he needed. He looked carefully through the accounts and they seemed healthy enough to at least approach the bank. He would do anything within his power to make Trev happy.

He then turned his attention to the print-outs he had on False Memory Syndrome, backing it up with reference to a website Carol had suggested. He was so engrossed in his reading, he hardly heard Trev come in until he heard him exclaim, 'Oh my God! You look so sexy in specs.'

Trev strode across the kitchen, put his arms round Ted's shoulders from behind and kissed the back of his neck. Ted looked up over the top of the tawny tortoiseshell frames, which the young woman in the shop had insisted were perfect to complement his dusty blonde hair and hazel eye colouring.

'Are they all right?' he asked anxiously. 'The young lady in the shop said they were fine, but you know I'm no good at anything like that.'

'If you give me that stern policeman look over the top of them, I might not be responsible for my actions,' Trev warned him, kissing him again.

Ted carefully unwrapped Trev's arms, kissed his wrists and pushed him gently but firmly away.

'Are you all right?' Trev asked, suddenly looking concerned. 'Not like you to say no.'

'It's not no, it's just not now. I need to read through some stuff for work, and to study these accounts in detail. If you want to join the grown-up world and go into business, we need to put together some sort of business plan, tonight, for me to present to the bank. After that, we'll see.'

Chapter Five

The local press had given some coverage to the safety advice to drivers, particularly to those who could be targets. Ted sensed, however, that they were waiting with bated breath for something a lot juicier, to splash all over their front pages.

With a reminder from the Ice Queen, Ted had called the local reporter to let him know in advance before the press release went out. He'd also taken the time to ask for his cooperation in giving it some prominence, if he could.

'I'll do my best for you, Ted, but you know that's not the sort of stuff that sells papers these days. Readers love to read about the ones who didn't get away, d'you know what I mean?'

'I really appreciate your help, Alastair, and you can be sure that as soon as there is any other development, you'll be the first to hear,' Ted had said, before he hung up and swore under his breath. Dealing with the press in general, and the local reporter in particular, always made him feel tainted.

The next attack, when it came, wasn't on their patch.

'Dover, boss,' Rob O'Connell told them at the morning briefing.

'See, I told you, he's a trucker. Plenty of ferries to the continent from Dover all the time. Second busiest port in Europe,' Jessica Vine said triumphantly.

She was a mine of general knowledge, largely thanks to her autistic younger brother Tommy and his obsession with Trivial Pursuit.

'Is there something we should know about you and this

obsession with lorry drivers, Jezza?' Rob asked her, but it was good-natured banter, an exchange of equals on the team. Nothing like the sort of sexist remarks Jezza had encountered in previous stations, which were simply not tolerated by Ted on his team.

'Why a lorry, though, Jezza?' Ted asked. 'I agree there's a possibility he uses the ferry, and the Shuttle to Europe, but why not just a car driver?'

'It could be a car driver. Maybe doing the booze run to Calais, then, perhaps, going on to somewhere here, with a boot full of drink for, I don't know, a get-together with some old mates? Some old forces mates if he is ex-military?' suggested Mike Hallam.

'Same knife again, Rob? Was the victim injured?' Ted asked him.

'Victim was too shaken up to have taken much notice of the knife, but again she was cut rather than stabbed. The wound needed stitches but it wasn't classed as a serious one.'

'So, one at a Channel port, one near the Shuttle terminal, and three on our patch. Does that mean Stockport is his home, or just somewhere he likes to stop off on his travels? In between checking the leads we've had so far, you need to get out round your contacts and see if anyone knows anything.

'Let's not assume anything at all, but there is still the possibility that our man may be ex-forces. If he's been a career soldier, he could have done around twenty or more years, which could put him around the mid-forties, as our man is said to be. He could also be a lorry driver,' Ted inclined his head towards Jezza in acknowledgement of her idea, 'but let's not get totally hung up on any of that, either. Try to keep an open mind.'

'Boss, I ran into Nat, that former witness, who now works in a supermarket. He was on an early evening shift while I was looking for digestive biscuits and brown sauce for the wife,' Virgil chipped in.

'Thanks for sharing that image, Virgil. I may never be able to look at a digestive biscuit again,' Jezza smiled.

'Try sitting up in bed with her while she's eating them,' Virgil grinned back. 'Anyway, part of Nat's duties include gathering up trolleys from the car park, so I asked him to keep a look out.'

Ted nodded and added, 'I hope you warned him that our man is dangerous? The last thing we need is a member of the public getting hurt trying to play the hero.

'Steve, how did you get on looking at bus routes? Anything there?'

'Too much, sir,' Steve replied. 'Because the attacks have all been early evening, there are still quite a few buses running. I've not really been able to come up with anything much that's conclusive yet, over the three separate locations of the attacks. But I'll keep working on it.'

'If he is a trucker …' Jezza began, before the rest of the team laughed and Rob said, 'Seriously, Jezza, what is it with you and lorry drivers?'

Jezza stuck her tongue out at him and said, 'Shut up and listen, you lot. Seriously. Just suppose he is a lorry driver. Perhaps he parks his rig somewhere near to where he attacks, then goes back there and drives off when he's finished.'

'Bloody hell, bonny lass, I think you've got something there. That's not a bad idea …'

Jezza cut him short.

'Before you say "for a woman", Maurice, let me remind you that I'm into kickboxing, not painting my nails,' she said scathingly, but it was clear the remark was light-hearted, despite her tone.

Ted let the exchange go. He knew the team needed a release from the tensions they worked under. He was pleased to see how much Jezza was now becoming one of them, both giving out and taking the banter.

'It's a good suggestion, one we need to look at,' Ted said.

'Find out where there's lorry parking close to where the attacks have been. Remember, if he drives containers, he may just be parking up his cab, which needs less room, of course. Ask around, see if anyone knows or suspects anything. Mike, don't forget to liaise with Inspector Turner for some extra officers from Uniform to help. And talk to the CSOs, see what they've heard.'

Police Community Support Officers were usually the first ones the public talked to about concerns or suspicions. They had their ears close to the ground of their communities and would often get wind of things before CID officers did.

'Rob, talk to Folkestone and Dover police, mention the idea to them, see if they've had any similar thoughts, or if it could be a possibility in their cases. And everyone, whenever you have time, ask your contacts if they know anyone who might just fit the profile, assuming he is local. But Maurice, that is not licence to go on a pub crawl,' Ted said with mock severity, knowing what Maurice was like if he got an excuse.

Maurice grinned at him innocently.

'Me, boss? As if!'

'Right, let's get on with it, see if we can come up with anything new. Rob, same as for Folkestone, can you make sure we all have the full details of the case in Dover. Maurice, have you got a minute, please?'

Maurice followed Ted into his office, shut the door behind them and sat down, vaguely wondering what he'd said or done wrong this time.

'I'd like you to come with me tomorrow morning for an appointment I've got. It's not strictly speaking to do with this case, only indirectly. I'm not sure how it's going to go, and I just basically need someone there to listen and say nothing.'

'You want me to look mean and moody then?' Maurice smiled.

'Something like that,' Ted grinned in reply. 'I may be taking us both on a wild goose chase, but it's just a loose end I want to tie up. It won't take us long. Thanks, Maurice.'

Another detail Ted had run down was to formalise what he had learned about the death of Kenny Norman. He'd contacted the police in Luxembourg for confirmation of the suicide and had been sent an official copy of the death certificate, which could now be put on the case file. The whole affair had been a tragedy which still played on his mind, and he was not quite finished with it yet.

Norman's accuser, Jenny Holden, had tried to see him again but been blocked by Bill at the front desk. She had, though, managed to get him on the phone and was still insistent that there must be a link between what she believed had happened to her all those years ago and what was currently happening. She was starting to make noises about a police cover-up and Ted was anxious to try to keep a lid on the situation.

If Pocket Billiards got hold of even a sniff of such a story, it would certainly not help their current enquiry. Nor did Ted want to see Kenny Norman's sister publicly dragged through all the unpleasantness which would follow.

'Ms Holden, clearly there are aspects of the case which I cannot discuss with you, because of confidentiality. However, I can assure you, and I do hope you will accept this, that I have carried out a thorough investigation, following what you told me. I can tell you that there was unequivocal evidence at the time that Mr Norman did not sexually assault you, which is why no charges were forthcoming. I also have categoric proof that he is no longer in this country and has not been for a number of years.'

'You would say that, though. You lot stick together, cover up your messes or any hint of police corruption,' her voice was rising, taking on a note of hysteria.

'I assure you, Ms Holden, that your complaint was thoroughly investigated and there was no case to answer against Mr Norman. And once again, I looked carefully into the information you provided to me. In light of information I received from another force, I was able to rule Mr Norman out as a suspect in this current enquiry. I'm sorry that's not the answer you were hoping for, but I would ask you to trust me on this. There is no question of any sort of cover-up.'

She was in tears and incoherent when she rang off, clearly not happy. With a sigh, Ted realised he was going to have to tell the Ice Queen about the whole incident, in case the first she saw of it was a sensationalist story splashed over the local papers. He did not, however, intend to mention his upcoming appointment with the therapist who had treated Jenny Holden. Ted didn't often play the maverick, but he just felt he needed to try to understand what had gone on.

'What an extraordinary case,' the Ice Queen commented as Ted filled her in, over a cup of her delicious coffee. 'I've never heard anything quite like it. You were quite right to inform me. It's precisely the sort of witch-hunt we want to avoid at the best of times, and certainly with an ongoing enquiry of this type.

'I will take the precaution of getting the Press Office to prepare a guarded statement, just in case we need it. And in terms of fire-fighting, Inspector, make time as soon as possible to buy your local reporter friend a drink. We want him on side, so that if this woman does contact him with the story, he will at least call you for a comment.'

Scorpion petting was higher on Ted's list of preferred activities than meeting Alastair, but he knew that her point was valid. He didn't think he would ever be best friends with the press, but of late there were signs of a working relationship slowly starting to build. It was probably worth quarter of an hour of his time and the price of a pint.

'So, what have you got for me, Ted?' the journalist asked, after he had downed nearly half his pint of lager top without pausing for breath.

Ted took a few swallows of his Gunner before replying. He didn't drink alcohol. The ginger beer, ginger ale and fresh lime mixture was the closest he came. He even insisted that the

Angostura bitters of the original recipe were left out of his.

'Nothing concrete just yet, Alastair. I just wanted to thank you for your help in putting the warning out to women drivers. Also to say that if there's anything you need help with, a quote or anything, at any time, just give me a call. I'll always try to make sure you get something no one else gets.'

It was purely flannel but it seemed to satisfy the reporter and he went on his way happily enough. Ted hoped he'd done enough to prevent any bad publicity they could well do without.

Before the team left for the day, Ted called Jezza into his office to run an idea past her.

'I've been wondering if we should try talking further to the victims,' he began. 'And I wondered if you would be interested in doing victim support training, with that in mind?'

'Permission to speak frankly, boss?' Jezza asked, her tone ironic.

Ted smiled at her.

'Considering you once pushed me face down into a puddle and sat on me, with no repercussions, I would hope that by now you know I'm a reasonable sort of person. By all means speak frankly; I would expect no less of you.'

'Is this just tokenism? I mean, as the only female on the team, I'm the one to send for the training?' she asked.

Ted looked at her, surprised.

'I must say I'm disappointed, Jezza. I would have thought that you knew I don't go in for gender stereotyping, certainly not intentionally. Nor do I approve of any kind of discrimination, and that includes positive discrimination.

'Is there some other reason, perhaps a practical one, why you don't want to do the course? If you're worried about getting someone to look after Tommy, it's a day course, not residential.'

Ted knew that Jezza often had trouble with childcare for her younger brother, who lived with her.

'Is this training compulsory?' she asked. 'It's just that, I'm not really the tea and sympathy sort.'

'Not compulsory at all, that's not how I work. I just thought it might be something which would interest you, and might be useful on your CV. If you don't want to do it, it's fine, and thank you for being honest.'

'No worries, boss,' she said as she got up to leave. 'Oh, nice specs, by the way.'

He had forgotten he had them on and felt slightly embarrassed at her comment. He was still disappointed by her response, though, and wondered if there was more to it than she had told him to date.

Although he was flat out on the sex attacks case, as well overseeing a few others, Ted had found time to go and see his bank manager, as he'd promised Trev. He was delighted to find that his loan application went through swiftly and more easily than he had feared.

His excellent credit rating went in his favour. He was never overdrawn, always living well within his means. He had a morbid fear of being in debt. Trev was always teasing him about how frugal he was. He would never have dreamt of taking on a loan for himself, but he was determined to help his partner buy into the business, if he possibly could. He knew he owed a lot to Trev. Their solid relationship helped Ted get through the toughest times at work. A lot of his friends and colleagues had been far less lucky in theirs.

'We'll have to tighten our belts,' he warned Trev when he got home for supper, after he'd been to the bank and signed the forms for the loan.

Trev laughed and hugged him. 'Ted, if we tighten them any more, we'll end up eating the cats. You're not exactly one to splash the cash. A two week self-catering holiday in Italy in the last - how many years? - is hardly extravagant living.

'But thank you so much for doing this for me. I promise

you I'm going to be grown up and sensible and really make a go of it. I'll be able to pay towards the loan, too. I'll be on more money soon. And I've got lots of ideas for bringing in more business, especially now I have a financial incentive to do so.'

'No more duvet days, if you're going to be a partner,' Ted warned him. 'Why not invite Geoff and Wendy round for dinner one evening soon, let them know the good news, then we can celebrate properly? I'll try to make a point of being here. It would be nice to have something to raise a glass about, with this case going nowhere fast.'

Chapter Six

It was an unprepossessing suite above a small shop, not far from the Merseyway Shopping Centre. Up a flight of uncarpeted stairs to a dismal landing, with other doors opening off it, and just a small brass plaque to show Ted which was the right door. No receptionist, simply a bell to ring by the outer door to announce their arrival, then a cramped, dark waiting room with no windows.

The usual assorted pile of tattered motoring and gossip magazines, plus the obligatory and much out of date torn editions of National Geographic, were scattered haphazardly on a low occasional table in one corner of the room. Ted and Maurice were the only people there. They took a seat, but were not kept waiting for long before the inner door opened.

'Inspector Darling?' the woman who came out asked, looking expectantly from one to the other of them.

Both men rose and Ted made the introductions.

'Please come in,' she said, and led the way into her office, which was tiny and a little claustrophobic. The only window, which had clearly not been cleaned in a long time, looked directly on to a blank brick wall at the opposite side of the pedestrian walkway outside.

The woman moved round to her own side of the desk, gesturing to a chair and pulling out another spare one, before sitting down herself.

She was, Ted, guessed, in her late forties, average height, well built. She had a round, open face, accentuated by the mousy hair pulled back into a French plait. It was the sort of face people may have found it easy to talk to. In the cramped confines of the stuffy office, Ted knew he would only ever be able to talk about official business.

'Thank you for agreeing to see us, Dr Cooper,' Ted began. 'As I'm sure you will be aware from the news reports, we're currently investigating a series of sexual assaults. The public have been coming forward to help us with our enquiries, which is encouraging. However, we have also been contacted by someone in respect of a historical rape allegation.'

The woman had steepled her hands in front of her mouth and was nodding encouragingly at him to continue.

'I must stress that I appreciate that neither of us can discuss any individual because of confidentiality issues which bind us both. But in light of what this person told me, I wanted to ask you about various techniques used to help people to recover memories, and how reliable they are as a general rule.'

Maurice was doing a good job of sticking to his brief and saying nothing, just being a solid, silent presence. The routine was, as Ted had wanted, not so much good cop, bad cop as talkative cop, ominously quiet cop. The woman was looking shrewdly from one to another of them.

'Am I to understand that you have reason to disbelieve what this person has told you, Inspector?' she asked.

'I don't really wish to go into any details of this individual case, Doctor. I'm just really asking you, in broad terms, if, in principle, it can happen that someone remembers something during a therapy session, perhaps believes it completely, yet it's later proved to be completely untrue.'

She leaned forward slightly as she asked, 'And you're asking me, specifically, because …?'

'Because I understand that you are someone in this town who offers some of the types of therapy which can be used to help recover memories,' Ted said smoothly.

Now she leaned back slightly in her seat, keeping one hand

by her face, an index finger to her cheek, thumb supporting her chin, while the other hand picked up a pen and began absent-mindedly to tap it on her notebook.

'It's true that I have been successful in using certain types of hypnosis, and other techniques, in helping people to discover things from their past. Memories which they may have kept buried because they were too painful to confront. These techniques are scientifically recognised and well proven. And, as with all things in my profession, their application is strictly regulated.

'But how reliable are they? Can it happen that the memory which is recovered is not accurate?' Ted persisted.

Maurice moved his bulk slightly in his chair and for a moment, the woman's eyes left Ted's face and moved to him. Then she looked back as she said, 'Nothing about the human mind is ever one hundred per cent certain, Inspector. I assume you're talking about False Memory Syndrome? It has happened; that much is well documented. My personal belief is that it rarely, if ever, happens with someone experienced, using recognised techniques and following carefully laid down procedure.'

'Someone like yourself, Doctor?' Ted asked evenly.

She studied him hard for a moment before replying, 'I believe so, yes. It is an area in which I have had some degree of success. In fact, I've written a book about some of my more interesting cases. The identities of the people involved are, of course, concealed, but I have written in depth about some of the results of my work.'

She swivelled her chair round, took a book from the shelves behind her, turned back and placed it on her desk, the title turned towards Ted and Maurice, so they could read it. *Behind the Barbed Wire,* Dr Heather Cooper.

'I called it that because sometimes, when memories are particularly painful, the human mind has a way of burying them deeply, hiding them away. I liken it to the rolls of barbed wire on top of a wall, to prevent anyone from getting in or out.

'Using various techniques, including different forms of hypnosis, it is sometimes possible to break through these defences. One can sometimes succeed in unlocking the hidden memory, and can then begin the process of helping the person towards recovery.

'But I'm not entirely sure that I see how this line of questioning is going to be of benefit to you in your current investigation, Inspector.'

It was time for Ted to deploy his secret weapon. He threw her his most disarming, boyish grin and said apologetically, 'Nor do I really, Doctor. I'm just trying to get my head round a few things, to see what lines of enquiry I need to follow up urgently and which I can possibly set aside for the moment.

'So, without going into specific details, could you tell me the kind of cases in which you've used these techniques successfully?'

'Well, considering your current enquiry, it's worth mentioning that one of the cases, one I go into in detail in the book, involved a historical rape allegation. The techniques I use can be very useful for that type of thing as it's often violence, particularly sexual violence, which can be buried the deepest.'

'And do you find generally that victims who are helped to remember such acts of violence are then motivated to go to the police about what has happened to them?' Ted asked.

Her voice was suddenly more guarded as she replied, 'Sometimes.'

'And have you ever had personal experience of memory recovery which has turned out to be false? Am I right in thinking that sometimes a history of drug or alcohol abuse, as well as other factors, can lead to false memories?'

'You're well informed, Inspector. You've clearly been doing your research. Are you implying that someone I have treated in the past has been shown to have had false memories?'

'I'm just talking in the broadest possible terms at the moment, Doctor, not in specifics. What you've told me is very helpful,' Ted said, turning on the charm once more. 'Are there any other times when you've had particular success with hypnosis?'

'Hypnosis is traditionally useful in tackling issues like smoking and weight problems. The techniques I use are particularly helpful at dealing with the factors which lead people to become addicted to tobacco, or indeed to food. I have also personally had a lot of success in helping people, especially impressionable young people, with misguided notions about their sexuality.'

Maurice straightened up in his chair and looked instantly alert, watching the boss's reaction. He could almost feel the suddenly charged atmosphere in the room.

'What do you mean by that?' Ted asked quietly, all hint of boyish charm gone, his normally warm hazel eyes suddenly flashing like shards of bottle-green glass.

She gave a small laugh.

'You know that sometimes, young people get a strange notion in their heads. They may, for some reason, start to think they may be gay, or bisexual, for example. It's often to do with peer pressure, and it seems to be getting more frequent. It seems to be increasingly the fashion for them to want to 'come out', as they call it.

'Under hypnosis, it may be possible to help them to realise that these ideas are unfounded, to guide them to a better understanding of who they really are. To help them to be comfortable with themselves as they are, without feeling the need to change.'

Maurice made to rise awkwardly.

'Thank you, Doctor, that's very helpful. We need to get going now, boss,' he said pointedly. 'Don't forget we have that other appointment to get to.'

Ted didn't move. His voice now was terse.

'Are you saying that when young vulnerable people entrust themselves to your care, you use hypnosis to try to influence their sexuality?' he asked coldly.

The woman gave a short laugh.

'That's really over-simplifying the issue, Inspector. Here, let me give you some leaflets about the sort of thing which can be done to help. It's nothing invasive, I assure you. I most certainly don't go in for the electric shock treatment you hear of in some countries.'

She shuffled some leaflets on her desk, took out two or three and slid them across the polished surface towards Ted.

Maurice had known the boss long enough to be getting seriously worried, seeing the tension showing along his jawline. It was time to stop playing strong, silent cop and get Ted out of there, quickly, before he completely lost it, which was looking increasingly likely. He stood up.

'Boss, really, we must go, we're running late for the next appointment. Thank you for all your help, Doctor.'

He gathered up the leaflets and put them in his pocket then attempted to take Ted by the arm. Ted's movement to shake his hand off was as fast as a whip-crack and Maurice could see the sudden alarm on the doctor's face.

'By what right are you even attempting to coerce young people into changing their sexuality?' Ted began, his voice still quiet but the tone now glacial.

Dr Cooper stood up abruptly, pushing her chair back first, putting more distance between her and Ted.

'I don't like your tone of voice at all, Inspector. Your attitude is becoming hostile and I would like you to leave, now. You've clearly come here with a hidden agenda, which is totally unacceptable, and I will be making a phone call of complaint to your superior officer.'

'Boss, we need to leave. Now,' Maurice said pointedly. 'I'm sorry we've disturbed you, Doctor. Thanks again for your help. Come on, boss.'

Maurice hadn't a clue what he was going to do if the boss refused to leave. He'd never seen him so close to losing control and he was desperate to get him out of there before he did. He was relieved when Ted finally ground out, 'Thank you, and good day,' before turning and marching out of the room.

Maurice hurried after him and caught him up as he strode outside. Ted glared at him and said warningly, 'Not one word, Maurice. Whatever you're about to say, just don't.'

Maurice moved to plant his not inconsiderable bulk directly in front of Ted, preventing him from walking away.

'With respect, boss, shut up and listen. You can't go anywhere, wound up like that, certainly not back to the nick. You're no use to man nor beast. There's a decent café just near here. I'm going to take you for a cuppa and then, when you've calmed down a bit, we can go back and face the music. I don't think she was kidding. I bet she's already on the phone to the Ice Queen.'

For a moment, Maurice wasn't sure whether the boss was going to walk away or thump him one. Even Ted seemed unsure. Then he relaxed visibly and gave an embarrassed grin.

'Yes, Maurice,' he said meekly, and fell into step with him, heading for the café.

Ted obediently took a seat while Maurice went to get their drinks. He came back with a steaming mug, topped with whipped cream, which he put down in front of him. Ted eyed it suspiciously.

'Hot chocolate,' Maurice told him. 'It works miracles. It's what I always get for my girls when they're upset about anything.'

Ted took a cautious sip, surprised at how good it tasted.

'Maurice, look, that should never have happened. I can only apologise. It's just …'

'Boss,' Maurice interrupted him, then went on, 'Ted. Look, I know how hard that must have been for you. But losing it like that? That's not like you. If the doctor does phone the Ice

Queen, she's going to go ballistic.'

Maurice was the only one of the team who had known Ted long enough and well enough to slip into first-name informality on rare occasions. Ted was so mortified by his own behaviour, he didn't even bother to pull him up on his lack of respect for their senior officer.

Just then the sound of Freddie Mercury singing Barcelona announced to Ted that he had an incoming call on his mobile. He looked at the caller identity on the screen and groaned.

'Speak of the devil,' he said, as he took the call.

'My office. As soon as,' was all that she said before she hung up abruptly.

'The royal summons,' Ted grimaced, making to stand up. 'Give me those leaflets, Maurice, I want to have a long look at those now I've calmed down a bit.'

'Finish your hot chocolate, boss,' Maurice told him, fishing them out of his pocket and handing them over. 'The condemned man's last nourishment.'

Making his way to the Ice Queen's office when they got back to the nick, Ted felt a touch of prophecy in Maurice's words. He knew he could be in serious trouble, with the first ever complaint of his career against him. He was facing possible suspension, a disciplinary hearing and who knew what else. He couldn't even justify his behaviour to himself. He had quite simply lost it and he shouldn't have.

The Ice Queen's tone was colder than ever when she called out to him to come in, in response to his knock. In the circumstances, Ted thought he'd better wait for her permission to sit down. It was not forthcoming, so he remained standing, not quite at attention, feeling more than a little awkward, and inwardly cursing his unaccustomed loss of self-control.

The Ice Queen studied him long and hard, her expression somewhere between annoyance and disappointment.

'I have to say, Inspector, that of all the officers in this station, you are the last one I expected to be the subject of a complaint from a member of the public.'

Ted decided it was probably safest to say nothing at all until asked for a direct response.

She regarded him a moment longer then said, 'I want you to go home, now, and stay on leave until Monday morning. You are not to make any contact with any member of your team, especially with DC Brown. I assume, from the description I was given, that was who was with you? I will brief the team on your absence, without giving the reason. I will then conduct my own enquiry into this matter and let you know my findings on Monday. Do not return to your office. Is there anything there which you need?'

'Everything is in my car, ma'am,' Ted told her, feeling wretched. 'Am I suspended?'

Again, the long look and the deliberate pause.

'Not suspended at this stage, no. I have so far managed to persuade Dr Cooper not to make the matter official, therefore it is something, at the moment, which I can deal with without having to pass it on to Complaints. But that still remains a possibility, depending on my findings.

'For now, go home, try to relax, and I will see you here at eight o'clock on Monday morning.'

Chapter Seven

It was rare for Ted to be home before Trev. His hours were often long and erratic, so it was usually Trev who did the cooking. It made a pleasant change for him to come home to delicious smells wafting from the kitchen.

'You're home early,' Trev said, crossing the kitchen to hug his partner and look over his shoulder at what was cooking. 'Mmmmm, Thai green curry? Is this a special occasion I've forgotten about?'

He glanced round the kitchen, spotting a new book, open on the table, with Ted's reading glasses next to it. Ted seldom read books; he hardly ever had the time. When he did, it was usually fiction, like his guilty secret pleasure of reading Agatha Christie and Ian Rankin. Trev could see that this was a hefty-looking non-fiction work.

'I'm doing some detective work here. You're home early, making your signature dish, and buying books. What have you been up to?'

Ted finished stirring his dish and turned to him with a self-effacing grin.

'I was sent home from school early for being naughty.'

'You're suspended?' Trev gaped in astonishment. 'What did you do?'

'Not suspended, no, just told to take a long weekend and not go back in until Monday morning. So I'm all yours for a couple of days, if you want to do something? Do you want tea? The kettle's just boiled.'

'Tea, yes, extra strong. I need it for the shock. Tell me what you did.'

Ted busied himself brewing up for Trev. Just then, his mobile phone, on the table next to his book, rang. Trev was nearer so he looked at the caller display, and handed it to Ted, saying, 'It's Maurice.'

Ted put a mug of tea down in front of him and sat down, but shook his head.

'I can't take it. Maurice is my witness and I'm not allowed to speak to him until the Ice Queen has completed her initial enquiries.'

Trev took a swallow of his tea, his eyes wide.

'I can't believe I'm hearing this. Tell me everything, from the start.'

'Just in brief, I went to see some sort of a therapist who reckons she can cure young people of being gay. I wasn't expecting that, I went to talk to her about something else. She just mentioned that side of her work. There are some leaflets there, with the book. It's one she wrote. I bought it on the way home.

'Look, would you mind if we talked about this later, over supper? I promise I will talk to you, properly, but right now, I really feel the need of an hour or so doing some Krav Maga.'

Of the four martial arts in which Ted had black belts, Krav Maga, the fastest and potentially most lethal of them, was the one he relied on when under the most stress.

'Where are you going?' Trev asked suspiciously.

At Ted's own club, training sessions were strictly controlled. On occasion, when he was in a bad place, he had a habit of venturing over the Pennines to another club where the rule book didn't exist and there was no referee.

'Don't worry, just my own club. No rough stuff, I promise. I just need a hard work out. Then we can eat and I'll tell you all about it.'

Trev wasn't happy, but their relationship was built on trust, and he knew that Ted wasn't lying to him. He also knew Ted always needed physical release when he was under stress. He didn't suggest going with him, either. Krav Maga was Ted's thing. If that's what he needed, Trev would let him go. He had an idea of his own of what he might be able to do to help, while his partner was out.

True to his word, Ted wasn't gone too long. He looked physically tired when he came back into the kitchen, dumping his kit bag in the hall on his way. Trev had cleared away the book and laid the table ready to eat when Ted got back home.

Trev looked at him anxiously.

'Are you all right?'

Wordlessly, Ted pulled up his sweatshirt, exposing his well-muscled torso, and did a slow pirouette.

'Not a mark, as promised,' he said, as he sank wearily into his chair. 'I just needed the outlet.'

'Sal phoned me,' Trev said, as he dished up the food Ted had prepared. 'The team are all worried about you. It seems Maurice has been sworn to secrecy and the Ice Queen must have put the frighteners on him as even he is saying nothing. I just told Sal there was some personal stuff you needed to see to and that you'd be back on Monday.'

'I hope I've not made trouble for Maurice,' Ted said, sounding glum, as he took his plate. 'And I hope he doesn't have any ideas of bending the facts when the Ice Queen talks to him.'

'Is it going to have to go to Complaints?' Trev asked him anxiously, sitting down with his own plateful.

'I won't know until Monday. The Ice Queen will do her bit, then let me know her findings. Which may mean I'm not going to be the best of company this weekend, so apologies in advance.'

Trev stopped eating and put his fork down.

'That's why I've arranged something for you, for the

weekend. Something I thought might help. I phoned Annie. She's got the weekend off, so I've fixed up for the two of you to go to Wales.

'You pick her up at nine on Saturday morning and I've booked the two of you in at a cheap and cheerful B&B somewhere unpronounceable, down in the Amman Valley, near where she's from. I thought perhaps a bit of mother-son bonding might help. She was absolutely thrilled at the idea. She's not been back to Wales for years. I hope that's all right?'

He sounded anxious again, not sure of Ted's reaction.

'That's kind, thank you for the thought. But I've got paperwork I want to go through, and I want to finish this book and look into what, if anything, I can do about this woman.'

'So do it in a different place. A change of scenery might help. Please do it, Ted. I think it might be good for you, and Annie was so pleased when I called her. She's really looking forward to spending some quality time with you. And you'll have all day tomorrow to sort out your paperwork.'

Ted was up at his usual time the following day, even though he was going nowhere. He consoled himself with the thought that at least he could dress as he pleased for a day of working from home, and for a weekend away. Now that he was resigned to the idea, he found himself quite looking forward to spending some time with his mother. She had been missing from his life for a long time and they were only just getting to know one another properly.

He wanted to give Mike Hallam a call, although he knew he shouldn't, and he thought it would be best to catch him at home, before he left for work.

'Mike, sorry to call you at all and especially at home. I expect you've been told I'm currently a pariah who's not to be spoken to,' Ted began, trying to keep it light-hearted.

'Are you all right, boss?' the sergeant's voice sounded genuinely concerned. 'Nobody's saying very much. The Ice … the Super said you were just taking a couple of days off. Trev told Sal it was personal stuff and Maurice said he's been told to saying nothing or the Super will have his knackers for a necklace.'

Ted had to laugh at the choice of expression, which sounded exactly like Maurice.

'I'm actually taking my mother away for the weekend, but there's more to it than that. I'll fill you in when I'm back on Monday.'

He mentally crossed his fingers, hoping he would be back with his team on Monday.

'This is asking a lot of you, and I don't want to compromise you in any way so I'll understand if you say no. But I'd really appreciate being kept in the loop if anything happens with this case while I'm away. Just a quick call or even a text. Not that I think you can't manage without me. I know you can. Just that, you know me, I like to be kept in the picture.'

'No worries at all, boss. I may have a chunk missing out of one ear but thanks to you, I still have an ear, which is attached to a head which is still on my shoulders,' Mike laughed. 'Have a good weekend, and we'll catch up on Monday.'

Ted rang off, hoping he was right. At least it was nice to be able to enjoy breakfast with Trev, for once. But after Trev had left for work, Ted was suddenly confronted with the prospect of a long day at home which he had not anticipated and was decidedly not looking forward to.

He started reading through the leaflets the therapist had given him, then, on an impulse, he took out his mobile phone, made a call and arranged a lunch date.

After a couple of hours of paperwork, he showered and dressed. He chose his relaxed chino suit and an open shirt, took the car and headed for a gastro-pub in Manchester. He had not been there for a few years and was, as ever, early for the meeting. He sat nursing his Gunner, looking around at his surroundings. They hadn't changed a great deal in the intervening years; they were just perhaps slightly more pretentious than he remembered.

When the man he had come to meet came in, Ted could see straight away that he had lost a lot of weight. Ted stood up and held out an awkward hand, but the other man put his hands on each of Ted's upper arms, lent forward and kissed him on the cheek. Even at that time of day, Ted could smell the alcohol on his breath, barely disguised by the scent of expensive aftershave. He noticed the tremor in the hands, too.

'Ted, it's lovely to see you again, after all this time,' the man said as he took a seat opposite Ted. 'How is that young man of yours? Tony, was it? Are you two still together?'

'Thanks for coming at short notice, Philip. It's Trevor, not Tony. And yes, we are very much still together. What about you? Are you with anyone?'

'Oh, one night stands are more my style since you, Ted. You broke my heart when you left me. I hope you realise that.'

He made the remark lightly but Ted could see the pain behind his eyes, and knew that he meant it. He'd always felt bad about the break-up. But as soon as he'd met Trev, he had hoped there would be a future there, although he was not optimistic, thinking that Trev was way out of his league. He had at least wanted to be free to find out.

'I assume this is more than a social call?' Philip continued, picking up the menu with a hand which shook badly. 'What can I do for you?'

As soon as they had ordered, Ted outlined his visit to the therapist and showed him the leaflets, particularly the parts offering a 'cure' for gay people, especially younger ones.

'Basically, it worries me that someone on my patch is doing stuff like this, potentially doing serious damage to vulnerable young people. I need to know if it breaks any laws, and if there's anything I can do about it.'

Ted noticed that Philip hardly ate anything once their food arrived. He was just picking at his fish, mostly ignoring the chips and salad which came with it. He was certainly a lot thinner than when they had been together.

'And you came to ask your former lover, a Crown Prosecutor for another division altogether, rather than talking to someone on your own patch, because …?' Philip asked shrewdly.

Ted grinned ruefully.

'Because I nearly lost it trying to talk to her myself and I'm currently under investigation by my Superintendent for possible misconduct.'

Philip reached across the table and put his hand on one of Ted's.

'I've missed that grin, Ted,' he said, and now there was an intense sadness behind his eyes. Then he withdrew his hand, seeming to shake himself, before pushing his plate away, barely touched. 'Leave it with me, let me see what I can find out. It's a new one on me, I'll need to look into it. Give me your phone number, I'll call you with my findings. Meeting up was a mistake, it just opens old wounds.'

Wordlessly, Ted took out one of his cards and handed it to him. Then Philip was gone. The encounter left Ted feeling subdued for the rest of the day, which just added to his anxiety over his fate. He decided that perhaps Trev's idea of going away was a good one, after all.

He filled his car up with fuel on the way home and carefully checked oil, water, windscreen washer and tyre pressures. The Renault was getting decidedly past its sell-by date so he tried to take care of it to the best of his limited mechanical ability. Any thoughts of replacing it would have to go on the back burner, now he'd taken out the loan to help Trev.

On an impulse, he drove to a store with a decent deli selection to pick up something for the evening meal, and added a bottle of good French wine for Trev. He assuaged his conscience when he found something suitable which was only a tenner for the lot. That wouldn't break the bank, nor stretch the loan any further.

'I know you're dying to get back to work, but I could get used to you being a house-husband and coming home to a meal on the table,' Trev smiled when Ted dished up the food and put the open wine bottle in front of him.

'I had lunch with Philip today,' Ted told him as he sat down.

'Philip?' Trev echoed. 'That's a blast from the past. You never said you were meeting him.'

'I didn't want to worry you.'

'Should I be worried?'

'No, of course not,' Ted said, putting a hand on his arm. 'It was business, nothing more.'

'Then I'm not worried. Go and have a fabulous couple of days with Annie, come back calm and collected, and I hope all goes well for you on Monday.'

Except that calm and collected was not at all how Ted arrived home on Sunday evening, much later than he had anticipated. After a pleasant time with his mother, visiting her old home area, the Renault had broken down in Welshpool, he'd had to call the AA to get it started again, and there'd been a long wait for a patrol.

'I didn't dare switch off again all the way home, not even when I dropped my mother off. I'll have to book a taxi for the morning. I doubt the car will start again and I'd rather not risk the bus at that time. I'll have to get the car into the garage sometime this week. It's due its MOT soon anyway.'

Trev folded him in a hug.

'It's going to be all right. All of it. The car will be fine, you'll be fine. Try not to worry. Get a good night's sleep and everything will be all right in the morning. You'll see.'

Chapter Eight

Ted was obsessively punctual. He always arrived early for any appointment, especially for anything as important as his Monday morning meeting with the Ice Queen. He booked a taxi for seven-thirty, allowing plenty of time for the barely eight minute drive from his home to the police station.

It all started to go pear-shaped when the taxi was late. After ten minutes, and several calls to the taxi office, Ted tried in desperation to start the Renault, which was having none of it, despite his best efforts.

The taxi finally arrived twenty minutes late, by which time Ted was furious and anxious in equal measure. It was still feasible to do it in the remaining time. Except, of course, as everything was conspiring against him that morning, whatever supreme being was in charge of such matters decreed that traffic would be backed up bumper to bumper practically the length of Hillgate.

Ted bottled out of calling the Ice Queen himself to say that he was running late. Instead he called the front desk, relieved to get the familiar tones of Bill on the other end of the phone. He asked him to inform Her Majesty that he was on his way, but stuck in heavy traffic. Luckily, Bill had already heard of a minor road accident in the area causing tailbacks, so he was able to convey the information to the Superintendent.

In the end, Ted's nerves couldn't take the confinement in the cab any longer. As they finally crawled towards Spring Gardens, he threw a note at the driver, asked him to unlock the

62

door, leapt out without waiting for his change, and sprinted for it. He would have bet that it was the biggest tip the driver would get that day, especially when he had arrived so late to pick up his fare and hadn't even come past the accident on his way, so didn't have that as an excuse.

Ted arrived, breathless and flustered, nearly half an hour late, at the Ice Queen's office, where he panted out his excuses, hoping she wouldn't leave him standing up this time. She waved aside his apologies and told him to take a seat. Ted was relieved to sit down, but more than a little concerned at how much his heart was racing. He was in peak physical form, with all the martial arts and hill walking he and Trev did together in every spare moment. He could only assume that it was the tension of the moment which was making his heart pound at such an alarming rate.

The Ice Queen studied him for a long moment. Ted was acutely aware that beads of sweat were rolling down the sides of his face and his shirt was sticking to him. His mouth was so dry he wasn't sure how he was going to be able to speak, when and if it was required of him.

'These are words which I never imagined myself saying, Inspector,' the Ice Queen began, her tone flat and formal. 'I have booked you on to an anger management course. It is this weekend, in Blackpool, and is residential. It begins on Friday afternoon and goes on until Sunday afternoon. It is not optional. You will attend all parts of the course, including the meals, which form part of the assessment process.

'In addition, you will write a letter of apology to Dr Cooper, and send the draft to me for approval before it goes out. You will then stay away from her. Completely. If, at a future stage, you continue to think she has anything to do with your current enquiries, or that she should form part of some other investigation, you will come and discuss it fully with me before you take any further action.

'Subject to your fulfilling these requirements, Dr Cooper

has agreed to let the matter drop, so there will be no need for me to refer it to Complaints. I will, of course, have to leave a report about it on your file, but I hope that will now be an end to the matter.'

'Ma'am,' Ted said tersely, feeling thoroughly ashamed of himself, but realising the outcome could have been so much worse.

'I spoke at length to DC Brown,' she continued, her voice thawing by a degree or two. 'I have to say, I do admire your ability to inspire such intense loyalty in your team members. He was utterly unshakeable in his account of what had happened, which differed significantly from that of Dr Cooper. It was largely that which led me to proceed no further. That and my knowledge and belief that this was an isolated incident in an otherwise unblemished career.

'So please let's have no more of such behaviour. Go back to your team, and I hope to have some news of progress from you shortly.'

Ted didn't dare say anything further. He was worried that his voice might be as wobbly as the rest of him was feeling as he stood up, so he simply nodded briefly and left the office. His legs were still rubbery as he climbed the stairs, much more slowly than usual.

All of his team members were already in and at their desks. They looked up expectantly when the door opened, then there were smiles all round as they saw their boss appear. Only Maurice knew exactly what had been happening, but the rest of them had sensed something serious was going on.

'Give me five minutes to brew up, then I'll be with you,' Ted told them, heading straight for his office.

Then, pausing, he turned and looked across the room. 'Oh, and Maurice? I owe you a pint.'

He hadn't managed any breakfast before he had left home that morning, feeling far too wound up to eat. Instead he'd brought a high-energy bar with him, which he fell on and devoured, suddenly feeling the ravenous hunger of relief from tension. He added an extra spoonful of honey to his green tea then went back out to the main office, thrilled to be back with his team.

'So, any progress? What's been happening?' he asked expectantly, as he perched on the edge of the nearest desk.

'Boss, I did some asking around at the weekend,' Sal began. 'I went to one of those vans that sells tea and burgers. I've noticed it's popular as a quick stop-off on the edge of town for delivery drivers. I found a couple of drivers who mentioned a man with a white Sprinter van they'd seen around a few times but didn't know much about. Nothing at all conclusive, but their descriptions roughly match our attacker, for age and height certainly. They both independently said he was a bit strange, aloof, didn't want to mix much when they tried to strike up conversation. It may be nothing, of course.'

'A Sprinter van, eh, Jezza? That's smaller than a lorry,' Rob said with a laugh.

'Yeah, but I know you men. You're always boasting it's bigger than it is,' she shot back at him.

Ted was just so pleased to be still leading his team he merely laughed along with the rest of them, before he said, 'Right, we need to track down this Sprinter van, see if it has anything at all to do with our case. Check with Traffic, see if they've had any incidents with a similar van. If it's even had a parking ticket on our patch, I want to know about it.

'Rob, talk to Folkestone and Dover, see if they've had any similar sightings. There's plenty of those vans about, but let's try to track this one down and rule it in or out of the enquiry. Do the sightings by these drivers coincide with the attacks on our patch, Sal?'

'One definitely does, boss. It was just after a big United match that everyone was talking about. One of the drivers tried to talk to Sprinter-man about the result, which was controversial. He said the man was very off with him.'

Ted shrugged.

'He may just not be into football. You all know by now it would be no use trying to talk to me about it, either. But let's check. If it is our man, a Sprinter van suggests deliveries of something. It would help us if we could pin down what they might be.'

'Could still be booze runs. Or cigarettes, coming over from France duty-free,' Mike Hallam said. 'You can certainly get a good few quid's worth of stuff in a van that size.'

'It could be people trafficking, too,' Jezza suggested. 'You'd certainly have to be some sick sort of individual to go in for that. And I hear that a lot of the people being smuggled get raped, and worse, on their journey. Maybe our man just gets so fired up with it all that he can't control himself?'

Ted groaned.

'I hope you're wrong, Jezza. Just when we thought this case was bad enough. If he really is involved in the filthy people trafficking trade as well, we desperately need to get him, and fast. But remember, let's not assume anything.'

True to his word, Ted took Maurice off for a pint at The Grapes at lunchtime. As well as thanking him over a drink, he wanted to give him a stern talking to for not telling the Ice Queen exactly what had happened, possibly putting himself in jeopardy at the same time.

'I stuck to the facts, boss,' Maurice assured him. 'You didn't go over the top. You were just being a good copper, trying to make sure no laws were being broken. She just touched a raw nerve with this gay stuff, you being the way you are.'

Ted had to laugh. Maurice had all the tact of a charging rhino and was about as politically incorrect as it was possible to be, but he was a sincere and kind-hearted man. He may not have been the sharpest knife in the drawer, but he was also a solid and steady presence. Some officers in Ted's position might have felt him too much of a plodder to bring much to the team. Ted, recognising his good qualities, was glad to have him.

'I appreciate it, Maurice. Just make sure you take care of yourself as well. Always.'

Ted had fired off a quick text to Trev as soon as he knew he still had a job and was more or less off the hook, but he was looking forward to seeing him that evening to tell him all about it. Trev was in the kitchen preparing supper when Ted got in, feeling tired but relieved that the day was over.

Trev greeted him with one of his famous hugs, but his face was anxious. Ted sat down at the table and filled him in on all of the Ice Queen's conditions, hoping to set his mind at rest.

'It means me abandoning you for another weekend on the trot, and I'm sorry about that. But I got off lightly, all things considering. I'm just glad it's all over.'

Trev sat down next to him and took hold of one of his hands between both of his.

'I'm glad, too. I know how worried you were. Now, I have something to tell you. But first, I want you to promise not to get angry with me.'

Ted was instantly on the alert. He didn't like the sound of this.

'I promise to try to stay calm, whatever it is,' he said guardedly.

'You know I told you Annie had the weekend off?' Trev asked, scanning his partner's face warily as he spoke. 'It was a bit of a white lie. She was on the rota, but I thought it would do the two of you good to go away together, so I phoned her boss and said she was off sick.

'Annie phoned me today, in a bit of a state. She's on a zero-hour contract – I didn't realise that – and she said they've taken her off the rota completely this week. She phoned her boss and was told they didn't know when they could give her any more hours. Now she's really worried about paying her bills.

'Ted, I'm really sorry, I thought I was doing a good thing but I've messed up completely and I don't know how to make it right.'

Wordlessly, Ted pulled his hand away, pushed his chair back, stood up and went out of the back door into the garden, shutting the door quietly behind him.

His silence worried Trev more than any words could have done. Absent-mindedly, he picked up the nearest cat and started to stroke it, standing up to watch out of the window as Ted strode about the garden. It was too dark to see his expression, but his whole body language screamed tension and barely suppressed anger.

It was several minutes before he came back in. Trev was still clutching the cat in front of himself, almost protectively. He noticed it was Queen, the most senior of their six cats.

Ted went over to him, gently took Queen from his arms, put her on the floor, then hugged Trev fiercely.

'I'm sorry. I reacted badly. I think the Ice Queen is right. I do need to learn some anger management. I was angry, for a moment. Now I've filed it under "wrong thing for the right reasons". I'll sort it. I'll phone her work in the morning, with my policeman's hat on, and thank them for giving her the time off to deal with a family crisis. That should do it.

'But please, promise me you'll run things past me first, when you have your next bright idea,' he added with an affectionate smile. 'What with the mortgage, the bank loan, and still paying for your bike, I couldn't afford to support my mother as well, if she did lose her job.'

Trev's relief was palpable as he hugged him back hard and kissed him. He hated being at odds with his partner.

'I really am sorry, Ted. I'm an idiot, I know. I take the piss something shocking with Geoff about the hours I work and it never occurs to me that other people can't do the same. I promise to try to be a grown-up from now on.'

Ted smiled indulgently and said, 'It's just as well I love you beyond reason.'

He was rewarded by seeing the way Trev's face lit up at his words, his intensely blue eyes sparkling. He didn't tell him anything like as often as he should do. He promised himself he would do better in the future.

Trev busied himself dishing up their supper then, as he sat down, said, 'What about Christmas? Do you want to invite your mother to have dinner with us?'

'I haven't really thought much about Christmas this year, with this case going on. Would you mind if I asked her?'

'Of course not. I really like Annie. It would be nice to see you two together for the festivities. Assuming you don't get called in to work, of course. Are you going to have your usual get-together for the team, and do you want me to bake for it?'

Ted's face clouded briefly. The previous Christmas had been a difficult one for him, with the loss of a valued member of his team. The memories were going to be hard to erase. But he owed it to the team to keep up the annual tradition. It was always a good morale boost.

'I suppose I should do. Yes, please. If I deprive the team of your mince pies, I might face a mutiny.'

'And are you going to invite the Ice Queen?'

He saw the face Ted pulled at the suggestion and added, 'You'll have to, for form's sake. You always had Jim Baker there. It would be too much of an obvious snub if you didn't invite your new senior officer. Besides, I'm dying to meet her, to see if she really is as glacial as you portray her. From the sound of it, she treated you reasonably fairly today. Perhaps I might get her to thaw out a bit more, over a plate of mince pies.'

Chapter Nine

Ted was anxious to sort something out with his car as soon as he could, preferably the next day. He was going to need transport for the weekend to get to Blackpool, for one thing. He was not looking forward to the course at all, viewing it as an ordeal to be endured.

It was not a police course. He might find himself the only copper there. He was dreading having to sit there and talk about himself to a roomful of strangers. Doubtless it would begin with the usual, 'I'm Ted, I'm a policeman and sometimes my job makes me angry.'

Then he thought that might sound as if he was trying to make excuses for himself and wondered how he could phrase it better.

'I get angry with some aspects of my job,' perhaps?

He shook himself to clear his head. He was over-analysing again. He knew it was a bad habit of his. It would probably be best just to turn up with no preconceptions. But first he needed reliable wheels to get him there at all.

He phoned his usual garage to come and collect the Renault to sort it out. They promised faithfully to be there for twelve-thirty, so Ted could slip away from work for half an hour. They were unusually late and arrived after one o'clock with barely an explanation, let alone an apology. It worried Ted how angry it made him feel. He never used to lose his temper so easily, not even with the most difficult cases he'd handled.

The man who collected it told Ted to call round before six

o'clock that evening and they would have an idea for him of what was wrong. They should also know by then what it was going to cost to put it right, and to get it through its MOT test.

When he got back to the station, he got straight on the phone to his mother's employers. Ted hated to use the police officer card but he didn't see what else he could do in the circumstances. He'd had a good time with his mother at the weekend. It had been nice to see some of the places from her childhood, many of which he'd heard her speak about but had never visited. It had certainly helped to take his mind off his own predicament.

He spoke to her line manager to thank her for allowing his mother time off at short notice because of a 'family crisis'. He wasn't sure he was entirely believed but he was pleased when, shortly afterwards, his mother phoned to say she'd been called into work to cover the hours of someone on sick leave. She also told him delightedly that she was back on the rota for the rest of the week. It was one small but successful result for him to chalk up and he felt badly in need of some success, no matter how minor.

Next he decided he'd better get the letter of apology to Dr Cooper written and sent to the Ice Queen for her approval. It would, at least, be one more thing to tick off his list, so that he could get back to some sort of normality. He kept the letter short, tried to make it sound sincere and emailed it to the Ice Queen. He felt like a schoolboy sending his homework to the headmistress. He wondered how many marks out of ten she would give him, or whether it would land him in detention.

Her response was swift and concise.

'Perfectly acceptable.'

Ted printed it out, then put it ready for the post that evening. He was just about to attack his paperwork mountain once more when there was a knock at his door and Mike Hallam came in.

'Have a seat, Mike. Do you want coffee? The kettle's just boiled.'

'Thanks, boss. Look, I don't want to pry or anything, I just wanted to make sure you were all right. After the weekend away and everything. Maurice clearly knows but he's saying nothing. It's probably none of my business …'

'I'm going to be away this weekend as well,' Ted told him with a conspiratorial grin, sitting down opposite him and taking a sip of his green tea. 'I've got to go on an anger management course.'

'You, boss? Bloody hell! But you're the most easy-going person I've ever worked with.'

Ted gave him the edited highlights of what had happened. He wasn't proud of himself. The more times he went over it, the more he was disappointed with his behaviour and particularly, his lack of self-control.

'I can see why you would find that hard to take. I think any of us might have reacted similarly. At least I hope we would. I'd like to think that if either of my kids told me they were gay, I'd handle it better than dragging them off to be brainwashed out of it. Is there anything we can do about the woman?' Mike asked.

'I'm under strict orders to drop it completely,' Ted said levelly.

Mike gave him a shrewd look.

'Which of course, you have done. Except …'

Ted smiled.

'You caught me out. I've asked a man who might know if there is anything about it which makes it a police matter. Thanks for your concern, Mike. I'm hoping to come back from the course all peace and light and Zen. Then perhaps we can finally get on with nailing this bastard for the sex attacks.

'In the meantime, I'm temporarily without wheels. My car broke down and is in the garage. I'm hoping to get it back tonight, but if not, it's buses and lifts for the moment. Unless I can scrounge a pool car, but I know they're in short supply and high demand.'

Ted's mobile rang, just as Mike was leaving the office. The number showed as Unknown. Ted answered with a guarded, 'Hello?'

'Hi, Ted, it's Philip. How are you, and how is young Tony?'

'Trevor,' Ted correctly automatically. He wasn't sure if Philip got the name wrong deliberately to try to annoy him or whether his mind was impaired by the amount of alcohol he clearly now consumed on a regular basis. He'd always enjoyed a drink when they'd been together, but from what Ted had seen of him on their recent meeting, it had clearly now gone way beyond that level.

'I've been looking into the little matter you brought to my attention. I've gone into it thoroughly, but at the moment, I can't see that it breaks any law that I'm aware of,' Philip began. 'There is still a possibility, of course, that professional standards of some sort may be being breached. I'm thinking particularly in relation to the ages of some of the people she sees.

'I would suggest, if you're determined to carry on with this, that you contact this woman's professional body and get their advice. I take it you've already looked into the various qualifications this doctor gives herself, to make sure they're genuine? If not, then there's your way forward.'

Ted surprised himself by swearing out loud because he should have done that first and foremost and he hadn't. He was not usually much of a swearer. When Philip gave a throaty chuckle and said, 'I always loved it when you talked dirty,' he fervently wished he hadn't. He was getting alarmed at yet more evidence of his current lack of self-control.

'Thanks, Philip, I really appreciate you taking the time to do this for me. I'm sorry to have troubled you with it and, well, you know, I'm sorry.'

He broke off awkwardly.

'Water under the bridge, Ted,' Philip replied, although there was the same sadness in his voice. 'I wish it wasn't so, but I accept that it is. You just enjoy your life with young Tony.'

'Trevor,' Ted sighed quietly, as the other man rang off.

Ted was in need of some cheering up after the call, so he headed down to find out if Kevin Turner was free to have his ear bent for a few minutes, under the guise of discussing the current joint enquiry.

'Anything your end, Kev?' Ted asked him as he took a seat.

'Sweet Fanny Adams,' he replied. 'We're still looking at every Sprinter van we see but nothing so far.'

'I want to try talking to the victims again, just to see if they've thought of any more details. I wondered if I could borrow Susan Heap to go with me? I've found her very good in tricky circumstances before. I asked Jezza but she doesn't think it's her sort of thing and I don't like pushing people into something they're not comfortable with.'

'I would have thought Jezza would frighten people, in the wrong mood,' Kevin laughed. 'She's certainly a feisty one. How's she settling into the team now?'

'She's fine. She gives as good as she gets. It's me that's on the short fuse at the moment,' he admitted, and proceeded to tell Kevin what had been going on. He watched his eyebrows climb steadily higher up his forehead at what he heard.

'Anger management issues? You, Ted? I would have thought the Dalai Lama would have needed that sort of help before you did. What's behind it all?'

Ted shook his head and sighed.

'I wish I knew. I think I'm losing it. Whatever it is.'

'Mid-life crisis?' Kevin asked. 'We've all been there. I'd offer to show you my tattoo, except it's somewhere a bit personal. The wife was furious. To make it even worse, I couldn't even remember getting it done, which shows you how drunk I must have been at the time! Pity you don't drink, you might find it would help.'

'I'll just have to get in a few more hours kicking people,' Ted smiled, referring to his martial arts. 'That usually helps. My car's off the road at the moment, too. I'm hoping to pick it up tonight.'

'Time you parted with that old relic, Ted, and got yourself something that doesn't need someone walking in front of it with a red flag. You'd be surprised at the development in cars these days. Some of them even have more than three gears,' Kevin mocked.

'You can scoff, but the seats are comfortable,' Ted retorted.

'Let me know if you need a lift anywhere in the meantime,' Kevin said more seriously. 'I can always try to find a car to pick you up, if necessary. At least, until the next round of cuts mean I'm reduced to sending officers out in response on bicycles.'

The news of Ted's car was far worse than he'd feared, and he had to take the bus home. When he got back and walked into the kitchen, Trev was preparing their meal.

'I didn't hear the car. Was it not ready?' he asked.

Ted slumped wearily down into a chair at the table, immediately assailed by cats vying for his attention and affection.

'They did manage to get it to start, eventually, but it then failed everything it needed to pass for the MOT test so spectacularly I think their pen ran out filling it all in,' he said glumly. 'When I asked them what it would cost to get it up to standard to pass, they just laughed at me.'

Trev gave him a sympathetic hug.

'So what are you going to do now?'

'I'm having to buy a replacement. I asked them what they had that was cheap and comfortable. They've got a little Renault for two grand, at one of their other branches. They're going to get it brought over and service it for me. I can pick it up tomorrow evening.'

'Another Renault? What model?' Trev asked, dishing up the meal.

'A black one. Runs on diesel,' Ted grinned.

He was about as interested in cars as he was in fashion.

Ted managed about three mouthfuls of his supper before his mobile phone rang. It was Bill, from the station.

'Sorry, Ted, but your man has finally done it, by the looks of things. Just getting reports of a fatality at a supermarket car park, a young woman in a car.'

'Shit,' Ted said, swallowing his mouthful and putting down his knife and fork. 'I've got no transport at the moment, so I'll call Mike Hallam in. He lives nearest to me and he can pick me up on the way. We'll go straight there.'

'There's more, too, I'm afraid,' Bill told him. 'Early reports say a witness has also been badly injured, but I don't have any more details for you at the moment.'

'Double shit. Give me the address and I'll get there as soon as. Is everyone else on the way that needs to be?'

'Got to go?' Trev asked, picking up Ted's plate and putting it in the oven to keep warm, as Ted got the details he needed.

'Sorry,' Ted said. 'Looks like our attacker has finally killed someone. I've no idea what time I'll be back. My supper might be frazzled by then.'

'D'you want me to make you a sandwich or something, to take with you?'

Ted gave a wry smile.

'The only good thing to come out of this shout is that, being at a twenty-four hour supermarket, I can always grab a sandwich if I get hungry. Don't wait up.'

With a parting kiss, he was already on his way out of the front door, on the phone to Mike Hallam, telling him he'd start out on foot and asking to be picked up on the way.

As he set off at a brisk walk, he next phoned Rob

O'Connell then Virgil Tibbs and asked them both to get there as soon as they could. He hadn't gone far before Mike's car purred up alongside him. Ted opened the door and got in beside his sergeant.

'I don't have many details yet, just a fatality on the car park, and a witness injured. We'll know more when we get down there. Thanks for picking me up, Mike. My car is also a fatality. I'm hopefully getting another tomorrow.'

'Well, that's good boss. What are you getting?'

'It's black and it runs on diesel,' Ted told him. 'I'm about as knowledgeable on cars as I am on computers. As long as it starts, it will be an improvement on the old one.'

There was a police car with flashing blue lights at the main entrance to the supermarket car park, one officer diverting traffic away, another rolling out the blue and white tape to cordon it off. Ted had his warrant card in his hand as he opened the window, although everyone in the station knew him by sight and he knew most of them by name.

'Evening. Any update?' Ted asked.

'Evening, sir. All I know at the moment is one fatality, one injured, possibly seriously. Fire crew and ambulance are still on the scene dealing with that one.'

As they drove on, Ted felt in his coat pocket for the familiar comfort of his Fisherman's Friend lozenges. They usually got him through dealing with fatalities and the post-mortem examinations which followed them. He slid one out and put it into his mouth as a precaution. He didn't bother offering one to Mike, knowing he didn't share his taste for the menthol sweets.

'Over there,' Ted said, rather redundantly, as Mike drove over to where they could see a fire appliance, an ambulance and another police car. They could see, too, that the scientific team had arrived and were setting up.

Ted and Mike got out and went first to the car. There was a young woman, still in the driving seat, but clearly dead. The car seemed to have pulled out of its parking place straight into a line of trolleys being wheeled back towards their shelter.

Ted made himself known to the senior fire officer on duty, whose men were working to free someone who appeared to be trapped between the car, the trolleys and the parked cars in the opposite row.

'Person trapped works here. He was collecting trolleys. Eye witnesses are saying he seemed to have realised somehow that the woman in the car was in some sort of danger and was trying to manoeuvre the trolleys to stop her from driving away, for whatever reason. There was a man in the passenger seat but he jumped out and ran off. A doctor came with the ambulance crew. She said the woman driver was dead. That's as much as I can tell you for now.'

The doctor had clearly heard herself referred to and came over, introducing herself and shaking Ted's outstretched hand.

'I'm afraid the driver was already dead when we got here. From the look of it, not as a result of the collision. From the quantity of blood, and its location, I'm imagining she was stabbed or possibly shot. I suppose that as she died, the car shot forward when her foot came off the clutch. Once I'd verified that she was dead, I turned my attention to the store employee who is seriously injured, but we've hopefully stabilised him. The fire crew are just working to free him.'

A staid, large estate car was just arriving and parking close by. The senior pathologist got out and headed over to them. Professor Elizabeth 'Bizzie' Nelson had not been long in the post but she and Ted had already become friends. In public, they were always professionally formal.

'Good evening, Inspector, what do you have for me?'

Ted took her to the car and showed her, leaving her to make her initial findings on the victim. Rob O'Connell and Virgil Tibbs arrived just as the fire crew freed the injured person from behind the trolleys, and the paramedics were transferring him to the ambulance.

Virgil glanced at the casualty as he went past and said, 'That's Nat, our witness from the Sorrento case. I hope he's going to pull through, he looks bad.'

Chapter Ten

Ted took control of the crime scene, put his team members on to gathering valuable witness names, then called the Ice Queen on her mobile to update her.

'I'll see what extra officers I can summon up for you. I'm presuming dog teams would be helpful, if your man has not long left the scene?'

'I'll take anything you can get us, ma'am. I also need Traffic to be on the look-out for white Sprinter vans in and around the area, just in case that is our man and he's trying to leave the location.'

'Leave that to me. I think I can call in some favours from Traffic,' she said dryly. She was married to a Traffic inspector. 'How is the injured witness?'

'No further details at the moment. He's being transferred to hospital. He didn't look good, from what I saw of him, but I don't know anything concrete. Professor Nelson is here, she'll let me know her preliminary findings shortly. At first glance it does look like death was due to a knife injury. The woman driver had already been dead too long for any resuscitation attempt by the time the ambulance got here.'

Ted went in search of the supermarket duty manager who was hovering about, looking green at the gills. Whatever his training had prepared him for, a murder in his car park was not part of it.

Ted approached him with his warrant card in his hand.

'I'm Detective Inspector Darling, I'm taking charge of this

enquiry, Mr …?'

'Er, Dixon, Dave Dixon,' the man wiped a clammy hand on his trousers before offering it to be shaken. 'I'm trying to get hold of someone from head office. I'm not sure what I'm meant to do. Should I close the store?'

'The main thing at the moment is to prevent panic, Mr Dixon. We can't let any more vehicles into the car park just at the moment, until we've secured the crime scene. We'll also be checking each car that's leaving, as we have a possible armed suspect to find. Other than that, you should try just to let people finish off their shopping and go home quietly.'

'Armed?' the man asked in alarm. 'You mean someone with a gun?'

He was looking wildly about him, as if he expected to be a target at any moment.

'We don't think that firearms are involved, so please try not to panic. Can you begin by giving me details of the employee who has been injured?'

'That's a terrible business. Is he going to be all right?'

'I don't have any further details at the moment, Mr Dixon. Can you give me his name, please?'

'It's Nat, Nathan. I can't remember his surname. I'm sorry. This has really shaken me up a bit. I've never encountered anything like this before.'

'Why don't you go and check your files, then you can give me all the information? We're going to need it. And, Mr Dixon? It's cold out here and the officers will have to be outside for some time, talking to witnesses. Perhaps a member of your staff might be able to bring them some coffee? Maybe a few biscuits? That would be very welcome.'

It was as much to give the man something to keep him busy as anything else. Ted could see he was in danger of losing it. He would be much better kept occupied.

'Yes, yes, of course. I'm sorry, I should have thought of that. I'll get on to it straight away.'

It was not long before a police dog van arrived. The Ice Queen had been true to her word. Ted was always a little wary around big dogs. Not being all that tall himself, the German and Belgian Shepherds the police mostly used looked huge to him and always seemed to sense his nervousness. He knew they were highly trained and perfectly safe, but the one that leapt out of the van now and came up to sniff at him seemed enormous.

'Evening, guv, what have you got for us?' the handler asked him.

'I don't know if you can help us. We've nothing belonging to the suspect, but he was briefly sitting in the passenger seat of the car and he legged it when the crash happened.'

'Don't worry, if there's any trace at all, Diesel will find it. He's the best. Aren't you, boy? Now come on, leave this nice inspector alone and let's get to work.'

The dog seemed to Ted to give him a scornful look. He half expected it to cock its leg and pee on his trousers. But it moved obediently away, started sniffing in the car then, with a small yelp of excitement, put its nose down and set off across the car park, the handler jogging in its wake.

Ted turned and walked back to the car, where Professor Nelson was just finishing up.

'So very sad, Edwin,' she said.

She was the only person who called Ted by his full name, except for Trev, on occasion, in a joking way. She only did it out of earshot of other officers.

'She looks young, no more than mid-twenties, I would say. We've finished with her, so she can be taken away whenever you like now.

'From what I've seen so far, it looks like a single stab wound from the left hand side, but of course, I'll know more when I do the post-mortem. I'm assuming you want something as soon as possible? If so, I could fit your lady in first thing in the morning? We're fairly quiet, and I could reshuffle my list.'

'Thanks, Bizzie, that would help. We're no doubt going to have to call another press conference on this, another plea for the public's help. So the more information you can give me, the better. What time?'

'You know me, I don't need much sleep so I'll be in early to start off. What about if you joined me somewhere around seven? Would that be all right for you?'

She'd taken her gloves off, and she shook Ted's hand as she spoke.

'I appreciate it, Bizzie, I'll see you then.' Ted was equally informal when there was no one close enough to hear.

As she walked off back to her car, Ted realised he had no transport for the morning. He'd just have to get up a bit earlier and walk down, then take a bus from the hospital to the station. He hoped the garage would have his replacement car ready for the evening. He needed to be independently mobile.

Two young women in the supermarket's uniform had appeared with trays of drinks and plates of biscuits. Their eyes were out on stalks as they moved round the car park handing them out to the police officers and to the Scene of Crime Investigators who were still there. It was just as well screening had gone up swiftly round the car. Ted wouldn't have wanted them catching sight of the young woman's body which was still awaiting collection. The coffee was not bad and brought welcome warmth. It was decidedly cold and damp to be working outside.

The dog handler arrived back before long and came over to find Ted, the dog once more sniffing round his legs. Ted hoped it was the inevitable smell of cats on his clothing which was capturing the big brute's interest, and that it wasn't eyeing up his leg for a snack.

'I think your man either had an accomplice who picked him up, guv, or he jumped on a bus. Diesel lost interest down by the main road, and there was a bus stop there.'

'Which service? What number buses stop there?' Ted asked.

'Didn't look, guv, not our remit,' the handler replied, off-handedly.

'Well, can you get back there and check?' Ted asked impatiently. 'It would be valuable information for us.'

The man shook his head firmly.

'No can do, guv. Diesel's got another shout. A missing kiddy on the other side of town and that takes priority. Sorry. Here's my card. Get one of your team to call me in the morning and I'll give them a detailed report of where we searched. But for now, your man's had it away on his toes, for sure. 'Night, guv,' he said, as he and the dog headed off back to the van.

Ted resisted the impulse to kick the tyres of the nearest vehicle. It was alarming how angry he kept getting, with each frustration he encountered.

It was getting late before Ted could stand most of the team down. They had initial witness statements from anyone who had seen anything, and contact details of others to follow up further the next day.

A couple of Sprinter vans had been stopped and searched in the area, with no results. He'd asked for two officers from Uniform to stay at the scene. With the supermarket usually open twenty-four hours, he didn't want people turning up and disturbing a crime scene. The manager had finally heard from his head office and been told to close the store exceptionally until morning, with notices posted to explain that there had been an incident.

There was no sign of Trev or the cats when Mike dropped a weary Ted off at his home. His supper was sitting on the table with a note: 'I rescued it from frazzling. Just whiz it in the micro if you want it hotting up,' followed by a row of kisses, which made him smile. He was too tired to eat, though. The events of the evening had rather taken away his appetite.

He took a quick shower to thaw himself out. The cold and damp seemed to have got into his bones and he felt chilled through. Then he went into the bedroom, lifted the duvet, picked up Trev's arm, which was draped across his side, and slid in as quietly as he could, so as not to disturb him.

Trev stirred and said sleepily, 'All you all right? Did you eat?'

'Too tired to be hungry. Go back to sleep. I'll have to leave early, I've got a post-mortem to go to.'

Trev lifted his head off the pillow. 'How will you get there? Do you want me to get up and take you on the bike?'

Ted smiled to himself in the darkness.

'I'd have more chance of waking the corpses in the morgue than getting you up early. But thanks for the offer. Now go back to sleep.'

It didn't seem long before an irritating and insistent muted buzzing from his mobile phone told him it was time to get up if he was going to get to the hospital on time for the post-mortem. He'd left himself enough time to eat a bowl of muesli and some wholemeal toast. He was hungry, aware of how erratic his eating habits were becoming. He wondered if that might, in part, explain his frequent irritability.

Ted found it quite pleasant, walking through the quiet, pre-dawn streets. Traffic was light and there were few people around at that time, until he got nearer to the hospital. That always seemed to be busy, like a mini town in its own right, with constant comings and goings.

Bizzie and her assistant were already well under way when Ted arrived, reaching in his pocket for a Fisherman's Friend, as he always did when entering the autopsy suite. He found post-mortems one of the worst parts of his job, somehow even worse than looking at bodies at crime scenes. It was all so impersonal, although Bizzie's brisk but respectful attitude always helped.

'Good morning, Edwin,' she greeted him breezily. 'As you can see, we have made a start. In fact, I'm very nearly finished. What I can tell you so far is that this poor young lady died from a single stab wound to the left side of the thorax, as I initially thought. The blade passed between two ribs and punctured her heart. The consoling factor is that she would have known very little about it. It would have been very quick.

'It's a long and narrow blade, double-edged, fairly fearsome. Seven inches long at least, going on the measurements I took of the wound, and I think, probably, handled with a certain degree of skill and accuracy.'

'Thanks, Bizzie. A seven-inch blade, definitely, if it's what I think it is. We're presuming this is the same man who has carried out the previous sex attacks, and two of the victims of those have mentioned a stiletto knife with a black blade. It's easy enough to pick up combat knives online these days, but to use one efficiently requires skill and practice. Our man has no previous convictions, not in this country, certainly, so I'm thinking he may be forces trained.'

'Which, I imagine, is worrying news for you? Presumably, her dying at the wheel is what caused the vehicle to shoot forward and cause the accident to the witness? How is he, have you heard?'

'I'll try to find out before I head back to the station, although doubtless I'll come up against the usual confidentiality barriers, despite him being a key witness in a murder case I'm investigating,' Ted sighed.

'Oh, I can help you with that,' the Professor offered. 'I'm just about done here, so I'm sure James won't mind finishing up for me. Come to the little cubby hole I affectionately call an office and I'll make some phone calls for you. They always tell me anything I ask. I use the excuse of needing to know who's heading down my way,' she laughed. 'I can even offer you some halfway decent coffee from my flask. I've given up risking the filth which comes out of the vending machine, outside canteen hours, unless I run out of my own.'

Bizzie was able to get all the information that Ted needed in a fraction of the time it would have taken him to cut through the red tape. Their witness, Nathan Cowley, had a fractured pelvis and thigh and had been operated on for internal bleeding, but was now stable and should make a good recovery, in time.

Ted was able to pass the information on to the team as soon as he got back to the station. Virgil, in particular, was relieved to hear that the man was going to be all right. He had spoken to him a few times in connection with the earlier Sorrento case in which he had been a witness, and had formed something of a bond with him.

'We now have a name for our victim, from the contents of her handbag, and she has been identified by her next of kin. Uniform notified them last night so we were able to get a swift ID and Professor Nelson was able to do the post-mortem first thing. Her name was Maureen O'Hara, aged twenty-four.' Ted wrote the name up on the white board, along with those of the rape victims.

'Like the film star,' Jezza observed, half to herself. No doubt another Trivial Pursuit answer she had memorised.

'Right, tasks for today. Mike, can you coordinate chasing up full statements from all the witnesses from last night, the shoppers using the car park, including those we didn't see. Track them through their car details. Virgil, you and I will go and see Nathan this afternoon, get his statement. I'll phone the hospital to check he's up to visitors, before we go.

'Steve, here's the number for the dog handler from last night. Get full details from him of where exactly the dog took him. Apparently it stopped searching near a bus stop. We need to know what services use that stop, and what buses had been there just before he got there. He'll give you timings. Again, it might not help. Our man might just have hopped off at the next stop, but we need to check everything, and I do mean everything.

'Jezza, you can talk to the staff at the supermarket. Start with the manager. It'll probably be someone different to the one on duty last night. I hope he's got some time off, he wasn't coping very well. Ask if anyone had seen anything, not just last night, but before then. Anyone hanging around, either in store or outside. You know the sort of thing. Anything. Is there any CCTV footage covering the car park? If so, we need to see it. Make sure it doesn't get recorded over before we do.

'Rob, Sprinter vans. Traffic didn't report anything which helped with our enquiry last night. Where could he have parked it, near to the supermarket? It wasn't on the car park, so if there was a Sprinter, and if it was connected to our case, where was it, and did anyone see it?

'Oh, and Steve, ask the dog handler how he got on with the missing child last night. It might not have been on our patch, but I don't like hearing about children being missing. I'd like to know there was a good outcome on that case, at least.'

Chapter Eleven

Ted wanted to try to visit Nathan Cowley in hospital later that afternoon, then he could get Virgil to drop him off at the garage afterwards. He was hoping his new car would be ready, so he could go straight to the judo club and meet Trev there. Trev would walk down, taking Ted's kit with him once again. Ted would be glad of a martial arts work-out to ease some of the tensions of the last few hours.

It was the one day of the week he always tried to get away at a good time, with the knowledge and support of the Ice Queen. The self-defence club for children which he and Trev ran voluntarily was having great success at reducing bullying in local schools. It was also an excellent public relations exercise, so she was completely in favour.

Ted and Virgil found their witness in a small side bay off a busy ward. Ted had asked to be able to visit him and had been told they could have some time with him but were not to tire him. The man was dozing when they were shown in, his face pale against the pillows, but he opened his eyes when the nurse told him he had visitors. He managed a wan smile when he saw Virgil.

'Mr Tibbs. It's nice to see you again.'

'Hello, Nat. This is my boss, Detective Inspector Darling,' Virgil told him. 'How are you feeling? You've certainly been in the wars.'

'There are a few bits of me which don't hurt, I think. I just haven't identified them yet. Are you going to sit down?'

Virgil found a second chair nearby and pulled it closer, as Ted sat in the one next to the bed.

'Is the young woman all right? The one in the car?' Nat asked anxiously. 'I keep asking, but no one will tell me what happened to her. I could see she was frightened, in some sort of danger. I tried to do something, but I'm not sure if I helped or made things worse.'

Virgil and Ted exchanged a look then Ted said, speaking quietly, 'I'm sorry to have to tell you that the young woman in question was killed in the incident.'

Nat looked stricken. Tears sprang to his eyes and started to trickle down the sides of his face onto his pillow.

'Was it my fault? Did I do the wrong thing? Did I make it worse? Oh God, I'm so, so sorry …

Ted always had a clean, neatly ironed handkerchief in his pocket, thanks to Trev. He took it out and passed it to the man in the bed. Nat tried to get hold of it, but it was clearly painful to try to lift his arms and his hand was shaking badly. Gently, Ted stood up and helped him to dry his tears.

'I'm so sorry. God, look at me, blubbing like a soft thing. I think I'm in shock. Christ, this is embarrassing,' he made a visible effort to regain control, then said again,'Was it my fault?'

'We haven't yet completed our enquiries into the incident,' Ted said guardedly. 'I can tell you that at this stage, we have no reason to believe that your actions had any effect on the tragic outcome. Are you able to tell us anything about what happened? Can you remember much?'

'It all happened so quickly. I was just taking a load of trolleys back to the trolley bay. I happened to notice the car, almost opposite where I was going. I saw a young woman get into the car, then I saw a man get in from the passenger side, very quickly. I could see straight away from her reaction that she was frightened when he got in. I've been keeping an eye out for anything out of the ordinary, after Mr Tibbs here told me about the attacks.

'I think she was shouting or screaming. I could see her mouth was open wide. I thought perhaps if I pushed the trolleys a bit nearer, I could stop her from driving off, at least until I could check if she was all right, and she knew the man. It could have been some sort of domestic, but it didn't look that way, from a quick glance.

'The car was facing out of the parking space. I could see that it would have to come out forwards as there was a vehicle behind it. I heard the engine start, I think, then suddenly it shot forwards. I'm not really sure what happened next. I just remember pain and confusion, then I was trapped up against some cars and I think I lost consciousness at that point.'

'Did you see the man clearly? Could you describe him at all? Anything you noticed about him could be helpful to us.'

Nat was looking tearful again, clearly shaken up.

'It was all so confusing. I noticed he had a hat on, like a fleece ski hat, that sort of thing. Dark. Dark clothing. I just saw the look on the young woman's face and she looked terrified, so I tried to do something. I made it worse, didn't I?'

The same nurse reappeared at that moment, looking disapproving.

'You really do need to leave now, gentlemen. Mr Cowley is clearly getting distressed, which won't help his recovery. Come back in a day or two, when he's a little stronger.'

Ted and Virgil stood up.

'Thank you for your help, Mr Cowley, and please try not to worry,' Ted told him.

As they turned to leave, Nat suddenly let out a distraught wail and said, 'Oh, God, the fish. What am I going to do about the fish?'

They turned back and looked at him. The nurse was looking from one to another, clearly not sure what he was talking about.

'The fish?' Ted queried.

Light suddenly dawned on Virgil's face, as he remembered a previous conversation he'd had with the man, some time ago.

'The tropical fish? In your friend's flat, where you've been staying? There's no one to look after them if you're stuck in here, is that it?'

Nat was nodding, tears once again running down his face.

'I'm so sorry, I've no idea why I'm being so feeble. Just what will happen to the fish?'

The nurse was busy checking his vital signs and making him comfortable.

'You're in shock and full of pain killers, so it's quite normal to feel a bit weepy,' she told him. 'You officers really do need to leave him to rest now.'

'Why don't you give me your address and your house keys and I can pop round and sort the fish out, if you tell me what to do,' Virgil suggested. 'I don't know anything about them, so you'll have to make it simple.'

'There's a full list of instructions next to the tank, and it doesn't take long. My friend left them there when he lent me the flat while he's away. You'd really do that for me? I'd really appreciate it. Thank you so much.'

The nurse found his keys for him and Virgil noted his address, then said, 'I'll come back tomorrow and let you know how I got on. Don't worry, I'm sure I can sort it. Then we can chat a bit more when I come again.'

'That was kind, Virgil,' Ted told him, as they crossed the car park. 'Above and beyond the call of duty.'

'Yeah, well, I like him boss, he's a nice bloke and he's been through so much. Do you think it was down to him that the woman got stabbed, though? Did it make our man panic?'

'I'm not sure what's motivating our attacker at the moment. If it was just panic, why not just run off? He had no real need to stab her. He's not doing it to protect his identity, either, as he's shown himself to all his victims so far. He may just be so hyped up that he has no control over himself.'

'Drugs?' Virgil suggested.

'It could be anything, including an abnormally high sex drive. We'll only know when we finally get our hands on him, and I hope that's going to be very soon. Especially now he's shown us what he's really capable of.'

They reached Virgil's black BMW and got in.

'So what car are you getting, boss?' Virgil asked him as he started his up and headed for the exit.

'I haven't seen it yet. I just know it's black and it's a Renault. Cars are not something that interest me much, it's just a way of getting around.'

'Not a new one, though?'

'No, I've just invested in a business opportunity, so a new one's out of the question at the moment.'

'Sorry, boss, I didn't mean to pry,' Virgil said hastily.

'It's fine, I didn't take it that way at all.'

'Do you want me to wait to make sure it's ready for you?' Virgil asked, as they pulled up on the forecourt of Ted's garage.

'There's no need, Virgil, but thanks. You best get round to see to those fish. Thanks for the lift, and I'll see you in the morning. If my new one's not ready, I'll get them to give me a courtesy car until it is.'

There was a small, shiny, black Renault Clio sitting waiting on the forecourt. A man came out with the keys and documents, which he handed to Ted.

'Here you go, Inspector, she's all yours. Fully serviced and valeted, half a tank of fuel and all ready to go. She'll do you well.'

It was the first time Ted had seen his new purchase. He wasn't going to bother making even a pretence of looking over it. The garage knew him well enough by now to know he knew next to nothing about cars. But he was a good customer, so he trusted them not to take advantage of his ignorance. Of course, the fact that they knew he was a policemen helped a lot.

The little car was certainly clean and it started straight

away, which was an improvement on his old one. Now he was in it and could see how compact it was, he hoped there would be enough room in the front for Trev's long legs, even with the seat pushed back as far as it would go. It was just as well they both preferred Trev's motorbike for longer journeys.

At least it would mean he was mobile for the weekend, to attend the anger management course in Blackpool. Encouraged by Trev, he was trying to keep an open mind and a positive attitude, but he really was dreading it. The more he read the agenda, the more his frustration levels rose.

'How to manage stress'.

Perhaps he could politely ask their latest target to stop abducting and raping young women. Appeal to his better nature. Or maybe he should make a television appeal to him to give himself up. That should work, he thought ironically.

'Learning not to take everything personally'.

The trouble was, Ted always did. He knew it was both a strength and a weakness. It gave him focus to solve crimes but at the same time, he felt deeply and on a personal level about every crime which happened, on his patch in particular. He was still not fully over the loss of a team member last Christmas.

'Appropriate ways to express your anger'.

That one made Ted laugh. He had always thought his martial arts gave him the right outlet for his and also helped with his self-control. He wasn't sure how far he might have gone, confronted with Dr Cooper, and that uncertainty worried him. He was glad Maurice had been there so he hadn't had to find out.

He was still seething at the thought of what she was inflicting on already vulnerable young people who might be struggling to deal with their sexuality. He had been lucky. His own father had simply accepted it when Ted told him, at a young age, that he was gay. Trevor's parents had reacted by throwing him out and cutting off all contact with him.

He still hadn't done a background check on the therapist, as

Philip had suggested. He made a mental note to do that the following week. He just hoped their attacker would lie low for the weekend while he was away, as the Ice Queen's instructions had been unequivocal. Whatever happened on his patch during the three days of the course, he was to stay in Blackpool, finish it, and get the required certificate to show that he had attended and fully participated.

The junior session was just getting started by the time Ted arrived and got changed. He loved working with the youngsters, hoping their self-defence training would not only protect them but make them better people. With luck, they wouldn't grow up to have anger issues, as the strict discipline of the dojo was teaching them how to keep control. He just wished it was currently working better for him.

Once the juniors had finished, he could at last burn off some energy and frustration with his own judo training session. He and Trev had first met at the judo club, when Ted had coached his future partner. Sometimes their sparring got a bit exciting, but there was always head coach, Bernard, to keep a lid on things.

Both Ted and Trev were breathing hard and sweating when they'd finished. They headed for the car so they could get home, shower and change and get something to eat. Ted was ravenous. Once again he couldn't remember if he'd eaten anything all day. It was getting to be a bad habit, which was certainly not helping.

'Well, this is cute,' Trev laughed, sliding his long frame into the front passenger seat. 'And dinky. At least it shouldn't be a target for car thieves or joy riders.'

'You can mock,' Ted retorted, 'it's all we can afford at the moment.'

Trev leaned across and kissed his cheek.

'I know, and I will never forget what you're doing for me. Oh, and I've got company for the weekend, while you're away.

I've got a hot date with a beautiful woman.'

'Willow?' Ted guessed, correctly.

Willow was a close friend of both of them, especially Trev, and they often spent time together. She was a model, now married to another model. He and Trev had been invited to their wedding but Ted's job, as ever, had prevented him from being there for most of it.

'Yes, Rupert's away on a shoot and she's at a loose end, so I invited her to come and stay. She has all sorts of fun planned for us. We're going to play badminton, going swimming, and she has a friend who's lending us a couple of young eventers so we can go riding.'

'I'm glad one of us is going to be having fun. The more I read the agenda for this course, the more I think I would even prefer to come riding with you, and you know my total lack of success with horses. You take care, with those wild animals. And promise me you won't tell Willow what sort of course it is I'm going on. I'm not exactly proud of myself.'

'Of course not!'

Trev laid a reassuring hand on Ted's arm as he drove, then leaned further back in his seat, casting critical eyes over his lithe form.

'I just hope I can still get into my breeches. It's ages since I wore them.'

Ted glanced at him fondly.

'You, put weight on? That'll be the day.'

Trev gave him a suggestive look, moved his hand to his thigh and said, 'Just in case, perhaps I better make an effort to burn off a load more calories when we get home?'

'Behave yourself,' Ted told him, trying and failing to sound stern. 'I've only just bought this car. I don't want to crash it already because you're distracting me,' although Trev noticed he did speed up a bit, without exceeding the speed limit.

Chapter Twelve

Ted somehow managed to survive the weekend and gain his certificate of participation in the course, which he could wave at the Ice Queen when he got back to work. It would have to stay on his file to show he had complied with the requirements of her investigation of the complaint. It was one certificate he was not proud of, because of the necessity to obtain it.

He arrived home late afternoon on the Sunday to find Trev and Willow blissfully splattered in mud from an exciting ride, sharing mugs of tea and slices of cake in the kitchen, still in their breeches. He gave both of them a hug and a kiss, made some tea for himself and sat down to join them, although most of their conversation went over his head.

He was pleased to see his partner having such a good time. Their backgrounds were completely different. Trev had grown up doing things that had never been, nor ever would be, on Ted's spectrum. Although Ted asked Willow to stay on for a meal, and to stay another night if she wanted to, she tactfully departed and left the two of them to catch up.

Apart from a brief nod and a 'Very good,' the Ice Queen made no further comment on Ted's course when he presented her with the certificate the following morning. They both hoped they could safely put the matter behind them and move forward.

The team had nothing new to report on the case, and were dealing efficiently with a couple of incidents from the weekend. Ted felt partially redundant, although aware that it meant his team members were good at their job and doing it well. In a strange way, he was pleased that their attacker had not resurfaced. He fervently hoped that he would be the one to collar him, when they finally got a breakthrough.

He spent the day catching up on witness statements from the various ongoing cases. He didn't make much headway on his routine paperwork, so he decided to take a stack of it home with him and see if he could make any inroads on it there. Trev was going to be home a bit later than usual as he was going round to see a friend who lived locally, helping to fix a motorbike. Ted hoped to be able to concentrate on his work, with no disturbances.

He had paperwork piled all over the kitchen table when he got home. So that he could work in peace, he had shut the six disgruntled cats in the sitting room. He didn't really need their help with a difficult case.

He was surprised when the doorbell rang. He wasn't expecting anyone, and they seldom had anybody drop in unannounced, especially in the evening. He just hoped it wasn't Jehovah's Witnesses. He wasn't sure if his newly-acquired anger management skills were up to being interrupted by them.

'Well, you're obviously not Trevor,' a somewhat disdainful voice greeted him when he opened the door.

Although he'd never met her, he recognised the unexpected visitor immediately by the rebellious, glossy black curls and the piercing blue eyes. Not unusually, she was taller than Ted. He knew she was only fourteen but she could easily have passed for closer to twenty.

He stood aside as he said, 'Come in, Siobhan. Is Trev expecting you? He's at a friend's at the moment, bonding over motorbikes.'

Trevor's sister stalked into the hallway and in response to Ted's nod, headed towards the kitchen at the back of the house.

'I thought I'd surprise him,' she said loftily, as they reached the kitchen. She looked round, appraisingly, then pronounced, 'Quaint.'

'Do your parents know you're here?' Ted asked her, shuffling papers out of the way and pulling a chair from under the table for her to sit on.

'The Olds are abroad, as usual,' she said with a shrug. 'I'm at boarding school, in Somerset.'

'And do the school know where you are?' Ted persisted.

Again, the arrogant shrug.

'I'm on an exeat, it's cool.'

Ted leaned against the sink, his arms folded, studying her.

'The thing about being a copper, which I am, Siobhan, is that you develop a sixth sense for when someone is lying to you. Like you are now, to me. Give me the number of someone in authority at the school and I'll contact them, let them know you're safe and will be going back tomorrow. Do you want something to drink, in the meantime?'

She peered at his partly-drunk mug on the table and asked, ' What are you having?'

'Green tea, but I'm not sure you'd like it.'

She arched an eyebrow at him. It was a gesture disconcertingly like one of the Ice Queen's.

'Are you always this patronising? And policeman-like? What does Trevor see in you?'

Despite himself, Ted threw his head back and laughed at her directness.

'Probably, and I have no idea,' he replied. 'I'll put the kettle on. Now give me that number, then after that, I'll call Trev and let him know he has a visitor.'

Ted was not surprised to learn from the school that unauthorised absence was not unusual for Siobhan. He used his police credentials to smooth feathers and assure the house parent he spoke to that she would be escorted back there the following day. Then he called Trev and simply asked if he could come back earlier than planned as he had a visitor.

When Trev asked who it was, Siobhan suddenly looked as young as she really was and mouthed to Ted, 'Please don't tell him, I want it to be a surprise.'

'It'll certainly be a surprise for him,' Ted said as he rang off. 'I think a visit from a younger sister he's never met before is the last thing he'll be expecting. How did you find out the address?'

'Pa can find out anything he wants to. He knows lots of Spooks. I saw the address in Her Ladyship's desk. I assume she'd been in touch about the heart condition.'

Her father was a top diplomat, with a knighthood. Trev had found out recently that his parents had had a daughter after they had thrown him out. His mother had come to see him, out of the blue, because his father had suffered a heart attack because of a condition which could be hereditary.

'What's he like, my big brother? I've never even seen a photo of him. I only knew I had one because Nanny would sometimes mention him after she'd had a bit too much port.'

'You look almost exactly like him,' Ted told her.

She also had the same poise and self-assurance. He could tell that her clothes were expensive. Her look was casually pulled together Boho that clearly cost a fortune. He dreaded to imagine the price tag of the long, soft, leather boots or the coordinating handbag. The cloud of pricey perfume which hovered about her reminded Ted of one which Jezza sometimes wore. Siobhan had clearly planned to stay over as she had a weekend holdall, which was also leather, looked costly and was stamped with her initials.

'I mean as a person. What sort of a person is he? The Olds refuse to talk about him at all. I don't even know if he was clear on the heart tests, like I am. I wanted to find out. And will he be okay about me? I mean, he's not resentful that the Olds had me, after they threw him out?'

'Your brother is one of the nicest, most generous people you could ever meet,' Ted told her sincerely, then he cocked his head as he heard the sound of Trev's big Triumph roaring into the driveway. 'You can see for yourself in a minute, once he's put the bike in the garage. And yes, he's fine, no heart condition.'

They heard the front door open after a moment, then a familiar sound which Ted knew was Trev dumping his helmet on the hall table as his voice called out, 'Hi, I'm home, so where's my mystery visitor?'

He came striding into the kitchen, filling the space, as ever, with his presence. Then he turned and saw his sister for the first time.

'Wow,' they both said, almost in unison.

The resemblance between them was striking. Siobhan had been conceived and born after their parents had disowned Trev when he told them he was gay. They had never yet met, nor had any other contact.

'Trev, this is Siobhan. Siobhan, meet your brother, Trevor,' Ted said, smiling from one to the other.

Trev was still in his leathers, which always made him look taller. He looked down at his sister, sitting looking up at him in nervous expectation, all semblance of being a sophisticated adult having disappeared at the sight of her good-looking brother. Then Trev was beaming and holding his arms out to her for one of his famous hugs and, shyly at first, she stood up and went to him.

'Hey, little sis, it's nice to meet you. It's like looking in a mirror!'

Ted knew that there was no way he was going to get any of his work done that evening, so he busied himself tidying it away into his briefcase, which he put in the hall ready for the morning. He'd just have to catch up tomorrow, perhaps go in early to clear his desk.

Trev had put a casserole in the oven before he'd gone out. There was plenty for an extra one and the two of them already seemed to be getting on brilliantly as they laid the table together, talking nineteen to the dozen.

When they sat down to eat, Ted went back into serious policeman mode once again.

'Siobhan, you're very welcome to stay tonight, but tomorrow, one of us will take you back to school. Trev, can you get the day off? You know I'm a bit up to my eyes at the moment.'

Siobhan interrupted as Trev was about to reply.

'There's no problem. I came on the train and I have a return ticket. I can go back by myself.'

Ted put his knife and fork down and looked serious. His voice had the quiet, measured tone which let his team members and even Trev know when it was not the right time to push their luck by arguing with him.

'Siobhan, let me just tell you a bit about my job. I spend a lot of my time looking at the bodies of young people, just like you, who think they're very grown up but who finish up in a ditch somewhere, strangled, maybe raped, when they go off by themselves.'

Trev put a restraining hand on his arm, but Ted shook it off and continued.

'I'm busy at the moment because we have a serial rapist on our patch. A man who overpowers young women at knife point, and who is getting increasingly violent with every attack he makes. He killed his last victim. I've had to deal with young runaways, sometimes not much older than you, who have left home, thinking it's a great adventure, and finished up on the streets ...'

'Ted, come on,' Trev told him. 'I'm sure Siobhan understands you're just telling her this for her own good. She did something silly, but she won't do it again, I'm sure,' he said, looking directly at her.

His sister was looking taken aback, eyeing Ted warily. Ted was breathing hard, clearly struggling for control.

Trev took hold of one of his hands and this time, Ted didn't shrug him off.

'Hey, it's all right, there's no harm done. I'll take Siobhan back to school tomorrow, no worries. It's fine. Now I'm a partner in the firm, I can take the odd day off when I need to, it's one of the perks.'

Ted nodded slowly and started to relax.

'Sorry,' he said. 'Sorry, Siobhan. It's just that, you think you're an adult but you're not, not in the eyes of the law. You don't realise the risks you're running. Trev will take you safely back. Take the car, I'll go in on the bus.'

'Are you kidding me?' Siobhan demanded. 'I've just discovered that my brother is totally ripped and owns a motorbike and you expect me to go back in your car? I mean, unless you have a seriously cool sports car, it's just not going to cut it, compared to turning up at school on a bike.'

Her words broke the tension and finally Ted produced the grin which always transformed him from serious policeman to almost boyish charm.

'There is no street cred of any sort in appearing in my little car, not even my new one, believe me. You can borrow my helmet and Trev can take you on the bike. Just promise me you will be more careful in the future. No more going off alone. Make sure someone always knows where you are and what time to expect you back.'

Trev and his sister had so much to talk about and were delighted to find they had a lot in common. Ted sat back and watched them as they talked, Trev occasionally chipping in an aside when Ted was clearly not sure what they were on about.

Siobhan told him she'd persuaded her parents to let her go to the Somerset boarding school so she could continue her passion for riding. When she mentioned having her own eventer, Trev's face turned wistful as he said, 'I used to event. I had a really good mare, Delta Fox.'

'Foxy? We still have her. She's retired now, but I learned to ride on her. My horse, Blue, is her last foal. But Her Ladyship makes me ride the school ponies.'

L M KRIER

'Polo ponies,' Trev told Ted, seeing that none of it meant anything much to him.

The conversation really highlighted for Ted the gulf between him and Trev in terms of their background and upbringing. Ted was a miner's son whose only attempt at riding, on a pony on Blackpool beach, had not been a success. His life had been a world away from the privileged circumstances in which Trev had grown up.

After Siobhan had gone to bed, Ted and Trev moved into the sitting room and sat together on the sofa, immediately invaded by the cats. Trev put his arm around Ted and hugged him close.

'Thanks for caring about Shewee, and thanks for letting her stay,' he said.

'Shewee?' Ted queried.

Trev laughed.

'That's what her school friends call her. She told me when you'd gone upstairs for something. She's quite a live wire, it seems. They like to slope off to the festivals, especially Glasto. It's the name of something the girls use to pee through if they don't want to sit on the seats of the Portaloos.'

Ted looked at him, horrified.

'She's fourteen and she's going off to the festivals? Trev, promise me you will have a serious talk with her on the way tomorrow. You know what my job's like. You know how often I have to deal with bodies, including girls just like her. Kids dead in skips, dumped in ditches.

'Look, I'm sorry I went off on one but you know that I've been dealing with so many young people meeting a bad end of late. I'd hate the same thing to happen to your sister. Make her see sense, Trev, otherwise some poor coppers somewhere might find themselves dealing with her body one of these days.'

Trev stood up and pulled Ted up by the arm.

'It's going to be a long day tomorrow, so it's time we were going up. Can you wake me when you get up, then I can make

104

sure Shewee is up and ready to leave at a respectable time. I imagine teenage girls take even longer in the bathroom than I do in the morning.'

'Just drive carefully and promise me you'll take a proper break before you head back. How long will it take you?'

'About four hours each way,' Trev said lightly then, seeing Ted's look, he added, 'well, maybe four and a half, if I stick to all the speed limits.'

'Make sure you do,' Ted told him sternly.

Trev laughed as they headed towards the stairs, then replied meekly, 'Yes, mother.'

As they reached the small landing at the top, they heard Siobhan call out from the guest room, 'Not too much noise in there now, you boys. Impressionable teenager trying to sleep in here.'

Trev let out a shout of laughter then called back, 'Go to sleep, Shewee.'

They were both in their bedroom now but as Trev was closing the door, they heard her call out again.

'Good night, John Boy,' then, after a brief pause, 'Goodnight, Grandma.'

Ted looked aghast as he started to undress.

'Grandma?' he asked. 'Is that how she sees me?'

Trev had already peeled his clothes off, scattering them randomly on chair and floor, before sliding under the duvet.

'She is so like me it's scary, especially as we've never met before. She's teasing you,' he told his partner. 'That means she likes you. She told me she did. And you're not remotely old enough to be anyone's granny. Why not come and join me and I'll prove it to you?'

Chapter Thirteen

Ted was up at six so he could get into work early to clear his paperwork before his day began. He was surprised to find Siobhan already in the kitchen, the kettle just boiling. She greeted him by thrusting a mug of green tea at him.

Seeing his surprised look, she said, 'I have to get up at sparrows' fart when I'm hunting or eventing. Trev's out of practice, but don't worry, I'll get him up and sorted in plenty of time.'

Then, more shyly, 'Thanks, Ted, for letting me stay over, and for making sure I get back safely. And I promise I'll be a good girl from now on.'

After the morning briefing, Ted went to find PC Susan Heap, who was going to accompany him when he went to visit the victims of the sex attacks.

'Thanks for this, Susan, I appreciate your help. It's nice to have someone with me. I'm not much good at this sort of thing. I never know what to say.'

'Oh, that's not true at all, sir,' she told him. 'You're brilliant with people, everyone says the same.'

Ted smiled.

'Well, that's flattering of you to say so. I just wish I could believe it was true. I don't have big feet but I always feel I open my mouth and put them both right in it.'

The victims had already been questioned at length by specially trained officers. To a degree, Ted knew that PC Heap was right. People would often talk to him, open up and speak of difficult things. His short stature and quiet manner seemed to encourage them, making him seem less threatening than other officers. At the same time, he was ruthlessly efficient when interviewing suspects. Some had made the mistake of underestimating him because he was small and seemed inoffensive.

Ted had made appointments to see the three women who had been attacked, starting with the first victim. It was a long shot that they would get anything out of interviewing them again, but sometimes, with the passage of time, more details emerged from victims' memories and it was a chance worth taking.

Their first call was at the home of Kathy Finn. She had told Ted that she was still off work, recovering. Susan Heap was in uniform, Ted had his warrant card in his hand when they arrived at the front door of a neat mid-terrace house, with a minuscule front garden.

In reply to their knock, there was the sound of bolts being drawn back and the door being unlocked from the inside. It was opened only as far as the short security chain would allow. All they could see was an eye and some wild-looking hair as a voice asked sharply, 'Yes?'

'Detective Inspector Darling and PC Heap, Ms Finn,' Ted said, holding up his warrant card to the door crack. 'I telephoned you and made an appointment.'

A pale hand appeared, took his card to examine it, then handed it back through the gap. They heard the chain being detached, then the door opened. The woman was wearing baggy sweat pants and an over-sized sweater. She looked painfully thin and rather cold, despite the central heating being turned up to tropical heat.

'You better come in,' she said warily, and indicated that they should go down the narrow hallway to a small kitchen at the back. There was a large blue Persian cat in the middle of the table, whose tail twitched at the sight of strangers. Kathy

Finn indicated that they should sit down and went to put the kettle on in a distracted fashion.

'Gilbert doesn't like people very much,' she told them, as the cat confirmed her statement by hissing menacingly at Susan Heap. It then turned its attention to Ted, sniffing at the sleeves of his trench-coat, which inevitably betrayed traces of his own cats.

'Gilbert? That's an unusual name,' Susan Heap commented, trying to break the ice.

'There was a Sullivan as well, but he got run over,' the woman told them. 'Do you prefer tea or coffee? Or something herbal?'

The cat had now abandoned hostility and was rubbing its head along Ted's sleeve. Ted very gently lifted his hand and started to rub his fingers against the top of its head, which sent it into a frenzy of purring and pushing.

'Anything at all, Ms Finn, whatever is to hand,' Ted told her, still stroking the cat absent-mindedly.

She produced a pot of something which was unidentifiable when she poured it out into three china mugs, which she passed round, before sitting down. She studied Ted for a moment then said, 'I've never seen Gilbert allow a stranger to touch him before.'

Ted gave her his most disarming grin and said, 'I'm a sucker for cats. We have six of them,' before switching into formal mode.

'Thank you for agreeing to see us, Ms Finn. I know you have been interviewed at length, but I just wondered if there was anything else, anything at all, which you could tell us. Perhaps some small detail you've remembered which could be useful in our enquiries.'

'I've been going over and over it in my mind ever since,' she told them with a slight shudder. 'I have terrible trouble sleeping, and when I do sleep, I have nightmares, reliving it over and again. That's why I'm still off work.

'Because I was the first, when he first got into the car, I thought that's all he was after. The car. It was a nice sporty Audi. He told me to shut up and drive where he told me to and I wouldn't get hurt. He let me see that he had a knife, and he pressed it against my side so I could feel it through my clothes. It left a small cut. Not serious, just a warning.

'I believed him, that's the stupid part. I thought that if I just drove him away from any people, he'd take the car and go. I was terrified, because of the knife, but I kept telling myself to stay calm, do exactly as he said, and I would be all right.'

She picked up her mug in both hands and took a drink of the hot liquid. Ted and Susan Heap took advantage of the pause to do the same. Ted still couldn't tell what it was that he was drinking. He was glad when the insistent head-butting of the cat meant he had to put his mug back down.

'Even when he made me turn off the road up a track to the back of beyond, I kept thinking it would be all right, it would soon be over, he just wanted the car.'

She made a harsh sound which could have been a laugh.

'The thing that was worrying me the most was the thought that I would have to walk back from there on my own in the dark, and that it would be scary. Then he told me to stop the car and get out. He got out too. I thought he was coming round to the driver's side to get in and drive away. But then he grabbed me, and he raped me.

'The police found the car, not far away. But I could never bear to see it again, after what happened. I sold it, cheap, for a quick sale. Too many memories.'

'I'm really sorry to ask you to go over it again, Ms Finn, but is there anything at all you can tell us about the man himself? Anything you may not have thought of at the time? Something, some feature, you've remembered since?'

'He was so ordinary,' she said. 'Medium height, no distinguishing features. What terrifies me most is that if I passed him in the street again, I'm not sure I would recognise him. The only thing I do remember is his eyes. They were dark brown. I always thought brown eyes were so warm, like melted chocolate. But his were cold. Cold and cruel. I'd know his eyes again, I'm sure.'

'Anything else at all? Any small detail?' Ted asked, his tone encouraging.

She shook her head.

'Nothing. His voice was English, no particular regional accent, just a hint of something I couldn't really pin down. He didn't say much. Again, I'm not sure I'd know his voice again. I'm sorry. I wish I could do more to help. When I think what happened to the last poor woman …'

'Here's my card,' Ted put it on the table in front of the cat as he stood up to go, leaving his drink largely untouched. 'If you think of anything, or if I can help you in any way, please don't hesitate to call me.'

'I said you were good with people, sir. And even the cat liked you,' Susan smiled as they got back into Ted's car.

Ted shook his head.

'I wish I knew the right things to say to someone like that. Will she ever truly get over it, I wonder?'

Their next visit was near the town centre. The second victim, Helen Lawrence, was back at work. She showed them into a small room at the back of the building, clearly the staff rest room, and offered them coffee from a machine which was giving off an inviting odour.

She looked calm and composed, neatly turned out, in the building society uniform, hair and make-up immaculate. She served them with coffee then sat down facing them.

'I'm not sure if I can help you any further, Inspector,' she began. 'I honestly can't think of anything I haven't already said to the other officers, and I do keep going over it in my mind to see if there might be something, anything, which I forgot initially. I'm anxious to help catch him, of course, so I am trying to remember details, although I don't really want to.'

'I appreciate you agreeing to talk to us, and I'm sorry for making you relive it. It's just anything at all you can think of which may help us to catch this man would be really useful to our enquiry,' Ted told her.

'I knew what was going to happen, of course. I'd heard about the first attack. He told me to shut up and drive and said as long as I kept quiet, I'd be unharmed. I knew he was lying, but there was nothing I could do about it. He kept the point of the knife pressed against my side the whole time. I could feel the sharp point, even through my clothes. I knew he would use it if I didn't do as he said.

'He didn't have much of an accent, certainly not a strong regional one I could recognise. He only said as much as he needed to, to tell me where to go and what to do. When he made me get out of the car, I suspected what he was going to do to me, so I tried to fight back. He hit me once, in the face, hard enough to knock me a bit senseless, for which I was grateful. I didn't know much of what was happening to me after that.

'He cut me again with the knife, although it wasn't serious. I realise now how lucky I was. I had all the tests. He didn't leave me pregnant, I don't have HIV or an STD, and I got my car back. I paid to have it not just valeted but steam-cleaned inside and out. Now I'm just carrying on as normal, because if I don't, then he's won, hasn't he?'

'Would you know him again?' Ted asked, handing her his card with his contact details.

'Only by his eyes,' she said. 'I'd know his eyes if I ever saw them again. They were dark brown but they were the coldest eyes I've ever seen. As if they were devoid of any humanity.'

Their third call of the morning was to a neat semi-detached house on a small estate. An immaculate sporty Škoda, in a metallic shade of electric blue, sat gleaming on the driveway. Ted knew from the case notes that it was the car in which Jayne Wright had been abducted. Clearly she, too, had decided to keep her vehicle.

The woman who opened the door was smartly dressed, in her early thirties, and smiled pleasantly at them as if they were expected for a social call. She showed them into a light and airy sitting room with a large bay window. Ted and Susan both declined her offer of a drink and sat down as she invited them to do.

'I just wondered if there was anything at all you could tell me, Mrs Wright, about the person who attacked you?' Ted began. 'I'm sorry to ask you to go over it all again, but really anything at all you may have remembered might be of help to us in our enquiries.'

'Oh, I'm over it now,' she said dismissively. 'I wasn't doing very well, but then I saw what happened to his latest victim and it made me realise how lucky I was. The physical scars have nearly healed, and the emotional ones will, in time. I'm trying not to let myself be defined by what happened to me. My husband's having a much harder time of it. He's finding it very difficult to come to terms with any of it.'

There was a catch in her voice and she paused to compose herself.

'I don't know if I can remember any more than I've already told the other officers. I knew what was coming, of course, as soon as he got into the car. He told me to shut up and do as he told me and I would be all right. I wasn't all right, of course, but I'm alive and I have the car back, as you can see, all cleaned and sterilised and good as new. I just don't know yet whether I will ever be able to drive it again. And I haven't been shopping since. Thank goodness for online ordering and home delivery. But I'll get over it. I have to.'

'Would you recognise the man again if you saw him?' Ted asked her.

'I'm not sure,' she said frankly. 'Everything about him was rather anonymous. He had almost no accent, which is rather unusual, don't you think? Most of us have something about the way we speak which betrays our origins. But his was very neutral. Average height and build, dark clothing. His eyes were dark, too, but they were cold. It's his eyes I have nightmares about.'

'Has that helped you, sir?' Susan asked him as they drove the short distance back to the station. 'Anything new there to give you a steer?'

'I'm not sure, to be honest, Susan, but at least I feel I've tried. Thanks again for your help.'

Ted called the team together at the end of the day, wanting an update. He was feeling frustrated and impatient with the apparent lack of any real progress by all of them, himself included.

'What have we got? Anything new? Steve, what about bus routes?'

'I did eventually get hold of the dog handler for the information, sir, although it took a while. And he told me the missing child was found safe, at least. She'd been in trouble at school so had gone to hide in a shed on her dad's allotment, but the dog found her easily enough. I have tried with the bus information, but our man could have gone almost anywhere. There's nothing conclusive in that direction.

'Look again,' Ted said, more shortly than usual. 'Check, double-check. There has to be something. Jezza, anything from the staff at the latest scene?'

'Nothing really, boss,' she told him. 'Now they're all so jumpy they're seeing suspects where they probably don't exist.'

'You be careful, too, don't go there after dark,' Ted warned her.

'Surely he won't come back to the same place? Not after killing there?'

'We don't know. We know practically nothing about this man, and that's what worries me. He's one step ahead of us all the time and we really need to up our game. All of us.'

113

Ted was bone weary when he got home, after more than twelve hours at work. Trev was in the kitchen, one of his Japanese motorcycle manuals open on the table. It was one of the languages he spoke and he liked to keep up the practice.

He stood up to give Ted a hug when he came in and said, 'Supper's nearly ready. It's just a quick pasta dish, I've not long got back. Hard day?'

Ted sank into a chair at the table, his face drawn.

'No progress,' he sighed. 'And I've been talking to the victims, which is never easy. How did it go at the school?'

'Oh, fine. I gave Shewee a long pep talk, and asked her house parent to contact me next time she's not toeing the line. Are you hungry?' Trev asked, standing up and starting to set the table.

'Not very, I think I'm too tired to be,' Ted confessed. 'I'll just have a bit, then I think I'd like an early night.'

'You need to eat something, you're losing weight,' Trev said, his voice concerned. 'Then I'll come up with you.'

'I really am tired,' Ted told him apologetically. 'Tired as in boringly in need of sleep tired. Sorry.'

'That's all right. We'll eat, then you can take a nice warm bath and I'll scrub your back, if you like. Then we can just go to sleep together, like a proper old married couple.'

Ted managed some food but opted for a shower instead of a bath as he was in danger of falling asleep in the water. As Trev slid up close to him under the duvet Ted said, 'Tell me all about your journey. And what the school was like. And what you think of your kid sister, now you've met her in the flesh.'

Trev had barely got past describing the first part of his journey to Somerset when he heard the soft sound of Ted's snoring. He kissed him gently on the forehead, closed his own eyes and tried to sleep.

Chapter Fourteen

Ted received two phone calls in rapid succession just after the morning briefing the following day. The first, totally unexpected, was from Trev and Siobhan's mother, Lady Armstrong, coldly polite, thanking him for taking care of her daughter. It was how he imagined she would sound when calling a hostess to thank her after a drinks party.

The second, not quite so unexpected but far more worrying, was from Pocket Billiards, the local reporter.

'Morning, Ted. I'm sitting on quite a story here and I hope you're going to be able to make it an even better one for me, with some nice juicy quotes,' he began.

'I doubt that very much, Alastair,' Ted said levelly. 'You should know by now that juicy quotes are not really my thing. But I'll certainly do my very best to help you, you have my word on that.'

He had sub-consciously picked up his pen and started doodling on a pad on the desk. Then he noticed how dark and aggressive his doodles were and realised the anger management course effects were already wearing off.

'I've had a phone call.' Then came a protracted pause for dramatic effect. 'From Jenny Holden.'

Ted managed not to swear out loud, but the point of his pen went through the top couple of sheets on the pad with a savage stabbing motion.

'I see,' he said cautiously.

'I can tell the name isn't unknown to you,' the journalist

continued. 'So what I'm going to need from you is a full response to the allegations she brought to me which, as you can imagine, include the possibility of a massive police cover-up into a serious sexual assault.'

Ted stood up and sent his waste-paper basket flying across the office with a well-placed kick. He took a deep breath to compose himself then said, 'Look, Alastair, this isn't something we can talk about over the phone. We need to meet face to face. I'm quite happy to answer your questions, as far as I'm able, and to give you a statement, but I will, of course, have to get clearance from higher up before I do.

'Are you free today? We could meet at The Grapes, perhaps? Over a sandwich?'

He noticed the familiar pause and added, 'On me, of course. Would twelve-thirty suit you?'

Knowing the reporter's unpleasant eating habits, he couldn't stand the idea of a full meal with him but thought he might just manage to keep his composure over sandwiches.

'I'll look forward to it, Ted, and I know you're not going to let me down on this,' came the oily response.

Ted's waste-paper basket was beyond resuscitation by the time he had kicked it several times round his office. It wouldn't be the first one he'd had to pay to replace. So much for the Blackpool course.

There was a timid knock at his office door and Mike Hallam put his head warily round the gap as he opened it.

'I come in peace, boss. Only, I heard the noise,' he said, looking at the mangled remains of the basket, 'and I see there have been casualties.'

Ted grinned sheepishly.

'Sorry, Mike. I was just arranging a meeting with my favourite journalist, and you know how much I look forward to those.'

He looked ruefully at the damage and said, 'That was just a bit of wishful thinking. I'll have to go and talk to the Super now, just to get my story straight before I meet him.'

The Ice Queen had already had a press release prepared, ready for if and when Jenny Holden decided to go to the papers with her story. They had known all along that it was just a matter of time. Ted wanted to go over it with her, just to check exactly what he could and could not say at his meeting.

'We knew this moment was likely to come, especially after the fatality. Coffee, Inspector?' she asked, lifting up the jug of the coffee machine.

Ted nodded his thanks. His discussions with the Ice Queen were not, and probably never would be, the relaxed sessions he'd enjoyed with his former boss and great friend, Jim Baker. But at least her coffee was much better than the evil black brew he used to serve.

'Of course, if the reporter were to get wind of the fact that the person Jenny Holden accused is now dead, I presume there would be nothing to stop him making that distressing part of the affair public? Including the circumstances of the death?' the Ice Queen speculated. 'I am already dismissing the hope that any sense of decency would stop him from doing that.'

'I imagine Jenny Holden will have told him Kenny Norman's name. It would be tragic, and wrong, if he were to go round to his sister's house, badgering her for a comment, but I fear that's what might happen,' Ted said in agreement.

'Unless, of course, you bring your not inconsiderable powers of persuasion to bear to stop him from doing so.'

Ted took a gulp of his coffee to buy himself some time. He wasn't entirely sure what the Ice Queen meant. She had a habit of giving hints that he was supposed to fathom out, so they could both legitimately deny any such conversation had ever taken place. Except that, sometimes, Ted was not entirely sure he had interpreted her meaning correctly.

'He's going to want something pretty big in exchange, if I ask him to ease off on the Kenny Norman line,' he said thoughtfully.

She was looking at him shrewdly over the top of her coffee cup.

'I'm sure that with the press release we've prepared, you can steer him away from naming the man and onto the bigger, wider implications of the case. Without, of course, being in any way indiscreet.'

It was at moments like these that Ted wished he was better at cryptic crossword clues. She was clearly hinting at what she did want him to tell the journalist, but he was not sure he had grasped the right end of the stick. If he got it wrong, it could be disastrous.

He wanted to make sure he arrived at the pub well ahead of the reporter so he could set things up. He was taking an enormous gamble, he knew. He hoped the journalist would react as he expected, and that he was intelligent enough to make something of the information which was about to come his way.

He also fervently hoped that he had not totally misinterpreted the hidden message from the Ice Queen. Ted was not hugely ambitious. He didn't mind if Detective Inspector was as far as he got in his career. But he would hate to slip back down the ranks, especially now he had taken on more debt, based on his current salary.

The Grapes was the local for the station and Ted was a regular there, despite not being a drinker. He ate there occasionally and liked to take his team there for morale-boosting purposes. He was greeted warmly by Dave, the landlord, who started preparing his Gunner without being asked.

'All set for your Christmas do here, Ted? Time flies, eh?'

Ted found a quiet table in the corner. Lunchtime trade was sparse, especially in the run-up to Christmas, when a lot of the regulars were using every spare minute for their shopping. He spread papers and a book around on the table, trying to make it look convincingly casual, then sat down and waited for Pocket

Billiards to arrive.

He found the reporter intensely irritating, not just because of his personal habits, but because of his obsequious manner. He had to admit, though, that he was quite good at digging out a story, and tenacious in going after the facts, even if he bent some of them slightly from time to time.

Under orders from the Ice Queen, Ted had been at pains lately to try to forge more of a working relationship with him. He was still not convinced it was working. Now would be his chance to find out. He was hoping to play the journalist on the end of his line like a fish. He just hoped that he would have more success than on the fishing trips of long ago with his father, up at Roman Lakes.

'Alastair, good to see you,' Ted said, trying to sound sincere, when the man arrived and held out a hand to shake his.

Ted always cringed at the contact, not knowing where the hand had been or what it had been up to.

'Sit down, I'll go and get the drinks in. Lager top? And what about a sandwich? What do you fancy?'

'I wouldn't say no to a steak butty, if we're just doing sandwiches,' he said hopefully. 'With perhaps a side order of chips? It's cold as a witch's tit out there today, fair works up an appetite.'

Ted headed back to the bar and ordered the drinks and Alastair's food. 'Can you give me the menu, Dave? I want to study it at length. And take your time with my next Gunner. In fact, if you needed to go and pick the fresh limes first, that would be fine.'

Dave looked shrewdly past Ted to the table, where the journalist was busy going through the paperwork left scattered there, as well as picking up the book to thumb through it.

'What are you up to, Ted?' he asked curiously. 'Whatever it is, your man has swallowed the bait, hook, line and sinker.'

Ted spread his hands in feigned innocence.

'Me? Up to something? Not at all. Just getting a bit absent-

119

minded in my old age. I keep leaving things lying about.'

Dave chuckled as he prepared the drinks and put them on a tray for Ted to carry over. He kept glancing across at the table, then said, 'I think you might be all right to head back there now. Tell me what you want to eat and I'll bring the food across.'

As Ted turned round, picking up the drinks tray, he saw Alastair hastily shuffling papers round on the table. By the time Ted walked back across, he was sitting with a studied look of innocence on his face. It didn't take a detective to see that everything had been moved.

'Here's your drink, Alastair, the food's just coming.' Ted put the tray on the next table and made a show of tidying things away. Just in case Alastair was more dense than he hoped, he surreptitiously pushed a brochure off the far side of the table so that it landed near his feet. As he moved the drinks across, out of the corner of his eye, he saw the man bend to pick it up and stuff it into his pocket.

'Right,' Ted said, sitting down and becoming business-like. 'This call you've had from Jenny Holden, and the information she's given you. Here's the official statement about it.'

He withdrew a sheet of paper from the stack and pushed it across to him. 'Now let me ask you something. Do you trust me?'

'More than I trust any other copper,' came the guarded reply, after a slight hesitation.

'That'll have to do,' Ted smiled. 'I hope you'll believe me when I say, the man whose name she no doubt gave you was eliminated from police enquiries for a very valid reason. But it's one which I can't share with you, because of confidentiality issues. That's why I need you to trust me on this. I've also made extensive enquiries and can assure you that he is no longer in the country and therefore is not implicated in any way in the current enquiry.'

He tried to hold eye contact with the other man to show his

sincerity, but Pocket Billiards' gaze had a way of sliding about all over the place.

'But there is another aspect to this and it's likely to be a much bigger story. Again, you'll just have to trust me when I say I'm going to do all I can to point you in the direction of where the real story is. I may need a little time. I also need to be able to trust you, in turn, that you will keep your source confidential. Otherwise the consequences for me could be very compromising.'

'Of course you can trust me, Ted. A journalist never reveals their sources,' he said smoothly.

Dave appeared at that moment with their food. They broke off their conversation until he had put the food on the table for them, after Ted had tidied everything away into his briefcase.

'I also need your word that you won't use the name Jenny Holden gave you in any way in connection with this case. All I can say to you is that it will be in your interest to let that line drop and wait a short time for me to get the information of a much bigger story for you. One which you can certainly sell to the nationals, if you play your cards right.'

He could see the avaricious glint in the journalist's eyes as he took a large bite out of the middle of his steak sandwich. The mustard which he had just drizzled over the meat squirted out of the bread and dribbled down the sides of his chin, apparently without him being aware.

Trev had remarked that Ted was losing weight. He risked not being able to eat anything if he had to watch Pocket Billiards eating for much longer, but he needed to be sure he really had taken the bait. He concentrated on looking at his own steak sandwich, cutting it up into manageable pieces, trying not to listen to the other man's noisy eating.

Alastair spoke with his mouth full, revealing bad teeth and partly chewed meat.

'Okay, Ted, I'll agree to that, as a gesture of good faith. But you better not be having me on about the bigger story. This is a good 'un that I could go with now. I'm counting on you to turn it into a better one.'

They ate in relative silence for a while, apart from the sound of the journalist's mastication. Then, with a carefully studied casual air, Alastair asked, 'By the way, Ted, if I wanted to ask around about something to do with people like you, where would I go?'

'People like me? You mean policemen?' Ted asked innocently.

'No, you know, gay people.'

'Ah, right. I don't know that there's much of a gay scene in Stockport, really. You might be better off going to Canal Street. You've got something with a gay angle that you're working on, then?' he asked, trying to keep a straight face.

They finished up their drinks and sandwiches. Ted endured another hand shake, then they went their separate ways. Ted went first to find the Ice Queen, to report in broad terms on how the meeting had gone.

'I'm playing the long game, ma'am, and I hope to heaven I'm playing by the right rules. But I have got his word, for what it's worth, that he won't name Kenny Norman or follow that line of enquiry. At least not for now. I hinted at something much bigger. I hope that was right?'

'I'm sure you handled the situation perfectly, Inspector. I have every faith in you. As long as you did not say anything in the least indiscreet in front of the press.'

'No, ma'am, I can assure you I didn't say anything indiscreet.'

Ted was about to leave then turned back to her and said, 'I should, of course, have said before now, but I always have a small get-together for the team and one or two others just before Christmas. It's on Friday evening, after work, in The Grapes, and I'd be pleased if you could come. With your husband, of course. Partners are very welcome. Trev bakes. It's worth coming just for his mince pies.'

'That's extremely kind of you. I would like that very much, and I'm sure Robin would too.'

When he told Trev about it later that evening, as they walked back from their martial arts session, he said, 'It was quite sweet really, she looked almost a little flustered, as if she hadn't expected to be asked. By the way, would you mind if I asked Bizzie to Christmas dinner as well as my mother? I'm not sure if she has anywhere to go and I'd hate to think of her being alone if not. And what about Siobhan? Will she be spending it with your parents, or should we invite her?'

Trev made a scornful noise.

'That's not how they do things. The Olds will be staying abroad for the social side of the festivities. They have a house here but they won't open it up just for Shewee. She'll be staying at school, but she'll have a far better time there than we could give her here, with plenty of riding, and hunting on Boxing Day, of course. But thanks for thinking of her. You caring about the waifs and strays is just one of the things I love about you.'

Chapter Fifteen

Their attacker had gone quiet for the moment. No more reported cases, not on their patch, not further afield. Ted fervently hoped the man had simply gone to ground for the festive season and that for once, he might get a quiet Christmas at home with Trev. Also, for the first time in many long years, with his mother.

Like Ted, Professor Nelson would be on call for Christmas Day so was not going to visit her mother until Boxing Day. She'd gratefully accepted the invitation to dine with them but had declined the offer to be collected. As she was on call, she told Ted, she wouldn't be drinking and would need her car with her.

Christmas Day was a Sunday, so Ted had planned his usual drinks get-together for the Friday evening, after work. After the morning briefing on the Friday, he asked Mike if the two of them could get together at lunch-time for a brainstorming session over a sandwich, and offered to go out and get something for them.

'I fancy a smoked salmon bagel. I've got a bit of an addiction for them at the moment,' he told him. 'Can I get you one?'

Mike made a face.

'I'm not much of a one for smoked salmon. Maybe some plain cheese?'

Ted had come in on the bus, leaving his car for Trev to pick up later on and bring in the buffet he had prepared. He would go and set it all up at The Grapes before Ted and the team adjourned there after work at the end of the day. As well as the team and the Ice Queen, Ted had also invited his old boss, Jim Baker, and the new woman in his life, Bella. Jim had headed the team for many years and was still held in high regard and affection by those who had served under him.

Ted had mixed feelings about the evening ahead. Part of him was looking forward to it, a chance to relax with his team in an informal setting. Part of him was dreading it. Memories of the team member they had lost last Christmas were still raw. That aspect would be hard for all of them.

'Plain cheese, or cheese with tomato?' Ted asked, waving two paper bags in front of Mike Hallam as they both sat down at Ted's desk when he returned from buying their lunch. 'Or both, if you like. I've got two salmon bagels. Trev says I'm losing weight and need to eat more.'

'I think we've all been forgetting the odd meal, working this case, boss,' Mike said, gratefully accepting both sandwiches.

'Is your wife coming this evening, Mike?' Ted asked him, putting coffee in front of his sergeant and making green tea for himself.

Mike grinned at him.

'She is. She's looking forward to it. And I'm glad you'll have the chance to see her back to her normal self, now she's better.'

'Is everything all right between you now, then?'

'Back to normal. No, better than ever, I would say. The person you saw last year is not the real Joan, at all. Neither of us had fully realised how ill she was. Now she's on medication to help her find balance again, she's back to being my missus. Just like the woman I married.'

Ted was pleased to hear it. He took a bite of his first bagel, washing it down with a gulp of hot tea, then sounded businesslike.

'Right, what are we missing about our man? I still favour

the ex-forces angle myself, but that's just a hunch. It's not just his knife use. He's pretty good at disappearing, too, and that's not as easy as people think.'

Mike smiled.

'You think ex-forces, Jezza's still convinced he's a lorry driver.'

'We could both be right, of course. Ex-military, now driving for a living? Mike, I'm not sure if it's even possible, but can you try to see if we can get details of ex-forces from our area who have been discharged and moved back here, particularly recently?'

'I'll try, boss, but I have a horrible feeling I'll be slapped down with the confidentiality card,' Mike said, with a sigh. 'Wouldn't it be great if we could all just work together to try to get the bad guys?'

'And let's not ease up on trying to identify the Sprinter van that's been mentioned. How can it just disappear off the scene, if it does have any connection?'

'At least we've wound up another couple of cases before Christmas, if we can't yet nail this one. His luck can't hold forever, boss. Sooner or later we'll get him, or someone else will.'

'I'd just like it to be us, Mike. It's our patch he's killed on, and there are three other young women here whose lives he's ruined.'

Ted finished off his bagel, then wondered if he really could manage the second.

'By the way, I wanted to ask your opinion. I was going to suggest we raise a glass to Tina tonight. Do you think that would be all right?'

'I think the team would really appreciate that, boss,' Mike said, then looked searchingly at him. 'And are you all right? It's not been an easy year for you, one way or another.'

'Me?' Ted queried, surprised. 'I'm fine. A bit tired, but then I think we all are. Looking forward to this evening.'

Trev had done them proud, as usual, with the spread. He loved cooking, especially baking, and his mince pies were legendary. Maurice was, as ever, first to arrive, with young Steve in tow, and headed straight for the buffet table. All the team members were there, some with partners. Ted was amazed at the transformation in Mike's wife. She was smiling and friendly, and found a moment to have a quiet word with him.

'I'm sorry about last year, Inspector. I wasn't well, not well at all. I think I came across very badly, and I just wanted to apologise. And to thank you for all your kindness to Mike, and in getting help for me.'

'You're very welcome, and please, call me Ted. It's informal this evening.'

Virgil Tibbs was there with his wife, who was pregnant with their first child. Sal was with his long-term girlfriend, Rob with his girlfriend, now fiancée. Ted and Trev had been at their recent engagement party, and they no doubt had another one to look forward to. Jim Baker seemed serious about his new lady-friend, Bella. They were both there. Jim had, as usual, greeted Ted with a handshake and a thump on the back. There was a great deal of affection between the two men, even if it was sometimes awkwardly shown by Jim.

The Ice Queen and her husband were the last to arrive, fashionably late. Ted had not yet met her husband, an inspector in traffic. He was as tall as his wife, slim, dark hair, greying at the temples.

'Ted, I'm so sorry we're late,' she began, her message clear. It would be first name terms for an informal evening. 'We got horribly held up in traffic, somewhat ironically. This is my husband, Robin, and this is Ted Darling.'

Trev had seen her come in and came over to join them, as Ted and Robin were shaking hands. Ted slipped an arm round Trev as he said, 'And this is my partner, Trevor. My boss, Debs, and her husband Robin.'

'Ted tells me you settled on the Ducati after you came to see the Hondas.'

The Ice Queen had previously mentioned to Ted having once seen Trev in his workplace when she was looking at bikes, without letting on who she was.

'Let me get you something to eat and you can tell me how you're finding it.'

Ted smiled to himself as he watched his partner deftly escort her away, in full charm offensive mode. The two of them were soon deep in conversation, dark-haired heads close together as they enjoyed some of the food and talked about bikes.

'So, how are you liking it, working for the Ice Queen?' Robin Caldwell asked with a smile. 'It's not entirely a fair nickname, you know. She's a pussy cat really. And she speaks very highly of you.'

'She does?' Ted gaped in astonishment. 'I always get the feeling she thinks I'm a complete idiot.'

Robin laughed.

'I probably shouldn't tell you this, and I will deny it was me if you ever breathe a word, but she was really apprehensive when she knew she was going to be your new boss. You come with an impressive reputation, too.'

Ted gazed across the room again, seeing his boss in a completely different light. It had never occurred to him that anyone might be in awe of him, certainly not the formidable Ice Queen. Then he nodded his head in understanding.

'So starting off by redesigning my wardrobe was her asserting her authority?' he chuckled.

Everyone seemed to be enjoying themselves. There was plenty of chatter and lots of laughter. The whole atmosphere was relaxed. Ted liked to see his team able to have a good time, especially in the middle of a difficult case. But there was something he felt he should do, and he hoped he could do it without putting a total damper on the evening.

'Can I just have your attention for a moment please, everyone?' he asked.

As usual, although his voice was quiet, it commanded respect and everyone fell silent, listening to what he had to say.

'I'd just like to thank you all for coming, and for all your hard work throughout the year. I wish you all a happy Christmas, and I hope at least some of us get to enjoy our Christmas dinner without being called out.

'This time last year was very hard for all of us who were on the team then. I don't want to rake over old wounds, but I would just ask all of you, please, to raise your glasses with me. To Tina.'

It was a moving moment. Even the newer ones present, Jezza, the Ice Queen, who had not known Tina, raised their glasses in silent acknowledgement.

After that, things started to wind down. The Ice Queen and her husband were the first to leave, full of effusive thanks, followed shortly after by Jim Baker and Bella. It just left the team members and their partners, who were collecting their possessions and getting ready to make a move. Ted and Trev stood near to the doorway so they could speak to their guests as they were leaving.

Jezza was the first of the team to need to go. Leaving her autistic younger brother with child minders was never guaranteed to be easy.

'It's been a great evening, boss, thank you. You really are the best boss I've ever had. I suppose a Christmas kiss is out of the question?'

The colour drained from Ted's face. Trev, standing right next to him, instinctively took his arm, as he looked as if he might pass out. Instead, Ted excused himself and blundered out of the room, through the bar, now filling with the evening's drinkers, and out into the street, Trev hard on his heels.

'What's wrong?' he asked anxiously. 'Are you all right? You look shocking.'

Ted was gulping big breaths of the chilly evening air, leaning back against his car which was parked outside, to make it easier for Trev to unload the buffet.

'It's what Jezza said. Just now. It just hit me. That's the last conversation I ever had with Tina. Almost word for word.'

Trev put his arms round him and hugged him close.

'God, I'm sorry, that must have been so hard for you. Look, why don't you sit in the car? I'll make your excuses to everyone. I'll say it was something you ate. Then I'll take you home. I'll ask Dave if I can come and clear up tomorrow.'

Seeing Ted was about to argue, he said, 'Go on, here's the keys. I won't be long, then we'll go home. Are you all right to drive? I've had a few glasses of wine, I wasn't expecting to be driving.'

Trev sprinted back up the stairs to where the team members were hanging round looking anxious, especially Jezza.

'Don't panic, folks,' Trev said reassuringly. 'The boss just felt ill suddenly. Something he ate, and not my cooking. He thinks it was a dodgy ham roll at lunch time. He's going to sit in the car for a moment, then I'll take him home. He said Merry Christmas, everyone.'

'Are you sure he's ok, Trev?' Jezza asked him. 'It wasn't me asking to snog him that made him feel ill was it?'

Her tone was light-hearted but Trev could see that she was worried.

Still reassuring everyone, Trev started to shepherd them all out of the door. Mike Hallam hung back, though he sent his wife on ahead, armed with the car keys.

'Right, Trev, it's just you and me here now so cut the bullshit. What's wrong with the boss?'

When Trev opened his mouth to reply, he interrupted, 'And don't say a dodgy ham roll. I had lunch with him and he didn't have ham. And he was fine all afternoon, after he'd eaten. So what is wrong?'

'He's all right, Mike, really. It's what Jezza said to him just now. It was almost word for word what Tina said to him, this time last year. The last time he ever saw her alive. It just got to him a bit. He's a bit tired, and a bit low over the lack of progress on this case. I'll take him home, he'll be fine. Thanks for your concern,' he waved away Mike's offer of helping to clear up, and went to explain to Dave.

Ted was unusually quiet as he drove them home, so Trev said nothing, just sitting quietly in the passenger seat. Once back at the house, Trev installed him on the sofa with the cats and put the news channel on automatically while he went to make them both a hot drink. He came striding back in rapidly when he heard Ted exclaim 'Shit!' and call his name.

'Police in Somerset have discovered the body of a teenage girl, believed to be about fifteen years old, in a field near to Glastonbury, scene of the world-famous festival. No information as to the identity has yet been released until next of kin have been informed, but the death is being treated as suspicious ...'

The two men exchanged stricken looks and both exclaimed, 'Shewee.'

Ted got up and went to his partner.

'Phone her,' he said. 'It won't be her. You'd have heard if she'd gone missing. It's not her.'

Trev had his mobile out and was pulling up his sister's number with a hand which shook visibly. He dialled the number then, when someone answered, he said, 'Shewee? Thank God! Are you all right? We just saw on the news ...' then, raising his voice, he demanded angrily, 'Shewee, are you in a bloody pub?'

He listened for a moment, then said, 'You are in a pub, I can hear from the background. Shewee, get a taxi and get back to the school, now. You frightened the crap out of us both. We thought you'd been murdered. It's just been on the telly that a girl around your age was found dead near Glasto. We were worried it was you.'

Ted held out his hand and said, ominously quietly, 'Give me the phone.'

Even Trev knew better than to argue with him when he used that tone.

'Siobhan? Give me the name of the pub you're in.'

There was a pause as she started to protest, then he said, 'I'm not asking you, I'm telling you. Give me the name. Then phone a taxi. You have ten minutes to get yourself out of there. I'm sending the local police round. You and I will talk again soon about this. Now get yourself back to school, and don't worry your brother like this again.'

'Are you really going to call the local nick?' Trev asked him, when he ended the call.

Ted sighed.

'I'm a policeman. I've just heard of an illegal act being committed, a pub allowing under-age kids onto licensed premises. I can't turn a blind eye. You should know by now, I'm on duty all the time. Every day. Even Christmas.

'It could so easily have been her, in that field. Your kid sister. Because some pub landlord somewhere is letting kids in to get drunk and get into all sorts of danger. So yes, I am going to send the local force round there, right now. And I really am going to phone Siobhan, and soon, to give her a sizeable piece of my mind.'

Chapter Sixteen

Being able to celebrate Christmas with his partner was never a certainty for Ted. He couldn't count the number of times an early morning phone call had taken him away and kept him absent for most of the day. He was on call and would go in as soon as he was needed. But for once, the morning was peaceful.

Ted woke up at his usual time, but stayed in bed for a while, revelling in the unexpected luxury. He kept reaching out to pick up his mobile phone to check it was still on and had a signal, hardly able to believe his luck that there had, as yet, been no call.

Trev was still dead to the world and wouldn't be stirring for a while yet. Ted carefully and quietly slid out of bed, pulled on sweat top, pants and slippers, and headed downstairs to make them both a tray of morning tea. It would be a rare treat for them to enjoy breakfast in bed together. Neither Trev nor any of the slumbering felines, dotted randomly round the bed, so much as moved a muscle. Only senior cat, Queen, opened one accusatory eye.

Ted had picked up almond croissants when he and Trev had gone into town the previous day, Trev to do the clearing up at The Grapes from the night before, Ted to call in at work to see if anything needed his urgent attention. It was always useful to have some quiet time at his desk to try to keep on top of the ever-mounting paperwork.

Virgil and Sal had both been on duty and at their desks on

Saturday, Christmas Eve. Ted went and sat with them for a moment to chat, reassuring them both that he was fine, once again blaming a dodgy ham roll.

'What's the latest on Nat Cowley, Virgil? And how are the fish doing?' he asked.

'He's still in a lot of pain, boss. He was worried about his job, but it seems the supermarket want to make a bit of a PR thing about him being a hero, trying to protect a customer. Get some free publicity out of it. So clearly they can't do that and then sack him for having too much sick leave.'

Ted frowned.

'I don't suppose there's anything we can do about it, especially if Pocket Billiards gets a whiff of a story. But it strikes me as a bit tactless to the family of the young woman who was killed.'

'As for the fish, I never realised how relaxing it is, just watching those little guys swimming about, without a care in the world. The wife's driving me crazy at the moment, all this shopping and nesting, so they're my sanctuary. My excuse to slip away for a bit and just chill out.'

Ted and Sal both laughed at the image.

'I'd make the most of it while you can, Virgil,' Ted told him. 'It's not a road I've been down myself, but I imagine that once the baby arrives, things will be even less peaceful.'

All was still peaceful in the bedroom when Ted went back up with a tray on Christmas morning. Fresh orange juice, croissants warmed under the grill, green tea for himself, and Trev's usual brew, strong, dark tea, with just a cloud of milk.

Trev opened one sleepy blue eye as his partner slid back under the duvet.

'No phone call yet? That's the best Christmas present I could have.'

'Play your cards right and you might get another one, as long as there's time before you have to start cooking.'

The kitchen was always Trev's domain, especially at

Christmas. Ted was put in charge of laying the table, then going to collect his mother. They would be eating in the living room for a special occasion, rather than the kitchen as they did when it was just the two of them. Bizzie arrived, under her own steam, with an expensive bottle of good wine for Trev and more home-made elderflower cordial for Ted, because he'd enjoyed it the last time she had produced some.

Earlier, Trev had phoned his sister and talked at length, before obediently handing the phone over to Ted, in full stern policeman mode.

After she'd listened dutifully while he read her the riot act, Siobhan said thoughtfully, 'Now I get it. What Trev sees in you. You really do care about people, don't you? My brother and I have never known much of that, with the parents we were saddled with. Merry Christmas, Mr Policeman.'

It made Ted feel surprisingly good. He did care. Sometimes he knew he cared slightly too much, which was why he took his job so much to heart.

'Merry Christmas, Siobhan. Try to keep out of trouble, and enjoy yourself.'

They made it through to the pudding before they were interrupted by a phone call, but it was the Professor's phone which rang. She excused herself, moved out into the hallway so as not to disturb the festivities, and listened to the details.

'Sorry to have to abandon you all, especially before the port and Stilton, but I have to go. Luckily, this one's for me, Edwin; you're not needed. Road traffic accident. From the sound of it, yet another drunken driver causing carnage. One young mother dead, two little children without a mummy on Christmas Day.'

She made her excuses and left. It wasn't long afterwards that Ted's mother's eyelids started to droop so he took her home. He still couldn't believe his luck that he and Trev had got to spend an entire Christmas Day, so far, without him being called away. He fervently hoped it would continue. He was going in to work on Boxing Day, at least for half the day, then it would be back to normal hours for most of the team. It was so nice to enjoy one quiet day, just like anyone else.

Boxing Day brought news of another attack, this time in Liverpool. Mike and Rob were on duty, and Rob was already on the phone to Liverpool when Ted arrived, getting further details. There had been a car theft and a sexual assault, but no serious injuries this time, although the attacker had used a knife to threaten his victim. There wasn't a lot they could do with the information until the following morning, when the team was back up to full strength.

'Taking his van to Ireland,' Jezza said decidedly at the morning briefing the following day. 'Trafficking something.'

The rest of the team made sceptical noises.

'You're obsessed with this lorry driver idea. Could be any number of reasons to be in Liverpool,' Mike cautioned her.

'But Jezza could just be right,' Ted said. 'It's worth a shot. So Rob, can you get your contacts in Liverpool to check with the ferries to see if there were any Sprinter vans booked on any crossings, either outbound or incoming. We've got so little to go on, we can't afford to turn our back on any lead. If they do come back with details, cross-check them against Shuttle traffic from Folkestone.

'And I still favour the idea that there is a forces connection, so let's find out where ex-service personnel congregate on our patch and get out there talking to them. Someone, somewhere, has a strong suspicion who this man is, and we need to know.'

'At least he may be off our patch for the time being,' Jezza added.

'Don't get complacent. He was there yesterday, but he might have arrived there coming back from Belfast, rather than heading over there. In which case he's had plenty of time to be back on our patch. Eyes and ears open everywhere, all of you. Jezza, you in particular, be careful. Don't take any avoidable risks.'

Ted thought he'd take a moment to catch up with the local

reporter next. He'd promised him a big story and wanted to make it look convincing that he was honouring his word. He was fervently hoping that Pocket Billiards had picked up the clues, as well as the dropped leaflet, and made some progress. If not, he would have to try again, using less subtle means.

The journalist was almost off-hand with him, not at all like his usual obsequious self. It seemed he could hardly wait to get Ted off the phone.

'I just wanted to wish you season's greetings, Alastair, and to say I've not forgotten about you. I did promise you information on a potentially very big story, and I'm just chasing down a few more details for you.'

'Great, Ted, thanks,' he said dismissively. 'As it goes, I got wind of something myself, something big, and it's keeping me a bit busy at the moment. But thanks for thinking of me, and I'll look forward to hearing what you have for me.'

Ted smiled to himself as he ended the call. It sounded like a result. He would just have to keep his fingers crossed that it worked out as he wanted it to and there was no fall-out.

Later in the day, on a whim, Ted made another phone call, then went back into the main office. 'It's still fairly quiet, so if you want to sort it out between you that half of you go earlier this evening and the other half do the same tomorrow? If that's ok with you, Mike?' he said.

'Fine by me, boss, good idea. Can we sort it out like grown-ups or shall we draw lots?'

'I'd really appreciate it if I could go a bit earlier, Sarge,' Jezza put in. 'I thought I'd got Tommy exactly what he'd asked for as his Christmas present but, apparently, it was the wrong colour so he had a bit of a meltdown. I promised to try and change it for him today, if I got time.'

Ted liked to watch the way his team worked together and supported one another. Jezza had had a shaky start, fitting in. Now the others knew more about her home circumstances, they were more supportive of her, without letting her take liberties.

'I'm off now, too, Mike,' Ted told him. 'There's someone I'd like to call on. But phone me if anything happens, or if you need me for anything. Otherwise, I'll see you in the morning.'

Ted pulled the car up outside the house in the quiet street where Kenny Norman's sister lived. He wanted to check that the woman was all right, living on her own as she did. He didn't want to give her false hope, but he did at least want to reassure her that he was doing all he could to keep her name, and that of her brother, out of the paper in connection with the current enquiry.

Although he was expected, Ted once again had to produce his warrant card and hand it through the narrow gap left by the safety chain. He was quick to reassure Miss Norman when she kept him waiting.

'You're doing absolutely the right thing, Miss Norman. Exactly the kind of safety measures we always try to encourage people to take, especially when they live alone.'

Once again, she led the way carefully down the hallway into the front room and immediately groped for the remote to turn off the television. Ted took a seat where she indicated and looked around the room, which he noticed was not all that warm with the frugal heat of just one section of a gas fire alight.

There were only three Christmas cards on the mantelpiece, and the remains of what looked like a Meals on Wheels dish, gone cold and congealed on the table laid for one.

'I just thought I'd call round to wish you seasons' greetings, and to let you know what was going on, with regard to our earlier conversation, Miss Norman,' he began.

'You are very kind, Inspector. Certainly the most considerate police officer with whom I have had contact.'

'As Jenny Holden threatened, she did go to the press about her allegations. Of course, I was not able to tell the local journalist anything at all about your brother. Even if I had been able to, I would have preferred not to.

'I think I've bought him off by sending him in a different direction altogether, for a bigger story. I thought I would just come and let you know in person, and to make sure you had my contact details, just in case anyone from the press ever does try to get in contact with you. Please free to call me, at any time, and I will do whatever I can to help you.'

'That is indeed kind, but surely above and beyond the call of duty?'

'I'm just trying to help, Miss Norman. It saddens me very much to hear how your brother was treated and I'm just trying, belatedly, to do all I can to make it, if not right, exactly, then better than it was,' Ted told her frankly. 'I don't mean to sound patronising, but are you on your own?'

'I am,' she told him. 'There was only ever Kenny for company, after our mother died. I've never been what you might call a joiner. Someone who signs up for every club and group going. So as you have no doubt deduced, you being a detective, from the small number of Christmas cards, my circle of friends has diminished over the years as my peers have passed on.

'Might I ask you an extremely personal, and therefore impertinent, question, Inspector?'

Ted was taken aback, not expecting her to even suggest doing so, but he said, 'Yes, of course, Miss Norman.'

'As I told you before, I no longer see very well, so I can't tell from your appearance. I do apologise for asking, but I'm sensing from your kindness and empathy that you are someone who understands what it is like to be different from others in some way.'

'I'm gay, Miss Norman,' he told her candidly. 'My partner is a much younger man. Even in these supposedly enlightened times, we still occasionally experience a degree of homophobia from some people. Including from those who should know better.'

'Thank you. And thank you for all your efforts for Kenny.'

139

She made to stand up to show him to the door but Ted stepped closer to shake her hand and assured her that he was happy to see himself out.

As he let himself out of the house, making sure that the door was securely pulled closed behind him, the mobile phone in his pocket began serenading him with the opening bars of 'Barcelona'. Ted took the phone out. The screen told him it was Jezza calling.

'Yes, Jezza, what can I do for you?'

'Boss ...'

Her voice was low and muffled with tears

Ted was instantly alert as he headed down the driveway to his car.

'What is it, Jezza, what's happened?' he asked anxiously.

'Boss, can you come and get me?' she sobbed. 'Just you? Please? Don't tell anyone else. Please, boss.'

'Where are you? What's wrong?'

He opened the car door and leapt into the driving seat, starting the engine.

'Tell me where you are, Jezza, I'm on my way.'

For a moment, he could hear only sobs. Then, her broken voice added, 'He got me, boss.'

Chapter Seventeen

'I'm coming Jezza, just tell me where to find you. I'll be right there. Is he still there? Jezza, please talk to me.'

Ted was racing the engine without realising, itching to be on his way, but not yet knowing where to go. Then he heard a noise as if the phone was being moved. A woman's voice he did not recognise said, 'Inspector? I'm with Jezza. She's been attacked, but I'm waiting with her until you get here. She wouldn't let me call anyone else.'

The woman gave him clear directions as to where to find them, then added, 'She's most insistent you come on your own first. She is injured but is adamant it's not life-threatening, and we have dressed the wound between us.'

Ted slammed the car mercilessly into gear and left rubber marks as he roared out of the quiet road, tyres squealing. Darkness had fallen and it was rapidly going cold and frosty.

It was not far to the location he had been given, near to Reddish Vale. Traffic was heavy near the exit from a busy supermarket, but there was no sign of anyone on the single-track road he took nearby, turning off the main road, following the unknown woman's directions. He slowed down as he started along the road, his eyes scanning anxiously for any signs of Jezza or the woman, either on the road or among the willow trees and undergrowth along the sides.

In the light cast by his dipped headlights, ahead of him, he saw a woman standing in the middle of the road, two enormous German Shepherd dogs by her side. He could just make out a huddled form on the ground at the side of the road near to them. Ted stopped the car and turned off the engine, switching on the four-way flashers and leaving the dipped headlights on to light his way.

He grabbed his torch and got out of the car, eyeing the dogs warily.

'Jezza?' he called.

'Here, boss.'

He didn't think he had ever heard such evident relief in anyone's voice. He started cautiously forward, pulling out his warrant card and holding it up towards the unidentified woman. Both dogs immediately began to growl and bark menacingly. The one with short hair was big enough, but the second, longer-haired one, appeared to be the size of a small pony.

'Perro! Sjambok! Lie down,' the woman ordered. Both dogs obeyed immediately. 'It's safe to come closer, Inspector, just please don't make any sudden movement, especially towards me.'

'Jezza, are you all right?' Ted asked anxiously, walking nearer.

As he approached, he decided the bigger dog wasn't the size of a pony at all. Up close, it looked more like a bear. But at least the two of them stayed obediently lying down as he approached, though both were rumbling under their breath.

He could see Jezza now, sitting at the edge of the road, her knees drawn up to her chest, one arm clasped tightly around them, the other holding her side. Her face was battered and bruised, streaked with tears, eyes puffy. There was no sign of her car.

'I'll call an ambulance,' he said, reaching for his phone. Both dogs immediately sat up and barked again.

'No sudden movements, please,' the woman reminded him, then again ordered the dogs to lie down.

At the same time, Jezza said, 'No ambulance, boss. Just you. He knifed me, but it's not serious. Olivia had a first aid kit.

As long as I hold this pad in place, it'll be fine. Just take me in yourself. Please, boss.'

'I must have come along just as the man was leaving,' the woman told him. 'I heard a car backing very fast down the track towards the main road. I've not touched her, just made sure she was able to dress the wound herself. I've tried not to get too close. Scene of crime, and all that.'

Ted looked at her enquiringly. She made a self-deprecating face as she said, 'I'm a crime fiction writer. Olivia Radnor. You may have heard of me?'

Ted shook his head, but his attention was focused on Jezza.

'I'm going to have to call the cavalry, Jezza, you know that. We need to get you seen by a doctor as soon as possible. They can advise if you need to go to hospital.

'Mrs Radnor, would you mind waiting here until someone arrives to take your witness statement, please? I'm sorry to inconvenience you, but we do need to take note of everything you can tell us, while it's still fresh in your mind.'

'It's Ms Radnor,' she corrected him. 'It really would be better if I take the boys home for their tea and someone comes to the house to interview me, if that's possible? I don't live far away. I've written all my contact details here, and I'll be at home all evening now.'

She handed him a card, which caused an increase in volume of the grumbling from the dogs, though they made no move, having been told to stay.

Ted nodded reluctantly, then, as she made to leave, he said, 'Please would you put the dogs on leads, Ms Radnor. I can see that you have them under control, but just in case we need to bring in police dogs to work the scene of crime for any reason. We'll also need to do a thorough fingertip search, so it would be better if your dogs don't wander everywhere and cause a distraction.'

'Of course, how stupid of me, I should have realised,' she

said, as she clipped the dogs' leads on and started to walk away, adding, 'I do hope you will be all right, Jezza. Do please ask someone to let me know how you are.'

Jezza mumbled her thanks. Her teeth were chattering with cold and Ted knew he should get her seen and treated by a doctor as soon as he could.

'I have to call back-up now, Jezza, you know that,' he told her again, his tone apologetic. 'Then I need to take you either to the station or to St Mary's, as soon as possible, whichever you prefer. It's your choice how we go forward with this. Is there someone you want me to call, to be with you?'

'The nick, not the rape centre. I don't want to go there. I want to be on familiar territory. And please call Maurice,' she said decidedly.

A seemingly unlikely but genuine friendship had grown up between Maurice, Steve, Jezza and her young brother, Tommy.

'Tom's with the child minder until seven, but could Maurice take Steve round to my place to take over until I get back? And can you ask him to bring me a change of clothes? Anything.'

Ted nodded his understanding. Maurice in fatherly mode would be a brilliant choice, if she had no one else to call on at short notice.

He phoned Maurice, gave him brief details and location, and swore him to secrecy. He didn't want word to leak out to the rest of the team too soon. When he called Mike Hallam and asked for two team members to come to the scene, he didn't tell them who the victim was. He didn't want them driving like lunatics and putting themselves at risk, knowing a colleague was involved.

Next he called the station to summon reinforcements, then turned all his attention back to Jezza. He crouched down so his face was at her level, but not moving too close.

'Are you sure the wound is all right? Is it still bleeding? What can I do to help?' he asked her quietly.

'What I really need right now is a hug,' she wailed forlornly.

Ted felt as if his heart was being torn out of his chest.

'You know I can't do that, Jezza. You know I shouldn't touch you.'

For a moment, her milky-blue eyes blazed with anger as she spat, 'I'm a bloody human being, not a scene of crime!'

Ted crouched a little closer. He had instinctively pulled on latex gloves before approaching, a reflex action for any crime scene. Jezza had dropped her chin and broken eye contact with him. As gently as he could, he reached out one gloved finger and tilted her head back up so he could see her eyes.

'Jezza, I know how you're feeling. Really. I do know,' he said gently, as their eyes locked.

Her own eyes suddenly widened in startled comprehension as she realised what he was telling her. Then, at the first sound of sirens in the distance, he continued, speaking softly, 'If you're sure, I can put you in my car and take you straight to the station. But I'll just have to wait until they get here,' nodding his head towards the approaching sounds.

'I'll get you the latest fashion in onesies from the car, then help you in there before they get here, so you don't have to see anyone. I'll start it up so you can have the heater on full blast. I don't want to take a risk with draining the battery, the way my luck has been running with cars lately. Then I'll take you in. You know the procedure. You'll be spoken to by specially trained officers, and you'll be in control all along of what happens.

'It's going to be all right, Jezza. And I promise you, we are going to get him.'

He got her carefully into his car, manoeuvred it as far to the side of the track as he could, then turned up the heater to maximum so she could benefit from some much-needed warmth.

Uniform officers were first on the scene in a patrol car. Ted got out to brief them and to tell them that he would be handing over to Mike Hallam as soon as he arrived.

'I don't know if there are any cars in the parking area at the far end. You might want to take a drive up there first. Send them on their way, if there are any. We don't need any rubberneckers. Then secure the scene from either end of the road, once you get another unit on site. And don't let anyone through, for any reason, not even on foot or bikes.

'My team and the Crime Scene Investigators should be here very shortly. I'll watch this end, you go and check the parking.'

Mike Hallam arrived next, with Rob, and parked his car behind Ted's. Ted quickly strode forward to meet them both, before they saw who was in the passenger seat of his car.

'I didn't want to tell you on the phone but it's Jezza. He got Jezza.'

Both men swore under their breath, then Mike asked, 'Is she all right, boss? Is she badly hurt?'

'She says not, but I want to get her to the station and checked out as soon as possible. She doesn't want to go to St Mary's. Here's the details of a passing dog walker who, luckily, stopped to help her. Rob, can you get round there as soon as you can and get a statement. And can you sort out trying to find Jezza's car. It's distinctive, so it might be spotted and we might just get our man that way.

'I better get going now. I'll need to let the Super know, for one thing. I know I can always trust you to do a thorough job but this time it's one of ours, so can you double your efforts on it, please? And keep me posted all the time.'

Ted got back into his car, put it into gear then backed carefully down the narrow road, hoping he wouldn't run into any of the reinforcements coming the other way at speed.

'How are you doing now, Jezza?'

'Oh, I'm having a bloody marvellous time,' she snapped back sharply, with a flash of the old Jezza, as she was when she had first joined the team.

'Sorry,' Ted said. 'I'm rubbish at knowing the right thing to say.'

'Well, can you just listen instead? There's something I want to say, but I don't want anyone else to know. I want to explain how it happened. How I let it happen to me.'

'No one is blaming you, Jezza, and you mustn't blame yourself. This isn't your fault ...'

'Boss, can you just shut up and listen? Please?' she asked, but her tone was lighter. 'I have been being really careful, I honestly have. I didn't park in a quiet corner, always where it was busy. And I was keeping an eye on anyone around me.

'I'd been into the store to change Tommy's present. I was just taking it back to the car. I saw a man at the car next to mine, just getting his keys out. He was really ordinary-looking. He was wearing a flashing Santa hat. He looked just like someone's dad. He smiled at me. I even smiled back ...' her voice broke slightly.

'I didn't give him a second thought. He didn't look like any kind of a threat. Then as soon as I unlocked and got into the car, he was through the door and into the passenger seat in a flash, and I could feel the knife up against me. I could feel the blade through my clothing.

'He told me to shut up, keep both hands where he could see them and do as he told me. He said if I did, he wouldn't hurt me. I knew he was lying. I knew what he was going to do. But I kept thinking if I did exactly as he said, it might be all right. He might not kill me, he might not even rape me. He might just take the car and let me go.

'I was praying in my head that that's all that would happen. And I was absolutely terrified. Too scared even to think about grabbing the spray Inspector Turner gave me. Or doing anything else. All I could think about was that he was going to rape me, and I was petrified. Because I've never had sex with anyone.'

147

She broke off again, with a small sob, before she added. 'Only my father.'

They were just pulling away from traffic lights. Ted let the clutch out too quickly in his shock at her words and stalled the car, then fumbled with the key to restart it. He had no idea what to say.

'It started on my eleventh birthday. He told me it was my special present, because I was a big girl now. It went on until I was sixteen, when I insisted on having a lock on my bedroom door. My mother knew, I'm sure. That's why she made him buy me the flat, to get me as far away from him as possible.'

She looked at him as she said, 'I'm sorry to dump all this on you, boss. I just needed to tell you that. Anyway, I was still hoping I'd be all right. I thought once we were out of the car, maybe I could do something. Kickboxing. Run away. Anything.

'I thought he'd make me get out my side while he got out of the passenger door and came round. Somehow he seemed to guess that I was planning to do something. When he told me to stop, he grabbed me, held the knife up against my throat, and pulled me out of the passenger door with him.

'There was just one moment when he didn't have the knife up against me. I took a chance on a kick. He must be trained. He moved faster than anyone I've ever fought in kickboxing. He grabbed my foot and pulled it up higher so I overbalanced onto my back. He leapt on top of me, kneeling astride me, and punched me a few times in the face. Then he cut me with the knife. Enough to draw blood. A clear warning not to try anything else.

'The rest you can imagine.'

They had arrived at the station. Ted parked as near to the entrance as he could. He always kept a spare fleece jacket in the car, and he it draped carefully around Jezza's shoulders now, over the disposable coverall he'd given her to slip on.

'I don't want anyone else to know that,' she told him,

anxiously. 'I just needed to tell you.'

'They won't,' he promised her. 'Now, this next part is not going to be easy, either, but everything is going to be all right. I promise you. It will be all right.'

Chapter Eighteen

Now she was in the coveralls and he wouldn't leave traces of his own DNA on her, Ted put a protective arm around Jezza's shoulders as he helped her into the station. He was careful to shield her from enquiring glances at the front desk.

A doctor had been called and she was already waiting. He handed Jezza over to her care and sprinted up to his office to make phone calls, taking the time to make himself some green tea. He had no idea when he would be able to get anything to eat or drink during the course of the evening ahead, so he wasn't going to waste the opportunity.

His first call was to Trev.

'Hi, it's me. I'm going to be late tonight. I've no idea how late. We've had another attack, so I don't know what time I'll get back.'

'Is the victim …'

'Alive, injured, but I don't think it's a serious wound. She's with the doctor now. I'll tell you all about it when I get back, if you're still up.'

'Wake me up if I'm asleep, if you need to talk about it. I'll cook you something I can heat up quickly for you when you get home.'

'I'm not remotely hungry at the moment,' Ted sighed wearily. 'Not sure I can even think of eating, certainly not yet awhile. It's a bad one. I'll explain everything to you when I see you, whenever that is.'

His next call was to the Ice Queen to put her in the picture.

'I'll come in,' she said at once. 'If something like this has happened to one of our officers, I should be there to show support.'

'Debs, knowing what our Jezza is like, she won't appreciate any kind of fuss,' Ted replied, wondering as he said it why he had used the familiarity. He was just too tired and too distressed to think of being formal.

'Well, please send her my best wishes, and if there is anything at all I can do to help in any way, Ted, you only have to call me again.'

Ted gave a small smile to himself as he ended the call. Personal feelings, rank, old awkwardness, everything was forgotten in the face of something like this happening to one of the team. He felt a moment's affection for the Ice Queen.

Maurice had just arrived when Ted went back downstairs, still carrying his mug of tea. He had a bag with him, Jezza's clothes, Ted imagined. He knew Maurice, the father of two girls, would probably have known what to bring. They went to stand together near the room where Jezza was being examined by the doctor.

'Bloody awful business, Ted,' Maurice said. It seemed that something as traumatic as what had happened to Jezza was drawing them all closer, blurring ranks, making them seem like a family, not work colleagues. 'How's she bearing up?'

'You know our Jezza. She's insisting on putting on a feisty front, but she's clearly devastated. Thanks for coming, Maurice. I know she has no family, but I didn't know whether if she had any friends nearby. Do you happen to know?'

'To be honest, from what Steve and me have been finding out, I'm not sure she has many friends. I think that prickly shell keeps most people away. That and the problems with Tommy, restricting her social life, poor lass.'

'How is Tommy? Will he be all right with Steve? I've no idea what time Jezza will be able to go home, nor whether she'll be up to dealing with Tom when she gets there.'

Maurice chuckled.

'I left Steve and Tommy playing some sort of game or something on the computer. I'm not sure if either of them even noticed I'd gone, and Tommy certainly didn't pick up on the fact that Jezza was going to be late. He and Steve are fine together, for hours at a time. They get on really well, especially when a computer's involved.'

At that moment, the door opened and the doctor ushered Jezza out, by this time wearing nothing but a clean, new coverall and paper slippers. Her clothes had been taken away for forensic testing. She looked pale and shaken, her battered face swollen and looking sore.

'Eh, bonny lass,' Maurice said as soon as he saw her, holding his arms out to her.

Jezza rushed forward to be engulfed by his hug while he gently soothed her as he would one of his own daughters.

'I've finished everything I want to do now, Inspector, so DC Vine can be questioned whenever you're ready. The knife wound is superficial. I have cleaned and dressed it with Steristrips, but it will require looking at again in a day or two,' the doctor told Ted, then added, 'Jezza, remember, we can either arrange to refer you to St Mary's for tests or you can see your own GP, when you feel ready. Goodbye, and good luck.'

'Jezza, if you feel up to it, we should arrange for you to be interviewed next, get all the information while it's still fresh in your mind.'

'Believe me, boss, it's not something I'm going to forget in a hurry,' she said dryly.

'Sorry, that was incredibly tactless of me,' he said contritely. 'Let me see what specially trained officers are available.'

'Bollocks to that, boss, I'm happy for you to interview me. And I'm happy to make it a taped interview. I know how much easier it makes it on everyone. But before I do anything else, I want to take a shower and get some clean clothes on. Did you bring everything, Maurice?'

'Well, my lasses are a good bit younger than you and I'm used to packing for them, but I think so. I couldn't find your Disney princess stuff but I think I've got most other things you'll need. I put a towel in, too.'

'You're a star, Maurice, and a good friend,' she said lightly, kissing him on the cheek, taking the bag and disappearing off to the back of the station, where there was a shower.

Maurice watched her appraisingly as she went.

'Typical Jezza. She's taking it too lightly, putting on too brave a face. Steve and I will stay over at hers tonight, whether she wants us to or not, just to make sure she's all right.'

'You're a good man, Maurice,' Ted told him warmly. 'Why don't you get yourself a drink while we wait? I imagine she'll be quite some time. I need to make a few phone calls and then see if there's a support trained officer available. Whatever Jezza says, I'd prefer to have someone there who knows what to say. I just open my mouth and put my foot in it all the time.'

'Boss, it's fine. You're fine. It's you Jezza wants to talk to.'

Ted looked hesitant.

'I'll just see if someone else is available. Just to be there. For form's sake. And in case I get it badly wrong. Can you wait here for Jezza, then see she gets a drink and let me know when she's ready to talk?'

Ted was pleased to discover that Susan Heap was on duty and had been called back to the station when he'd rung through with news of the attack. She'd done the victim support training so she would be the ideal person to have with him while he interviewed Jezza. Now he'd heard what Jezza had told him, he understood why she had been reluctant to go on the course. It would clearly bring up issues she was not yet ready to deal with.

He called Mike Hallam next for an update and was pleased to hear that Jezza's car had already been found.

'Undamaged, keys still in it, just parked up in a quiet road on the other side of Heaton Chapel,' Mike told him. 'A passing patrol car just happened to spot it. The officers had had the call to look out for it. They're arranging to get it brought in for examination, but they say it looks fine.

'Rob's been to interview the writer woman. He said to tell you thanks for warning him that she was Dances with Wolves. Those big dogs scared the crap out of him. Anyway, we've got her statement in the bag.

'There's not much else we can do here now. Uniform are staying on to secure the scene and the investigators are still working on site, but I think we'll stand down now, boss, if that's all right with you? We'll just call at the supermarket on the way back, on the off chance there might have been witnesses to the abduction.'

'Yes, wind it up there, Mike, and we'll see you in the morning. I'm just going to interview Jezza formally, and Maurice is here, looking after her.'

'How's she doing? I mean, I can't even begin to imagine, but is she holding up all right? How's the knife wound?'

'She's a bit too bright, I would say, Mike. The doctor says the wound isn't serious. She's putting on too brave a face at the moment, which is worrying. Maurice and Steve are going to stay with her and Tommy tonight, to make sure they're all right, so they may well be in late tomorrow morning.'

Susan Heap had arrived back and was setting up an interview room for them. Jezza had finished her shower and arrived back looking remarkably relaxed, wearing the sweat pants, hoody and trainers which Maurice had found for her, smelling of soap, shampoo and toothpaste.

'Not at all sure I'm comfortable with the knowledge that you've been rummaging round in my underwear drawer, Maurice,' she said lightly, 'but thanks for that, and for the rest of it. You brought me just the right stuff.'

Maurice was right. She was very brittle behind the façade she was putting up. He had made her a hot chocolate drink, his stock answer to all moments of stress, which she cradled in her hands as they all sat down in the interview room.

Jezza took a large gulp of her drink, then began, 'I've thought of something about him. Something distinctive. Like the others said, it struck me that he didn't really have any kind of regional accent, which is a bit unusual. He could have blended in anywhere. Certainly nothing I could recognise, and I'm not bad on accents, from the drama training.

'But when he was telling me what to do, he said if he saw me trying to signal for help in any shape, form or way, he would see it and then he would hurt me.'

She saw the blank looks of the others and went on impatiently, 'Shape, form or way! Nobody says that. Everyone would say way, shape or form. Someone might recognise that, might know someone who says it that way round. Maybe it's a regional peculiarity. It might lead us somewhere.'

Her face was full of hope as she looked from one to the other of them. Her eyes were shining, and Ted realised it was partly due to tears threatening to fall. She was close to falling apart, he could see. What she was offering them was so tenuous that he couldn't actually see at the moment how they could use it. But she so desperately wanted it to be of use. He tried to formulate the right words.

'That's great, Jezza, it's something to go on, more than we've had before.'

His words rang hollow, even to his own ears.

'Well, I'm bloody sorry I didn't spot a distinctive tattoo, or manage to get a look at his driving licence while he was raping me!' Jezza shouted angrily, then her voice broke and the sobbing began.

'Perhaps we should take a little break, sir?' Susan suggested tactfully, nodding at Ted and Maurice to leave, while starting to console the now shaking and weeping Jezza.

'I knew I'd make it worse,' Ted said glumly, as he and Maurice went outside. 'I'm just not sure what we can do with the information. We can hardly put out a media appeal for anyone who knows someone who says shape, form or way, instead of way, shape or form, can we? We'd be flooded with calls, and not just from Honest John. Is it really that unusual?'

'It might help, though, boss. I've never consciously thought about it, but it's certainly not how I would say it. We could at least give it a go, even if it only throws up Honest John.'

Like most police stations, they had a local confessor, who rang up to lay claim to any crime he got wind off. Their own one was nicknamed Honest John because of his habit of punctuating his sentences with, 'Honest, it was me.' In reality, he was a sad and lonely depressive, housebound because of his clinical obesity, with no criminal record of any kind, despite his frequent confessions.

'And stop beating yourself up, boss,' Maurice told him. 'Don't take it personally. She needed to let go, she was too wound up. Better to let it all out now, with Susan, than trying to bottle it all up until later. We can do something with the info. All our heads will be a bit clearer by tomorrow. We're all in shock. With the team all together, we can think of what to do next.'

Susan put her head round the door then and said, 'Jezza's ready to carry on.'

When they went back inside, Jezza gave them both a wan smile and squeezed each of their hands as they sat down with her.

They went slowly and patiently over everything that Jezza could tell them. Then Ted told her the car had been found safe and was being recovered back to the station for testing. Jezza shuddered visibly.

'I'm not sure if I ever want to see it again. I just need to get Tommy's present back from it, as soon as possible.'

'Don't let him win, Jezza,' Ted told her earnestly. 'Do like one of the others did. Get the car cleaned, valeted, steam-cleaned, whatever it takes. But keep the car. Don't let him take that away from you. For now, Maurice is going to take you home, then he and Steve will stay over, so you're not on your own tonight.'

'I'll not be in tomorrow, but I should be in the day after, with any luck,' she said confidently, back to the Jezza they knew.

'I don't think so, DC Vine,' Ted told her firmly. 'You need to see a doctor and get yourself signed as fit to work before you come back. See that you do, please. And take your time. You've been through a terrible ordeal. Be nice to yourself.'

Ted couldn't remember when he had last felt as low and dispirited as he did going home, once Maurice had taken Jezza back to her flat. It was all he could do to start the car, drive the short distance back to the house and put it away in the garage.

It wasn't quite as late as he had feared. Trev was watching a foreign film, layered in softly purring cats, as usual. He looked up as Ted came into the sitting room, brushed cats aside to make some space and held out an arm for his partner to come and join him on the sofa.

'Food, talk or hugs first?' Trev asked quietly.

'No idea,' Ted sighed. 'I just want it all to be over, and to get this sick bastard put away. But we're still going round in circles, getting nowhere fast.'

He paused, then said, 'It was Jezza, this time.'

He didn't often talk much about work at home, although he knew he could trust Trev completely. This was just something too big to handle on his own. He would need his partner's support more than ever. It was only with Trev that he could begin to discuss his feelings of helplessness and inadequacy, with no result even in sight. Only Trev knew how much he was still hurting about the loss of Tina last Christmas and how all this was stirring up those barely-healed emotions.

'God, that's awful. Poor Jezza. How is she?' Trev asked as he hugged him close. 'And how are you? I know how hard you take things. Talk to me.'

Ted was an excellent listener but was never good at talking, especially about his own feelings. He would never share with anyone, even Trev, all of what Jezza had told him that evening. But he did need to talk. He needed to try to make sense of how useless the case was making him feel. He started, hesitantly at first, but he did manage to vocalise some of his sense of frustration and failure.

When he seemed to have said all he could manage, Trev kissed him gently and said, 'You should try to eat something. I made leek and potato soup. Have a bit of that. Then you need to sleep, if you can. Get an early start in the morning, come at it with fresh eyes. It will be all right, Ted.'

'That's what I kept telling Jezza. It'll be all right, we'll get him. The trouble is, just at the moment, I have no idea how.'

Chapter Nineteen

Ted slept fitfully on and off and woke early, anxious to get back to work to see if he and the team could finally make some progress.

After he'd showered and had a light breakfast, he phoned Maurice to see how Jezza was.

'She says she slept, boss, but I'm not sure I believe her,' Maurice told him. 'She insisted on getting up, so I've just made her eggy bread for breakfast. It's the girls' favourite.'

'That sounds good, I think I might come round,' Ted said wistfully, realising that his own round of wholemeal toast lacked the same comfort factor. 'Is she going to be all right, on her own? Has she got anyone she can call to be with her?'

'She's called a friend who has to be in work this morning but says she'll be able to travel over this afternoon, then she can spend the night. You know Jezza, boss, she keeps saying she's fine, she'll be all right on her own. I don't know whether to believe her or not.'

'Well, if she's in the least bit worried about being on her own, either you or Steve stay with her, and the other come in. And tell her that from me. I'll hopefully see one or other of you at the nick shortly. Thanks, Maurice.'

As soon as he disconnected the call, his phone rang and it was the Ice Queen.

'What is the latest news on DC Vine?' she asked.

'I've just checked with DC Brown. He says she seems fine, but it's hard to tell with Jezza. She likes to put up a front.'

'I'd like to have a word with you and your team this morning, please. Can you let me know as soon as everyone is in?'

'Will do,' Ted said, as she was still being reasonably informal.

She'd spoken twice without calling him Inspector, as she usually did almost every sentence. It wasn't quite as relaxed as their almost intimate conversation of the previous evening, but it was less stiff than she was capable of being.

For some reason, Ted couldn't get the image of eggy bread out of his head as he left for work. His father used to make him something similar, covered in sugar and cinnamon. He decided to make a detour via a supermarket to pick up something sweet and sticky on the way in, as well as making a few enquiries.

He went to the store where Jezza had told him she had been abducted the evening before. They hadn't yet started in-depth enquiries there, looking for witnesses, although Mike and Rob had called in, and an area car had patrolled round the car park, on the lookout for anything suspicious.

Ted went to the customer service desk, showed his warrant card and explained that they would need to see any CCTV coverage of the car park for the previous day, up to and including the time Jezza was abducted. He made an appointment for someone to go in and talk to the manager later that day.

As he was leaving, he turned back and asked, 'What do you have that tastes a bit like eggy bread? You know, French toast? With cinnamon?'

The young woman on the desk gave him a strange look as if she suddenly doubted he really was a policeman. Then she clearly remembered her training and how she should always try to help the customer, no matter how strange their request.

'What about a cinnamon Danish?' she asked helpfully. 'We have them on that aisle, just over there.' She pointed in the right direction, clearly not sure if Ted would be up to finding them on his own.

Ted took a quick bite out of his purchase when he got back to his car, but decided it didn't quite cut it. He'd got his mouth ready for a certain nostalgic taste and that wasn't it. He set it aside on the passenger seat.

He was in work ahead of his team, although Mike Hallam wasn't far behind him.

'How's Jezza this morning, boss, have you heard?'

'Maurice says she's pretending to be fine, but I can't imagine she is for a moment. He's looking after her like a proper dad. He was making her eggy bread when I phoned.'

He couldn't quite keep the note of envy out of his voice.

Mike chuckled.

'He's a good soul, is Maurice. Not the best copper on the force, but he's a kind-hearted man. If I was ill or hurt, I'd want him in my corner.'

'The Super wants to talk to the team first thing, so can you let me know once everyone's in? I'll be battling the paperwork, while I've got a quiet moment.'

Mike raised an eyebrow and Ted added, 'A bit of a pep talk, a morale booster, I imagine. It didn't sound like anything more sinister than that.'

Ted phoned down to let the Ice Queen know when everyone was in, then went out to talk to his team, perching on the edge of a desk, as he usually did. When she swept into the main office, her commanding presence had its usual effect on everyone, including Ted, as they all shot to their feet.

'I just wanted to say a few words to you all about what happened last night. Our job is hard at the best of times. When something happens to a friend and colleague, it's harder still. I don't need to tell you that the man we are currently seeking is highly dangerous, and ruthless.

'I know you're already working flat out to get this attacker. I just wanted to remind you about responsibility, and following the rules. Look after one another, whenever you can, but remember, there is a correct procedure to be followed, in everything.

'I don't want any of you,' her eyes went from one to another of the team, lingering just a moment longer on Ted, 'to do anything dangerously heroic in trying to tackle this man by yourself, should you come across him.

'Carry your radios. Keep in contact, with your team members, with the station, at all times. At the first suggestion of a sighting of this man, call for back-up. And do not in any way attempt to apprehend an armed and dangerous suspect single-handedly. You may think of it as bravery. I would consider it reckless negligence, and it could well result in disciplinary proceedings.

'Do I make myself abundantly clear to everyone?'

There was a unanimous murmur of 'Ma'am', except from Steve, who was clearly so in awe of his senior officer that he managed only a small strangled noise, rather like a squeak.

'Thank you. I won't delay you any longer. Inspector, when you have finished your briefing, would you come down to my office, please.'

When she'd left, Rob O'Connell asked, 'Boss, should we do something for Jezza? Send her something? Flowers, maybe?'

'She won't want a fuss,' Maurice warned them. 'She's spent all her time telling me how fine she is, that's why I didn't stay with her this morning. You know what she's like.'

'A card, at least,' Rob persisted. 'If we do nothing, she might think we're just not bothered about her. I know she was a complete pain in the backside when she first joined the team but, well, I think she's kind of grown on us all.'

'If you think she'd like a card, that sounds fine. Sort it out. I'll chip in and sign,' Ted told him.

Sal took a call, listened for a moment, then said to the team, 'Just getting details of a burnt out van, found up at Whitehill. Not got all the facts yet, but it's possibly a Sprinter.'

'Get forensics onto it. I want every square inch of that

vehicle going over. I want to know everything about it. Who owns it, where it's been. It's just too much of a coincidence not to be connected with the case,' Ted said, a note of hope in his voice. 'Our man might just be getting worried, and that's when he'll start to make mistakes. He may have decided the van was too hot and tried to get rid of it.

'In the meantime, we need to check for witnesses at the supermarket, and to view any CCTV footage of the car park. I've got rough details of where Jezza was parked, so let's just hope it was within camera shot. Mike, can you sort it all, please.

Ted filled the rest of the team in on all the details of the attack on Jezza. He also mentioned the one possibly distinguishing factor she had picked up on.

'He says shape, form or way, where most people would probably say way, shape or form. Is that regional? Ring any bells? Steve, can you check on the Internet, just in case it's a known regional variation. Anyone here heard it before?'

There was a general shaking of heads and Mike said reflectively, 'It's not something I've heard before, certainly. It is distinctive.'

'Right, that's encouraging, it suggests it is unusual. I'm a bit worried that making it public will open the floodgates without getting us anywhere, but it's worth a shot,' Ted replied. 'I'll talk it over with the Super, see what she says.

'And remember what the Super told you all. Look out for yourself, and for one another. Stay in contact, and absolutely no heroics, from any of you. This man is armed and dangerous.'

'Says the man who once single-handedly disarmed a nutter with two machetes,' Maurice said, loud enough for the boss to hear, which provoked general laughter.

Ted grinned guiltily.

'All right, you got me on that one. But at least I'm martial arts trained to deal with an armed attacker. And remember, I was very nearly on a disciplinary because of it.'

The thing Ted liked best about bearding the Ice Queen in her den was the coffee. This time she greeted him by placing a freshly brewed cup in front of him when he came in after knocking, then asked him to sit down. It was a promising start.

'I hope I made myself clear to the whole team, and to you in particular, Inspector,' she began. 'I know that, in the past, you have done some things which would not now be considered as compliant with the regulations. I hope you will bear that in mind.'

'Understood, ma'am,' Ted assured her, then went on to share what Jezza had told him about the attacker's figure of speech.

'It's certainly not something I can recall having heard before. I would suggest you ask your friend on the local paper to give it a mention, to make it public together with the latest e-fit of the suspect. I presume that it will be updated, on the basis of DC Vine's statement?

'It will give you the chance to offer him a small exclusive. Tell him we're not yet releasing it to any other news source. He hasn't done anything with any other information which may recently have come his way, up to now, has he?'

When Ted shook his head at her loaded question, she continued, 'Then this will be a nice little snippet for him, to keep him on side.

'What is your feeling about our man? Is he local, do you think?'

'Gut feeling? He clearly has some ties to Stockport. It's where he keeps coming back to, and as far as we know, it's the only place where he's attacked more than once. Of course if some of his victims are illegal immigrants, which is an idea we've discussed in team briefings, then they, of course, would not report crimes committed against them.'

'If he does have a Stockport connection, then that's even more reason to try a piece in the local paper, to see if anyone recognises either his picture, or details of how he speaks. I'll leave it up to you to contact the local reporter.

'And speaking of DC Vine, as we were, I imagine she is planning to come back to work soon, raring to go? I hope you will ensure that she has nothing whatever to do with the current enquiry, on her return. I'm sure you will have plenty of other things to occupy her time, but clearly we cannot take any risk of a failed conviction because a victim was involved in the case at any stage. Not to mention the emotional damage to her that continued exposure to aspects of the case is likely to cause her. I suppose I should consider temporarily transferring her, but I suspect she will feel better with the first senior officer and team she has ever made much of a connection with.'

'I've already told her as much, and reminded her that she will need to be certified as fit for work before she returns. I'll also give her details of the counselling available to her. At least I can assure her, from personal experience, that it is useful.'

'Remember to do a full return to work interview, with notes on her file. By the book with this one, Inspector,' she told him. 'By the book.'

Jezza took just two days sick leave, then phoned Ted at the end of the second day to tell him she would be back into work the following morning. As soon as he started to protest, she interrupted, 'Honestly boss, I'm fine, and it's in the interests of my sanity. There's only so much Jeremy Kyle I can watch without going completely mad. And my doctor has cleared it. I have a certificate to prove it.'

Reluctantly, Ted agreed, and asked her to come in slightly early for a return to work interview, before the morning briefing. She showed up, still looking bruised and battered, but bright and breezy, although how much of it was a front, he couldn't tell.

'It's nice to see you back, Jezza. First, I must tell you that the Super has made it perfectly clear we must proceed by the book. That will mean you taking no part at all in this enquiry, not even attending briefings about it.'

Jezza snorted defiantly.

'That's ridiculous. I can't keep going off to powder my nose any time someone wants to mention something to do with the case.'

'It's either agree to that or I will have to put you on enforced sick leave,' Ted warned her. 'And the Super has already made mutterings about a possible temporary transfer for you if you don't agree. I hope you know that I and all the team care about you, Jezza, and would like to keep you here.'

Blushing slightly, though still looking mutinous, Jezza agreed but asked, 'Can I at least just stay at my desk, if I don't take any part? After all, if I have to keep trotting in and out, it won't be good for the knife wound, will it?'

Ted hid a smile and tried to sound serious as he continued, 'I'm going to give you details of someone who can help you, if you need to talk about what happened, at any time.'

He picked up a card and held it out to her. She made no move to take it.

'It's someone who helped me a great deal, so I know that her help is valuable. How are you doing? Really?

'It's going to sound crazy but ...' her voice caught, and she needed a moment to recover her composure. 'In a way, it's slightly easier to deal with an attack by a complete stranger than ...'

Ted nodded his understanding, still waving the card at her. She took it reluctantly, and put it in her pocket.

'Right, you sit in the briefing like a wise monkey. Not one word. I just have to make a quick phone call then I'll be right there.'

When his call was answered, he said, 'Got a small, but exclusive piece for you, Alastair, if you're interested?'

'Always interested in anything you put my way, Ted. What's it about?'

'We've got an updated e-fit picture of our attacker, together with a piece of information which might possibly help identify him. I'll email everything to you, and hope you can put it out there for us, as soon as possible. We're not releasing it to anyone else at this time.'

He cut the call off abruptly when he'd had enough of the obsequious thanks. At least the piece would appear rapidly on the paper's website then, later, in the print edition. It might just bring them a lead.

Sal had an update for them at the morning briefing, in the shape of the preliminary forensic findings on the burnt out van, which was confirmed as a Sprinter.

'Stolen near Levenshulme nearly nine months ago, running on false plates, so we don't have a record of the current owner. Early tests show substantial traces of human urine and faeces in the back, as well as dog urine and faeces. So maybe transport for dog fighters, as well as people trafficking?' he speculated.

Organised dog fighting was something they'd had trouble with in the past on their patch.

'Not just human trafficking, but the puppy trade as well,' Jezza chipped in, then, seeing Ted's stern look, she opened her eyes wide in feigned innocence. 'What? I'm suffering from post-traumatic stress. I've started talking aloud to myself.

'Seriously, though, boss, one of the advantages of all that daytime television is that I saw something yesterday about the puppy trade. Dodgy breeders in Europe who put fake microchips in pups' necks and issue false passports for them, so they come into Britain without the proper vaccinations. And giving mongrels some stupid fancy so-called breed name then charging the earth for them. Then there's all the puppies coming in from the Republic of Ireland, bred on puppy farms there. That's very big business.

'So we need to look for dealers in the pet trade? To see if they've perhaps used our man as a courier? Steve, can you ...'

'On it now, boss,' Steve replied, his fingers flying over his keyboard. Then he exclaimed, 'Blimey! There's serious money in this racket. What am I bid for a Vizslapoo?'

Chapter Twenty

Pocket Billiards had published the update Ted had given him on the paper's website and social media pages almost immediately and, as Ted had feared, the phones started ringing. From the number of calls they were receiving, he began to wonder whether the phrase was as unusual as they had thought. It seemed as if everybody knew someone who said shape, form or way, instead of the other way round. Everyone from the milkman to someone's dentist was said to use it.

Kevin Turner had made some of his officers available to help with the deluge of phone calls. It was not just answering them, it was the necessary legwork of following up each call, to see if there was anything at all which gave them a link to their attacker.

'Reminds me a bit of the A6 murder trial,' Kevin Turner said, as he and Ted caught up over coffee in his office, which was even more compact than Ted's. 'I've read a lot of books on those old disputed cases. Some of the prosecution case against Hanratty relied on him supposedly saying have a kip rather than a sleep. Same sort of thing, I suppose. At least if we get it wrong, they don't swing for it any more. And I honestly can't imagine anyone in this nick altering statements to put the right phrase into an innocent person's mouth. Not these days, at least, although maybe in the past.'

'Our man's phrase is slightly more unusual than kip, though. Or at least I thought it was, until every man and his dog started phoning in saying their neighbour uses it all the time. What I really want now is a tip-off on someone who says it like that and who drives a white Sprinter van, while delivering dogs. Wearing a flashing Santa hat.'

He didn't quite get all he wished for, but after Sal took one call, he went into Ted's office and said, 'A possible, boss. Some people bought a puppy online and went to pick it up from a delivery driver at a motorway service station. He had a Sprinter van, which had quite a few dogs in travel crates in the back.

'They said they remembered distinctly that the man told them a couple of times that he was just the delivery driver and he wasn't responsible for the dog's paperwork or vaccinations or anything else in any shape, form or way.'

Ted looked up hopefully.

'Description?'

'Medium height, average build, mid to late forties. Wearing a dark winter hat and dark clothing. No particular accent that they noticed, just that unusual turn of phrase. They said it stuck in their minds as they'd not heard it said that way before, and he used it more than once.

'The dog they collected was very ill when they got it home. They had to take it to the vet who found that its papers and microchip were both false. It cost a fortune to get it put right, and it had to go into quarantine, as it had come into the country illegally.'

'Right, well, the dog aspect doesn't concern us. You'll need to liaise with Trading Standards on that, I imagine. I'm not sure who else, you'll have to find out. But get round and see the buyers, Sal, as soon as possible. Get every bit of information you can on where they bought this dog from, how they got in touch, where the pick-up was. Let's see if we can find Mr Shape-Form-or-Way by this route.'

Ted followed Sal out into the main office and saw Jezza standing in front of Steve's mapping diagram, where he had been trying to establish links with bus routes, locations of the attacks and where the cars had been abandoned. It was up on the wall next to the normal white board with all the details, including the victims' names and dates of the incidents. Jezza's own name had now joined the others.

'Jezza, haven't you got some work to be getting on with?' he asked pointedly. 'If not, I can soon find you some.'

'I was just wondering what day of the week the Folkestone and Dover attacks were, boss. Something else I remembered from the programme I was watching. The dog smugglers like to travel at the weekends. There are no Trading Standards or Animal Health Agency staff on at the ports then, apparently, so it's a piece of cake getting dogs through with dodgy paperwork.'

'We're already looking at the dog trade angle, but you're not involved in this case at all,' Ted reminded her then, in a softer tone, 'but thanks for that. They were both weekends, as it happens.'

Ted had been keeping an anxious eye out on the local paper, and the nationals, for anything leaking out about the work of Dr Heather Cooper, after his meeting with Pocket Billiards. When it did break, it was bigger than he had dared hope. It formed a sizeable spread locally, with the nationals braying headlines like 'Dodgy Doc's Disgrace.'

Pocket Billiards was a good journalist, despite his other less desirable habits, Ted had to give him that. He'd certainly had a field day, checking into her background, and had found out that, amongst other details, her 'doctorate' referred to a PhD which she had started but never completed.

He'd also followed Ted's advice of asking around, probably Canal Street and The Village, and had found a couple of teenagers whose parents had taken them along to the therapist to be 'cured' of being gay.

Jenny Holden was identified only as JH, but her story was given in detail. There was no mention of Kenny Norman's name, Ted was pleased to discover. It was just reported that she had accused 'a Stockport man', who had later been entirely cleared by the police of any involvement in either the historical allegations or the ongoing enquiry.

It was an extremely effective hatchet job, all perfectly ethically done. Ted was not surprised to read that Heather Cooper herself had been 'unavailable for comment', her consulting room locked up with no explanation, and she appeared to have 'left town without leaving contact details.'

Ted's mobile rang while he was reading. He answered it without even looking at the screen.

'Ted? It's Philip. I take it you had a hand in what I'm currently reading in the press? If you did, I love you for it. The world is better off without someone like that, messing with the heads of impressionable young people, just at a time when they need help and support.'

He ended the call before Ted had chance to say anything. There was clearly still a lot of raw feeling there. He wished there was a way to make it better, but he decided that picking over the past to put things right was not always the best thing to do.

Ted was so engrossed in what he was reading that he barely noticed his office door open until he found the Ice Queen towering over his desk. He leapt up anxiously, trying to read her expression, looking at her over the top of the reading glasses he was wearing.

She sat down, without him saying anything.

'So,' she began. 'Our Dr Cooper was not what she seemed to be. And you said nothing to your press contact about any of this?'

'Not a word, ma'am,' Ted replied, with a clear conscience. 'In fact, I didn't know about the phony qualification.'

'Probably just as well, in view of how your discussion with her went when you didn't know,' she said, but her eyes had a mischievous twinkle as she said it. 'What I really need to know is whether there is likely to be any fall-out which we will have to deal with. Do you think the press in general will be happy to let the unfortunate Mr Norman remain anonymous? It is to be hoped so, for the sake of his sister.'

'I doubt they'd do it for that reason but yes, hopefully they'll be more interested in trying to track down anyone else with a story to tell after a visit to the Dodgy Doc.'

She seemed satisfied and went on her way, leaving Ted to try again to clear his paperwork backlog. He wished there was some of it he could delegate, much as he hated to hand work on. At the moment he felt he was drowning in it, and Ted hated to feel he was drowning.

He was interrupted once more by the phone on his desk ringing.

'Ted? Bill. You have a visitor.'

The duty sergeant lowered his voice slightly as he added, 'It's Jenny Holden again, in a right old state. She's insisting on seeing you. Can you come down?'

Ted sighed quietly. It was about the last thing he needed, but he was clearly going to have to go and sort it. He had known she was likely to be devastated by some of the revelations about the person in whom she had put so much trust.

'Is there an interview room free? Can you get someone to put her in there, with a cup of tea, and I'll be right down. I don't suppose you could spare me Susan Heap or someone? I'd just feel happier with someone with me.'

'You know how stretched we are, Ted. Could your young Jezza not do it?'

'I can't let her get involved in the current case at all ...'

'It's not connected to your current enquiries though, is it?' Bill cut in, his tone reasonable. 'This is historic stuff, and not even true at that, as it turns out.'

'You're right, as usual, Bill. I'll see who's free and come down in a minute.'

Jezza was working at her desk. Sal was the only other one

in the office, still manning the phones with the endless calls about people allegedly using the catch phrase.

'Sal, could you come down and sit in with me, please, while I talk to someone? It's nothing to do with this case. I don't know if you've seen the local paper? It's related to their lead story. The woman referred to only as JH is downstairs wanting to talk to me. I'd prefer not to do it alone and Susan Heap's not free.'

'The Dodgy Doc?' Sal queried. 'Is there something in it for us, then?'

'It's complicated. One of her former patients, or clients, or whatever they are, one who made serious allegations, is downstairs. She wants to talk to me and I'd just prefer to have a witness. She's apparently in a bit of a state. There are things she clearly wasn't aware of, and it must all have come as a considerable shock.'

'Er, hello, boss?' Jezza said pointedly. 'Apparently invisible female officer here, ready, willing and available for all chaperone duties.'

Ted hesitated.

'Jezza, I just think this could be something you might want to avoid …'

She was already on her feet as she said, 'You've already said it's got nothing to do with the current case. So whatever else it is, I have a medical certificate to say I'm fit to do it. Shall we go?'

A constable in uniform was waiting with Jenny Holden when Ted and Jezza arrived. Ted thanked her as she left, then he and Jezza sat down opposite the woman. She looked pale and distressed and her hand, trying to hold the cup of tea she had been given, was shaking badly whenever she attempted to lift it to her mouth.

'It was all lies,' she began as soon as they sat down, her voice anguished. 'Whatever that woman did to me, however she made me believe what I did believe, it was just lies. How was she able to carry on doing stuff like that, for ten years or more? When she wasn't even qualified?'

'Ms Holden, I haven't had the opportunity to look into Dr Cooper's background ...'

'Doctor? Quack, more like,' she spat. 'How could it happen? I was alone with her; I trusted her. She hypnotised me and planted all sorts of stuff in my head ...'

'Again, I can't really comment at this stage. It's not something I know enough about. There will certainly be a full investigation into what went on ...'

'Oh God, poor Kenny,' she suddenly wailed, looking more distressed than ever. 'None of it was true, was it? I said all those things about him. Dreadful, dreadful things. Then when the police wouldn't take any action, I did something really shocking. I thought he was guilty and the police were just covering up, for some reason. That's what I went to the papers about. The supposed cover-up. Now I know what really happened. Kenny was innocent all along. It was her. She made me believe he was guilty.'

She leaned forward in her chair, making earnest eye contact first with Ted, then Jezza, then back to Ted.

'But I really believed it. I honestly did. I was convinced that Kenny had raped me.'

Ted sensed Jezza shifting uncomfortably in her seat next to him. He inwardly cursed his stupidity and thoughtlessness for having brought her in on the conversation, particularly without warning her exactly what the subject matter was.

'Ms Holden, I accept that you firmly believed what you were saying. It's unfortunate that, because of confidentiality, the police were not able to share information with you to explain why they had been able to establish, beyond any doubt, that Kenny Norman was innocent. I can assure you categorically that there was no cover-up.'

She was crying now, noisy sobs. Wordlessly, Jezza took a packet of paper handkerchiefs out of her pocket and handed them to her.

'I have to make it right. I have to find Kenny and beg him to forgive me. He was always so kind to me. You said he was out of the country? I can remember where he used to live. I'll go there, see if his mother is still alive, or his sister. I'll tell them how very sorry I am for all the terrible things I said and did, and ask them to please let me get in contact with Kenny and tell him myself.'

Ted cleared his throat awkwardly to buy himself some time. He realised that he was rapidly getting out of his depth, still desperately trying to keep control of a situation he didn't feeling qualified to handle.

'Ms Holden, perhaps it might just be better to leave it all in the past? Kenny and his family knew he was innocent. I think they probably accept that you had, er, various problems in your private life which may have led to you behaving as you did ...'

'But I can't just put it in the past,' she sobbed. 'Apart from the terrible damage I did to Kenny, and to his family, I spent six months of my life in prison because of it. I have to start trying to put it right.'

Nothing Ted tried to say could shake her resolve, even when he pointed out she was not supposed to contact the family at all. She left the station stating her intention to try to track down Kenny Norman to begin to make amends.

'Jezza, I'm so sorry, I shouldn't have involved you in that ...' Ted began awkwardly as they started back up the stairs together.

'Forget it, boss, it's fine,' she reassured him. 'It's my job. I can't just stop working on anything which reminds me of what happened to me or I wouldn't be very good at it, would I?'

Ted hesitated in his office, the phone in his hand. Whatever he did at the moment seemed to make a bad situation worse. He thought he better phone Kenny Norman's sister, though, just to let her know that Jenny Holden might turn up on her doorstep.

'I haven't, of course, told her anything about what happened to your brother, Ms Norman. But I thought I better warn you that she may well try to contact you. She may even be on her way there. It is, of course, entirely up to you whether or not you choose to tell her what happened.

'Thank you for calling, Inspector, you really are most kind. I did hear on the local news about the so-called doctor Jenny went to see. Kenny never blamed Jenny, you know. That's the sort of man he was. He kept saying that she was easily led. That's why she got into trouble with drink and drugs and whatever else it was.

'It would have been easy to plant the germ of an idea in her head and she would have believed anything. She was, what's the word they use nowadays? Suggestible. Yes, that was it. Suggestible. If someone she trusted told her that any factual historical event never happened, she would believe it.

'If she comes here, I will probably tell her the truth about Kenny. I think she deserves to know. I will also, of course, tell her that he never blamed her. That he forgave her. It was just his experience at the hands of the police which destroyed him. Perhaps that might give her some peace. And then perhaps we can all leave the whole dreadful episode in the past, where it belongs.'

Ted was relieved to get home at the end of a long day. Trev had not been in long himself. Now he was a partner in the business, he was trying to build it up, taking on more service contract work. He was feeding the cats in the kitchen. The oven was on and something inside it was smelling good. Their self-defence and martial arts clubs were on a break over the holiday period so they wouldn't be going out.

They exchanged a hug and Ted said, 'I hope your day's been better than mine. If ever they make putting your foot in it an Olympic sport, I'll be the team captain. I seem to have done nothing but all day.'

'I've been madly busy all day, like a proper grown up,' Trev grinned. 'Makes me realise how much of a skiver I was when I was just a wage earner. Supper won't be long. It's just heated up left-overs, I'm afraid. I can't be a high-flying businessman and a brilliant cook at the same time. Do you want to put your feet up for ten minutes before we eat?'

'If I do, I'll just fall asleep. I'll lay the table, keep myself awake ...' he was interrupted by his mobile phone's Freddie Mercury ringtone.

'Bill again, Ted, sorry to disturb you. We've just had a call about a suspicious death. A young woman, found by her flatmate, hanging from her bedroom door. I thought you'd want to know straight away, only I knew the address as soon as I heard it. I don't have a formal ID yet, but the address is Jenny Holden's.'

Chapter Twenty-one

'So sorry, I have to go,' Ted told Trevor apologetically. 'A suspicious death. As it happens, it's someone I was speaking to this morning, it seems. I've no idea how long I'll be.'

'I'll keep some food for you. Have you at least time for a cuppa and maybe a sandwich?'

Ted shook his head.

'Got to go. I'll be back as soon as I can.'

Rob O'Connell was on call for the evening so Ted phoned him and arranged to drive by his house to pick him up. No sense in both of them having to get their cars out. Bill had given Ted the address and it was not far.

There was already a Uniform presence and Ted could see from the vehicles outside that one of the younger pathologists on Bizzie Nelson's team was also there already.

Ted and Rob pulled on shoe covers and latex gloves before entering what was at this stage a potential crime scene. The flat in question was on the third floor, at the top of the tall, narrow building, with a dimly-lit, creaking staircase.

A distraught young woman was being consoled by one of the first attending officers out on the landing. Another officer was at the open door to the flat, controlling entry. Although Ted knew every officer in the station by name as well as by sight, for form's sake he produced his warrant card before he stepped carefully into the small space of a cramped and cluttered hallway.

'It's the room at the far end, on the right, sir,' the constable on the door told him. 'The pathologist is already there.'

Ted and Rob made their way down the passage. Clearly, housework had not been a favourite occupation of either Jenny Holden or her flatmate. The whole place stank of stale cigarette smoke and old beer.

The body had already been cut down and was lying on the floor just inside a door which opened on to a dingy and untidy bedroom. James Barrington, the pathologist, was examining it. There was what appeared to be a bathrobe cord round Jenny Holden's neck, her tongue protruding between her teeth, her face discoloured.

'Evening, Ted,' James said in response to Ted's greeting, without looking up from his work. 'On the face of it, this is a simple suicide. I've seen nothing suspicious at all so far. Recent, too. I'd say she'd only been dead an hour or so when the flatmate found her. She cut her down and made a half-hearted attempt to resuscitate, but it was far too late.'

'I was speaking to her only this morning,' Ted said, trying not to look at the body but finding his eyes were compulsively drawn to it, despite his best efforts.

Instinctively, he put a Fisherman's Friend lozenge in his mouth and let its menthol fumes help to disguise the inevitable smell from the body.

'It's all such a mess, a real tragedy. You've probably seen the papers. This was the young woman involved in the historical rape allegation.

'Rob, can you get a statement from the flatmate, please? We'll clearly need to talk to her again, probably tomorrow, when she's recovered from the initial shock, but find out what she can tell us for now.

'When can you fit the post-mortem in, James, any idea yet?'

'We're just a bit snowed under at the moment, Ted. The Professor's had to take a couple of days off as her mother's had a fall, so there's a slight backlog. As this isn't looking like anything suspicious, can I provisionally say early afternoon tomorrow? But if I find anything on the body which makes me think there may be more to it, I promise to let you know and to bump her up the list.

'There's a note, which should simplify things, I imagine. Stay where you are, I'll pass it over.'

He straightened up and went to a dressing table, of sorts, underneath the window. Every inch of its surface area was covered in cosmetics, dirty coffee mugs, and a layer of dust. Ted took out an evidence bag from his pocket and held it open so that James could drop the note straight into it.

It wasn't long. He scanned it quickly. Jenny's handwriting was a childish scrawl, her spelling was poor, but the meaning was clear. Ted couldn't help thinking to himself that Jenny Holden had clearly been much better with figures than with words.

'I been thinking so much about what I did to Kenny. I never meant for it to happen. I beleived what I said, what that woman made me think. Im sorry for Kenny for everything. Sorry. And sorry Rhona. Luv you x'

'Thanks, James. Let me know a time for tomorrow when you can and one of us will be there. I'll just check with the flatmate if this is Jenny's handwriting. But as you say, it looks straightforward at the moment. Still a tragic loss of a young life, though.'

Rob had taken the flatmate into the kitchen, where the Uniform constable had made her a cup of tea. She offered to make some for Rob, and for Ted, when he came in, but both declined when they saw the dirty dishes piled up in a bowl of greasy, grey water.

Ted looked enquiringly at Rob, who made the introductions.

'Boss, this is Jenny's flatmate, Rhona Wesley. Rhona, this is Detective Inspector Darling.'

'You've had a terrible shock, Miss Wesley, and I don't want to bother you more than I need to for the moment. I wonder if you could just take a look at this note for me and tell me if you recognise the handwriting?'

He let her take the note to examine, protected as it was inside the evidence bag. The sight of it brought fresh tears to her eyes.

'It's Jenny's writing. She wrote it,' she confirmed. 'I didn't see it when I went in. I was too busy trying to get Jenny down and see if she was ...'

Her voice broke on a sob.

'Would you happen to have anything else she may have written, which we can take for comparison?'

The young woman rummaged through papers scattered over the kitchen table, which was in as much of a state of disorder as the rest of the flat.

'Jenny drew up a rota about who should do the cleaning and the washing up,' she said, finding a rough timetable, scribbled on the back of a large envelope. 'We were always arguing about who should do what. As you can see, we argued so much it never got done, except when we had visitors.'

She started to cry again as she handed it to Ted. He put it into another evidence bag and transferred both to his pocket.

'We're possibly going to have to bring in more officers to do a thorough search of the premises in connection with what has happened,' Ted told her. 'Do you have somewhere you can go and stay tonight? You might, in any event, not want to remain in the flat on your own, in the circumstances.'

'Definite suicide, boss?' Rob asked, on the way back in Ted's car.

'Looking like a certainty, but we won't really know until the post-mortem. For now we'll carry on treating it as a suspicious death. By the way, your Sally's an RSPCA officer, isn't she? I wondered if you could possibly ask her who we need to talk to about this puppy smuggling angle for our attacker? I'm more interested in getting our man for the rapes, of course, but we should try to help mop up other offences arising out of our own investigation, if we can. As long as they don't take priority.'

Rob was recently engaged. He had joked that his fiancée's work with animals made her hours every bit as anti-social as a copper's were. It should at least mean that their relationship shouldn't suffer the same fate as that of many others in the force, solely on the basis of his hours.

Yet again Ted arrived home late, finding his appetite had all but deserted him and all he really wanted to do was to sleep.

'You need to eat something,' Trev told him anxiously. 'You are losing weight, you know, and you haven't got it to lose. Try to eat a bit at least.'

Ted did his best. The food was delicious, as usual. He just couldn't get over the fact that he felt he was in part to blame for Jenny Holden's death. He should have seen that she was fragile, should somehow have realised what her likely reaction would be to the news of how Kenny Norman had ended his days.

He put his knife and fork down apologetically, with less than half of his plate cleared.

'It's good, it really is, I've just gone past the point of being hungry. Sorry. It was a particularly tough one tonight. Someone I'd been talking to only this morning, who went on to hang themselves this afternoon.'

Wordlessly, Trev moved closer and hugged him. Ted appreciated the warmth of the spontaneous gesture, so typical of his partner. But somehow, the way he was currently feeling, even one of Trev's hugs wasn't making him feel much better.

It was another night when what sleep he did manage to snatch was fitful, his dreams troubled, disturbed by overwhelming feelings of guilt. He kept waking with his heart racing, asking himself over and over if he could have handled things differently. If somehow he should have acted in a way which would have prevented a young woman ending up dead by her own hand. He was also worried at the prospect of telling the Ice Queen of the latest development, and how she would react to the news.

Another early start. Another hastily-eaten round of toast. He knew Trev was right. His belt was already fastening a notch tighter than it had before and was starting to feel loose again. He promised himself that if he could only make some sort of progress on the latest case, he'd take Trev away somewhere nice for a weekend. Somewhere simple, which wouldn't cost a lot, as he was keeping an even closer eye than usual on his finances. Just a little B&B, with some good hill walking and delicious food nearby. It was what they both needed.

The Ice Queen was also in early. All credit to her, Ted thought, she led by example. He knew some bosses who rolled in when they felt like it and spent their time navel-gazing and pushing paperwork. But she always put in a full day to match that of any officer under her command. He gave her just enough time to get her coffee machine on the go before he knocked on her door.

'A suspicious death last night, I hear,' she began, sorting out mugs, nodding at Ted to sit down.

Hesitantly at first, he began to tell her everything he knew leading up to, and including the death of Jenny Holden the previous day. She served coffee as he did so, then sat down opposite him, her expression reflective.

'I see,' she said in a neutral tone. 'A tragic and most unfortunate incident. I imagine that, as one of the last people to see her alive, you may well be called to give evidence at the inquest. You'd better prepare your notes on your conversation with her. Was someone with you at the time?'

'Yes, ma'am, DC Vine sat in on the conversation.'

'Very good. Get her to prepare her own account of what was said and let me have both copies by the end of today, without fail. I need hardly add that the two of you should not discuss the matter at all.'

They both paused to drink some of the coffee. As usual, it was excellent and Ted was grateful for the warmth and the sweetness of it, as he'd added extra sugar, feeling the need of a boost. It was some small degree of comfort.

He had groaned inwardly when the Ice Queen mentioned the inquest. He had realised, of course, that he would almost certainly be called as a witness. But the coroner was by no means his biggest fan. He was a dry as a stick solicitor who liked everything to be done to the letter. He disapproved of Ted's relaxed style in everything. Even the Ice Queen's insistence that Ted wear formal suits instead of his preferred smart casual soft chinos had not altered the coroner's opinion. Ted had strong suspicions that he disapproved of his sexuality, as much as anything.

'I want to state at the outset that you have my full support. But we do now need to talk damage limitation. It's essential that you are entirely frank with me at this stage, so that I know what we are dealing with. Can you assure me once more that you said nothing at all to the local reporter which set this unfortunate series of events in motion?'

Ted swallowed more coffee before he formulated his response. 'I said absolutely nothing at all to him.'

'I'm sensing a but? I hope you know by now that you can trust me. But I do need to know the full facts in order to manage the situation.'

'I met Pocket Billiards in The Grapes, to give him the press release about Jenny Holden's historical allegations, as we discussed. It's just possible that, when I went to the bar to order food, he may have seen a book which I was reading. A book by Heather Cooper, about some of her cases involving hypnosis, which mentioned Jenny Holden's case, though not her name.'

'I see,' she said again. 'Anything else?'

'It's also possible that he may have picked up one of the leaflets I collected when I visited Ms Cooper. The ones where she was offering a cure for young people with mistaken ideas about their sexuality. Her words, definitely not mine.'

They both paused for more coffee. Wordlessly, the Ice Queen stood up to refill their cups. That usually signalled that they were in for a long session.

'So, just to recap, the reporter may have seen that you were reading a certain book, which is on sale to the general public, which was written by Ms Cooper? And he may possibly have picked up one of her own leaflets, which she presumably made freely available to anyone? But you had no form of discussion on any of it?'

Ted shook his head.

'None at all. The only other thing was that on another occasion he asked me where he could find people like me to talk to. Again, his words. Meaning, he told me, gay people. So I suggested he went to Canal Street. That's as far as it went.'

'So Jenny Holden only found out, when his articles broke, that her memory may have been a false one? And that it may have come about in her sessions with someone she discovered through the article had lied about her qualifications? At what point did she learn what had happened to the unfortunate Mr Norman?'

'When she came to see me yesterday, she was devastated to have learned that her allegations were definitely false. She said, and I accepted, that she firmly believed they were true. She was desperate to try to put things right. Clearly, I couldn't tell her what had happened to Kenny Norman, but she needed answers.

'She knew where he used to live, of course, although she had never been near. She told me that it was a condition of her release from prison that she stay away from the family. She said she would go round there. I try to dissuade her but she was determined. I phoned Miss Norman to let her know. She said she might tell Jenny the truth, and tell her that she and her brother had forgiven her, hoping it might bring her some peace of mind.

'I suspect I may have mishandled the situation. I should perhaps have done more.'

The Ice Queen drank her coffee as she looked at him thoughtfully.

'I think, Inspector, that sometimes you are inclined to take things rather too personally, too much to heart. It is a good quality, up to the point where it starts to affect your judgement. From what you have told me, and I see no reason to doubt your word, I cannot see how you could have handled this any differently.

'Heather Cooper was extremely convincing, certainly when I spoke to her, at length. We will need now to carry out a full investigation of the work she was doing and whether or not she was properly qualified to carry out any of it. This is not an investigation which you will take any part in, for obvious reasons.

'Knowing you, I assume you checked at the time of your unfortunate encounter with her that the so-called treatment she was offering was not illegal in any way?'

When Ted nodded without speaking, she continued, 'Then we will need to carry out an in-depth examination of everything else she did, and there may well be a prosecution to arise out of it all.

'Concerning your discussion with Ms Holden and the later tragic event, subject to seeing notes from you and DC Vine, I cannot at this moment see how you are culpable in any way. If it's of any consolation to you, I suspect I might have handled matters in a very similar way myself.

'My advice to you would be to forget about this for the time being and concentrate on the ongoing enquiry. Try not to let it prey on your mind. And thank you for your honesty.'

For some reason her words brought Ted close to tears. He excused himself hurriedly and took himself off to the gents. He was not yet ready to face his team for the morning briefing. He decided instead to text Mike Hallam, asking him to start without him.

It was easy for the Ice Queen to tell him to forget about it. As far as he was concerned, Ted had the death of a vulnerable young woman on his conscience.

The only thing he could do for now was to get his head down and work even harder on his current case. If he could at least start to see a result in that, it may possibly allow him to feel slightly less guilty.

Chapter Twenty-two

Trev was surprised to get an early evening phone call from Maurice Brown. He knew and got on with all of Ted's team, but he was not particularly close to Maurice and hadn't given him his mobile number, as far as he could remember. Maurice must have got it from Sal.

'Trev, it's Maurice. Is the boss there?'

'He's not back from work yet, Maurice,' Trev told him. 'Have you tried his mobile?'

There was a pause, then Maurice said carefully, 'He's not been in work all day. We haven't heard anything from him and his mobile seems to be switched off.'

Again the hesitation, then, 'I'm a bit worried about him, to be honest, Trev. He doesn't seem himself. He was like a zombie all day yesterday. Hardly said two words to anyone and the ones he did say were grumpy. Not like him at all. He's been like that a few days now, ever since that young woman hanged herself.'

Trev felt his stomach tightening with anxiety, hearing Maurice voice exactly what he had been feeling.

'This case is really getting to him, I know. He's not been sleeping or eating very well. Then we had a bit of a scare with my sister recently. She's always going AWOL from school, apparently, and a young girl turned up murdered in the same area, which shook us both a bit. And you know what he's like, Maurice, he just shuts down sometimes, even with me. Are you sure he's not just gone off following a lead by himself?'

'I'm not trying to scare you, Trev, but I really am worried about him. It's not at all like him to be out of touch with the team. We usually get a text if nothing else. Have you any idea where he might have gone? Somewhere he might go just to give himself some space, do some thinking? I know it's only been today but he's been pretty low at work for a while.'

'He's been the same at home,' Trev admitted, starting to get seriously worried now.

He'd always thought of Maurice as not particularly sensitive. If even he had noticed it, then things were clearly not right.

'I'm not much good at a lot of stuff but I'm a good dad, and I know when someone is hurting,' Maurice said, as if reading his thoughts. 'And the boss is hurting, more than he's letting on to anyone, maybe even to you. I just wonder if we should go and look for him?'

Trev noticed the 'we' and felt grateful that Maurice obviously cared so much.

'I know a few places he might go. The car's not here, so he's out somewhere. Just hang on a sec, Maurice, let me see if he's gone out in his work clothes.'

Trev sprinted up the stairs to the bedroom, keeping the call connected. Ted's work suits were still hanging in the wardrobe, with his trench coat and smart shoes, but his hill-walking fleece jacket was missing and so were his walking boots. Ted had, as usual, left quietly before Trev was even awake, so he'd been unaware that he had not gone out dressed for work.

'Maurice? He's gone out in his walking gear, so I have some idea of where he might have gone. I'll take the bike and see if I can find him. Can you keep trying his mobile, let me know if you track him down?'

Trev could see that Ted had not even taken any equipment with him. His rucksack, even his day pack, were both still in the wardrobe, and his good waterproof was hanging there. Wherever he was, he was going to be wet and cold if he was outside somewhere, with what the weather was like out there.

'Trev, I'm coming with you. I'll be there in ten minutes.'

'I'll be quicker on my own, Maurice, honestly …' Trev started to protest.

'We'll go in my car. When we do find the boss, and his car, you're going to need to drive him home, make sure he's all right, and you won't want to leave the bike in the middle of nowhere. I'm on my way.'

'You'll need walking boots, and outdoor gear,' Trev warned him. 'And a torch.'

'I've got no proper boots, but I'll manage. It's not the north face of the Eiger and this is the boss we're talking about.'

His words made tears spring to Trev's eyes as he ended the call. He tried Ted's mobile himself but it went straight to voicemail. As Maurice had said, it seemed as if it was switched off.

He kept thinking that Ted would walk through the door at any minute, laughing at him and Maurice for worrying like a pair of old mother hens. He didn't really believe it, though. He quickly checked that his own rucksack had everything he needed – fresh water, first aid kit, an extra fleece, space blanket, Ted's waterproof, some high-energy bars. He just had time to fill a flask of Ted's green tea with honey when he heard Maurice's car pull up outside. He pulled his boots on and hurried out to meet him, climbing into the passenger seat and throwing the rucksack into the back.

'I think the rape victim getting killed, near to Christmas, has really got to him, Trev. It brought it all back, you know, what happened last year. With Tina. And then that poor woman hanging herself, not long after she'd been talking to him. But I've been worried about him for a good few days now.

'We need to start off with where he and I went last year, after it happened. After Tina was killed,' Trev told him, directing Maurice out towards Marple Ridge.

There was no sign of Ted's car there, near the track where

they had walked and eaten fish and chips for comfort food, so Trev continued, 'Saddleworth next, then. It's where he sometimes goes when he's brooding over a difficult case.'

There was no sign of Ted's Renault there, either, in any of the parking places he usually used. When he was struggling with a case, Ted would sometimes visit the scene of the infamous Moors Murders, to help focus his thoughts. Trev tried his mobile again, with the same result.

'He's probably sitting at home by now, wondering where I've gone,' Trev said, trying to make light of it.

Maurice looked at him seriously as he said, 'I think we both know he isn't, Trev. Right, so where next?'

Trev got back into the car next to Maurice once more.

'Where we should probably have gone straight away,' he said, as they drove off, Maurice following his directions.

Ted's was the only car in the otherwise deserted car park near to Hayfield. It was getting late, it was dark and cold, and an incessant drizzle was making it feel even colder.

'Are you sure you don't want to wait in a pub somewhere down here, Maurice?' Trev asked him, pulling on a fleece hat and slipping his head torch over it. 'This is a good walk even in the daylight on a sunny day, if you're not much of a walker. It's not going to be a picnic in the dark, in this weather.'

'You're going to need help when you find the boss. I'm not up to much in the hills, but I'm the best you've got at the moment. And I'm first aid trained, at least, in case there's any call for that,' Maurice told him. 'So let's save our breath for walking, shall we?'

He took a Maglite out of his pocket, falling into step beside Trev, as they headed up towards Kinder Downfall.

Trev hadn't been joking when he'd said it was not going to be an easy walk for Maurice, ill-equipped and inexperienced as he was. It wasn't long before he was grumbling at every step.

'Why can't the boss just go out and get pissed, like any normal copper would in the circumstances?'

Trev paused a moment to let Maurice get his breath back, and to take off his shoes to adjust his socks, which had slipped down below his heels.

'Because he doesn't touch the stuff. Because his father was an alcoholic,' Trev replied patiently, with just a hint of reproach in his tone.

'Yeah, sorry, Trev, I forgot. Shall we go on?'

'We have no choice. If I were you, I'd save your breath for walking. We still have quite a way to go, and we've got the steepest part of the route in front of us.'

They could both hear Ted long before they came in sight of him, even above the noise of the waterfall and the sound of Maurice's increasingly laboured breathing. The night was inky black up here, visibility reduced by the cold, driving rain which was being blown sideways by a strong wind. From the rocks up above them, they could hear Ted's good tenor voice singing clearly. But like a tape on a loop, it was just a fragment of a song, sung over and over again.

'What the hell?' Maurice asked, between rough, rasping breaths.

'Bohemian Rhapsody,' Trev told him tersely, 'the bit leading up to 'I sometimes wish I'd never been born at all',' he added, as he peered anxiously upwards through the enveloping dark, waiting impatiently for Maurice to recover enough breath to continue.

'Go on, Trev, don't wait for me. Get up there, for God's sake, before he does something stupid.'

Trev was desperate to do as Maurice said. But he was also an experienced hill walker, too much so to leave anyone as inexperienced and badly equipped as Maurice to struggle on alone in the darkness. And he knew Ted would skin him alive if he let anything happen to one of his precious team members. Ted would be all right, Trev told himself repeatedly, as long as he just kept on singing.

'I'm coming, Ted, hang on in there,' he said under his

breath, grabbing Maurice's arm and half-hauling him up the last few metres of the stiff climb, trying to close his ears every time Ted got to the line, 'Goodbye, everybody, I've got to go.'

They finally saw Ted's silhouette in the beam of light from Trev's head torch, which he had dipped to the maximum so as not to startle or dazzle him. Ted was sitting on one of the furthest rocks, his legs over its edge, dangling into the void beside the waterfall.

'Hey, you,' Trev said quietly, as he approached slowly and carefully. 'You're late for supper.'

Ted turned his head and Trev could make out in the light of the torch that his expression looked bemused. He could see, too, that Ted was shivering with the cold. He had no waterproof on, his fleece jacket looked wet through, and his blonde hair, the shade of dusty over-ripe corn, hatless, was plastered to his head by the rain.

'Sorry,' Ted said, 'I think I lost track of time a bit. I needed to think.'

He looked past Trev to Maurice's looming figure and asked, his voice puzzled, 'Maurice?'

'Now then, boss, it's a strange place to be giving a concert. Why don't you come back down with me and Trev?'

Trev was gradually moving carefully closer, his face anxious. He had no idea what was going through Ted's mind. He just wanted to get him away from the drop.

'I think I lost my way a bit, too,' Ted said, in a small voice.

Wordlessly, Trev reached out and folded him in a careful hug, helping him to his feet, guiding him away from the edge of the waterfall, and sitting him down on a rock. He peeled off Ted's wet fleece and helped him into a dry one. Then he got his space blanket out and wrapped it round Ted's shoulders. He and Maurice sat down on either side of him, their closeness adding to the essential warmth to thaw him out.

'It's going to be all right now. We're both here, we're going to make sure you're all right. Have some tea to warm you up, then Maurice and I are going to get you safely down from here,' Trev told him, as Maurice nodded in agreement.

Then Trev said again, more firmly, 'It's going to be all right.'

'That's what I keep saying,' Ted sighed. 'I keep telling everyone that. But it isn't. It's not all right at all. I don't know if I can go on. I don't know if I can do it any more.'

Trev and Maurice exchanged anxious looks. Ted's voice was so forlorn, small and hollow. Trev had seen him low many times before, because of the nature of his job, but he couldn't recall when he had seen him as down as this.

'Come on, Ted, we need to get you down from here and into some dry clothes,' Trev said, the note of concern in his voice unmistakeable. Still Ted seemed reluctant to make a move.

'Why don't you two go on down? I'll be fine now. I'll just finish my tea to warm up, then I'll follow you down.'

Again the two men exchanged glances. There was no way they were leaving him there alone, not now they'd found him and seen the state he was in. Maurice decided the situation called for drastic measures.

'Bloody hell, boss, stop pissing about and come on. I'm freezing cold and wet through and I want my tea, even if you don't. And while you're fannying around up here singing whatever shit it is, I'm freezing my nadgers off and I want to go home, right?'

Ted blinked at him in surprise, rain streaming down his face, running off the end of his nose. If anything could get through to him in his present state of mind, it was his unfailing care and compassion for others, especially his team members.

'Sorry. Sorry, Maurice, you're right, we should go now.'

He got uncertainly to his feet as Trev slipped an arm round him to help and support him.

It took far longer than it should have done to get him back down to the car park. It was a walk Ted had done countless times before. This time he was hesitant and stumbling, confused and disorientated. Trev was getting increasingly concerned with every unsure step Ted took, but after what seemed like an eternity, they finally reached the car park. Between them, they bundled Ted into the passenger seat of his own car, then Trev turned to Maurice.

'Thanks so much for your help, Maurice. Clearly, he's not going to be in work tomorrow. I'll phone the Ice Queen, but can you let the rest of the team know he's not well. I think he'd prefer it if they didn't know what happened this evening.'

'I'm not stupid, Trev. What happened here stays between us. I'll tell the team the boss has a bug and he just happened to contact me to let me know.'

'Thanks again, Maurice, that's kind.' Trev took a step forward and Maurice immediately recoiled suspiciously.

'You aren't going to hug me or anything, are you?' he demanded warily. 'Only, no offence or anything, but I'm not into man hugs.'

Despite the seriousness of the situation and the stress they were under, Trev had to laugh.

'Don't worry, you're definitely not my type. No offence. I was just going to offer a handshake.'

Maurice nodded in relief and gripped his hand.

'That's fine. You take good care of the boss, now, and for God's sake get him to see a doc or a shrink or something. Good night now, safe home.'

Ted was shivering and subdued in the passenger seat as Trev slid the driver's seat back as far as it would go to accommodate his long legs, then started the engine. He would put the heater on as soon as he could, to try to dry Ted out a bit and warm him up. He put out his hand and took hold of Ted's, squeezing it gently. It was freezing cold and somehow felt fragile in his grasp.

'Are you all right now? You really had me worried up there, sitting so close to the edge like that. I thought ...' there was a slight catch in his voice, then he continued, 'I didn't know what you were going to do.'

Ted seemed to have to make an effort to come back from a distant place before he could reply. When he squeezed Trev's hand in response, it was firmer, more positive.

'You thought I was thinking of jumping?' he asked in surprise. 'No. God, no. I'm so sorry, Trev, I didn't mean to scare you. I would never do that to you. Honestly. I wouldn't. I just got very low, thinking of all the people who might still be alive today if I hadn't got things completely wrong. I just lost touch with everything else. Sorry.'

'You should maybe see Carol again, just for a few sessions,' Trev suggested carefully, knowing how much his partner hated to be pushed into anything. 'And we need to get you checked out by a doctor tomorrow, just to make sure you're all right.'

'I'm fine. Don't fuss,' Ted replied, but his tone was gentle. 'A hot shower, a bit of food and hopefully some sleep and I'll be right as rain by tomorrow. I'm sorry I scared you.'

Trev knew there was no point in arguing at the moment. But he had no intention of leaving it at that. He was determined to make Ted see a doctor, by any means at his disposal. Tonight's performance had scared him, more than he liked to admit, and he didn't want to see it repeated.

Chapter Twenty-three

Ted snapped awake at his usual time. He must have been asleep, although he wasn't sure for how long. It didn't seem long enough. He seldom had need of an alarm call. His internal clock was finely tuned to his normal routine.

Faint street light filtered into the bedroom through the curtains and in it, Ted could see that Trev was also awake. His head was propped up on his hand and he was watching Ted closely, his expression still anxious. Trev leaned closer and kissed his partner gently.

'How are you feeling?'

'Did I wake you? Sorry.'

'You've been tossing and turning half the night. You must be exhausted. You need to see a doctor, and you need to sort out some more sessions with Carol, as soon as possible. Phone her now.'

'I can't phone her at this time in the morning,' Ted protested.

Trev leaned across him and picked up Ted's phone from the bedside table. It was still switched off, as Trev had insisted. He turned it back on, noting how many missed calls there were, then handed it to his partner.

'Busted,' he said. 'I know you have her work number stored, which goes to voicemail out of hours. Call her now, ask for an appointment,' he ordered, handing Ted the phone.

When Ted hesitated, Trev said, his tone serious, 'We can't go through this stuff again, Ted. You need help, professional help. I'm here for you, I love you, I'll support you. But this isn't something we can deal with between us. Please phone her.'

Ted knew he was right. He and Trev were seldom at odds, but Trev had moved out once before when Ted was in too dark a place for him to handle. He couldn't risk that happening again, so he meekly dialled the number and left a message for his therapist, asking for an urgent appointment for more counselling.

'I hope you're not even thinking of going into work today? You really scared me yesterday. I think you scared Maurice, too. You definitely need to see a doctor, as well as Carol.'

'I think if I just rest a bit, I'll be fine,' Ted said evasively. 'I'm sorry I scared you. I honestly wasn't going to do anything stupid.'

Trev sat up a little straighter and looking at him directly.

'Doctor, Ted. Promise me.'

Ted made a face.

'You know our GP was as much use as a chocolate teapot when you had that scare over your heart. I'll get five minutes' attention and a bottle of pills.'

'I can't take today off, or I would take you myself. I've just landed us that big new courier fleet service contract, and I need to be there to do the work. So I need to trust you to do as I ask.'

'I'll phone and see if I can get an appointment,' Ted promised him.

The reason their partnership was so solid was that Ted would do anything to make Trev happy. He always backed down when necessary. It wasn't weakness on his part. It was a measure of how much he cared, and wanted the relationship to work.

Trev kissed him again.

'I'll go and make you some tea. Try and get some rest. Do you want anything to eat?'

'No food yet, thanks. I'll get up and make myself something later on. But a cuppa in bed would be nice,' then, as Trev slid out from under the duvet he added, 'I am all right, you know. I promise.'

'If you say so,' Trev said doubtfully. 'And don't go looking at your phone for missed calls. They can wait for a day. Maurice is going to tell the team you're off with a bug and I'll phone the Ice Queen later, tell her the same thing.'

Ted knew he couldn't go the whole day without checking his messages, and suspected he wouldn't make it to mid-morning before he called Mike Hallam for an update. For now, it felt wonderfully sinful to be cosy and warm in bed, sipping his tea, listening to Trev in the shower, getting ready to go to work. At least he wasn't singing, Ted smiled to himself. For all his many talents, Trev couldn't hold a tune to save his life. Not that it stopped his enthusiastic attempts, particularly when he was slaughtering the Queen hits that only Freddie Mercury could really pull off.

Ted was surprised to hear the doorbell, just before Trev left for work. It was rare for them to have callers at that time of day. He could hear muffled voices downstairs when Trev opened the door, so he got out of bed, pulled on a sweat shirt and pants over his nakedness, slid his feet into slippers and went downstairs. He was surprised to see his mother in the hallway, talking to Trev. He shot an enquiring look at his partner.

'I wasn't sure if I could trust you,' Trev confessed. 'So Annie's here to babysit, and to make sure you make that doctor's appointment.'

For the briefest moment, Ted felt a flash of irritation. He hated fuss of any kind. But he had lost all contact with his mother for a large part of his life. Maybe it would help him now to spend a bit more time with her.

'Don't you have to be at work?' he asked her.

'Not until this afternoon. When Trev phoned me and said you weren't quite yourself, I wanted to come and look after you. Trev says you haven't had any breakfast yet. Shall I make you something? What about some eggy bread? It was always your favourite.'

Ted smiled nostalgically.

'Dad always used to make that for me, when I was little.'

'I taught him how,' she said, a touch of sadness in her voice. 'Go and sit down and I'll bring you some.'

Trev looked pleased with himself as he kissed them both fondly.

'My work here is done,' he said as he pulled on his leathers and headed for the garage.

True to his word, Ted tried to phone his GP's surgery to get an appointment, after he'd enjoyed his breakfast and the novelty of having his mother to look after him. The number rang constantly engaged and when he finally did get through, it was to discover that there was no appointment available to him until the following evening. He booked it, because he had promised Trev he would, but he very much hoped he would be back at work and feeling much more like himself by then.

He was itching to get his phone out and check in with Mike, but his mother kept him occupied, and topped up with tea, so he didn't have a free moment to do so. She didn't press him at all to talk about what was wrong with him. She just accepted his explanation that work had been getting on top of him and he just needed to rest and recharge his batteries.

She made him an early lunch, as she had to leave for work. As she was getting ready to go, Ted was surprised to hear a car pull up in the driveway. His mother answered the door and showed Professor Bizzie Nelson into the sitting room, where Ted was comfortably installed on the sofa with his feet up.

He got to his feet when Bizzie came in but she waved at him to sit down again. He noticed she had a medical bag with her, though not the big one which went with her to the crime scenes they worked on together.

'I have to go to work now, Teddy, but Bizzie kindly said she'd look in on you,' his mother told him as she gave him a kiss.

Ted had only recently felt comfortable about any intimacy with the woman he thought had abandoned him as a child. He had to admit to himself that it had felt good, having his mum to look after him when he was feeling down. A bit of nostalgia provided just the healing effect he needed.

Bizzie perched on the sofa next to him and regarded him thoughtfully, as if he was one of the corpses on her autopsy table.

'Trevor told me a little bit about yesterday, Edwin,' she began. 'I imagine you haven't done anything about a doctor's appointment yet?'

Ted started to explain about the long wait for an answer, and the appointment for the following evening, but she cut across him.

'Will you allow me to check your blood pressure and your heart rate?'

Seeing his surprised look, she said, 'I may spend all my time with the dead these days, but I would just remind you that I do have a medical degree and I did a rotation in a hospital casualty department in my younger days.'

Meekly, Ted pushed up his sleeve and held out his arm for her to slip the cuff on, then pulled up his sweatshirt so she could listen to his chest.

'Have you been out running this morning?' she asked him when she had finished.

Ted shook his head in surprise.

'In which case your heart rate is ridiculous and your blood pressure is in danger of damaging my equipment.

'What I propose to do now is to take you to the hospital's A&E department to get you some pills to stabilise things. It's not strictly correct procedure, but if I can't pull a few strings and jump a few queues where I work, it's a poor lookout.'

'It can't be that bad,' Ted protested. 'I'm fine, really. I was just feeling a bit down and I got a bit too wet and cold out on

Kinder yesterday.'

The Professor gave him another long look.

'We haven't known one another long, Edwin. But in that time, how many times have I told you how to do your job?'

Ted looked taken aback.

'Well, never …'

'Precisely. So please don't tell me how to do mine,' she told him brusquely. 'You are not seriously ill, yet. But you do need something to bring things back to normal levels. I would advise that we do something today, rather than waiting until late tomorrow. Once we get you started on some medication, you should be perfectly able to resume your duties. I would also strongly advise you to get some emotional help.

'You're clearly under enormous strain at work. I understand how this current case is stressful for you, and for your team. If it was anyone else other than you, I would tell them to relax with a good bottle of wine, or maybe even enjoy a spliff or two. But knowing you, and especially how much you take things to heart, I think you may just have to admit defeat and get some pills from your doctor.'

'I have rung for an appointment,' Ted assured her. 'I'm all right, though, I just made a bit of a fool of myself yesterday. It was nothing. I was just being maudlin.'

'Let me tell you about when I had a breakdown, at Cambridge,' Bizzie began, then, seeing Ted was about to interrupt, she held up a hand to stop him. 'And please don't tell me you think sitting on top of a mountain singing in the pouring rain is normal behaviour for a rational police inspector.

'I'd led a relatively sheltered life when I went up to university. I was bright, talented, top marks in everything, always. One of my tutors took a particular interest in me. Encouraged me, spent time helping me with my work. With the benefit of hindsight, it was inevitable that things developed the way they did.

'He swore undying love. Told me he and his wife were no

longer intimate. He said he would wait until I graduated before leaving her, as it wouldn't look right before then, him having a relationship with a student.

'Then one day I happened to see them together, quite by chance, somewhere he would not have expected to bump into me. Him and his wife. The one he said he no longer felt anything for. I saw the affectionate gestures. The protective way he helped her out of the car. I didn't need my medical training to notice that she was pregnant.

'I reacted not dissimilarly to you. I must have visited every bridge in the region, wondering whether it would be cowardice or courage to throw myself off one. I spent hours humming the duet from The Pearl Fishers, as it was his favourite. I've had a particular aversion to Bizet ever since. I felt all sorts of emotions – guilt, fear, utter helplessness.'

She saw the recognition in Ted's eyes and said, 'I see those feelings are not unfamiliar to you. I pulled back from the abyss and threw myself into my studies, graduating with some of the highest marks ever. You have a partner who adores you and a mother who loves you. Don't let them down, Edwin. Allow yourself to be healed.'

'Did your feelings include a strange desire to cry at inappropriate moments?' Ted asked her, his voice husky.

She patted his hand awkwardly.

'All perfectly normal, I assure you. Now, let's get you to A&E and onto some pills as the first step. Do you want to change first?'

Ted was impressed with the way Bizzie had him whisked into a cubicle in record time when they got to the hospital. When a young registrar came in to see him, the Professor was at her most formidable.

'I'm Elizabeth Nelson, Professor of Forensic Pathology, practising from this hospital, and this is my very good friend, Detective Inspector Darling. I've brought him here in a proactive role. As you will see, when you check his heart rate and blood pressure, if you don't do something with him now, I will be seeing him in my drawers downstairs,' she said, with a wicked twinkle in her eye.

'I know this should be a GP matter but he can't get an appointment within a sensible time-frame, so I've brought him here because I don't want to have to carry out a post-mortem examination on him just yet. He's under considerable stress at work at present.'

Ted opened his mouth to protest but it was as much use as trying to use a stinger to stop a steamroller. When the registrar finally managed to get a word in edgeways, he said, 'Perhaps you would wait outside, Professor, while I examine the inspector?'

'I'm the senior pathologist for this area. I can assure you, there is nothing at all of the male anatomy which I have not seen, many times over. But to spare your blushes, Edwin, I will wait for you outside. Take good care of him, Doctor,' she said as she swept out.

Once again, Ted submitted meekly to having his heart and blood pressure checked and tried to answer as honestly as he could the questions the registrar put to him. He admitted to feelings of anxiety, of not being in control of situations. But he went on to point out what his job was like and why the current case was proving particularly hard for him.

He was finally allowed out, armed with a prescription and advice to take things as easily as his job permitted, to see his own GP as soon as possible and to restart counselling sessions as soon as he could.

He found Bizzie in the waiting area, and the two of them headed in search of the car, pausing to pick up his pills from the hospital dispensary on the way.

'I'm sorry to inconvenience you still further, Bizzie, but could we possibly stop somewhere on the way back? I'd like to get something really nice so I can make Trev a special supper, by way of an apology. And could you possibly help me to select a good bottle of wine? It's not something I know much about, and I want it to be something out of the ordinary.

'I really need to make things up to him. I know I frightened him yesterday, so I'd like to do something nice for him. You're very welcome to join us, if you'd like to. It's the least I can do, by way of a thank you for your kindness. And I've been so self-absorbed I haven't even asked how your mother is.'

'Mummy's fine, thank you, unstoppable. I've arranged to have carers going in several times a day, but doubtless she will scare them all away, as she usually does. And you have no need to thank me. It's what friends are for, and I consider you and Trevor to be good friends. I will never forget your kindness in including me for Christmas lunch. That meant a great deal to me.

'And as for joining you this evening, don't be ridiculous. You certainly do have a lot of making up to do with Trevor, and you definitely don't need me in the way of that.'

Chapter Twenty-four

'Have you had your morning pills? And have you got the others with you to take at lunchtime?'

For the second day running, Trev was awake at the same time as Ted and fussing over his proposed return to work.

'Yes, and yes,' Ted assured him, his turn to be bringing morning tea up to his partner in bed. 'And I've washed behind my ears and got a clean hanky.'

He leaned over to kiss him and added, 'I will be all right, honestly. Now my heart has stopped going like a trip hammer, I feel a bit more rational.'

Ted had half an hour at his desk to make a start on the accumulated paperwork, before the rest of the team arrived. He began by catching up on missed phone calls and emails. There were several logged calls from the local reporter. He would need to give him a ring at some point, to find out what he wanted.

Mike Hallam was the first of the team to arrive. Seeing the boss back in his office, he went in, after a peremptory knock at the door.

'Morning, boss. How are you feeling? Not another dodgy ham roll?'

'Just one of those twenty-four hour bugs, I think, Mike. I'm fine now, itching to get back to the case. Any further developments?'

'Sal's got a few things for us. He told me last thing yesterday so we've not updated the board yet. I thought it would keep for this morning's briefing. We've got the sniff of a lead, at least.'

The rest of the team were just coming in. Steve was there, but so far there was no sign of Maurice. Ted knew they always arrived together, sharing Maurice's car, now that Steve was lodging at his house.

'Where's Maurice?' Ted asked, but at that moment DC Brown walked through the door, or rather he limped painfully through it.

'Takes me a while to get up the stairs at the moment, boss,' he growled. 'I've got bloody sore feet, with blisters all over them.'

Mike Hallam laughed, 'Yeah, and he won't tell the rest of us how he got them, boss, although there have been a few colourful suggestions.'

Ted felt a pang of guilt, realising it was no doubt from Maurice's unaccustomed climb on the Dark Peak, in totally unsuitable footwear.

'I'll buy you a pint at dinnertime, Maurice, help ease your pain,' he promised.

He would have said lunchtime in Trev's company, but to Maurice, the midday meal would always be dinner.

'Okay, so, fill me in, what have we got? And Jezza, you're not listening to any of this, right?'

'Doing my knitting and painting my nails, boss,' she assured him.

'Boss, yesterday I went round to see the dog dealer, the one who arranged the sale of that puppy to the couple who met Mr Shape-Form-or-Way. I don't know much about keeping dogs, but to me, the place looked like a shitheap, pardon the expression. I've already spoken to Rob's fiancée and she's arranged for the RSPCA to go round there with some police back-up, and someone from Environmental Health, at some point. In light of what I found out, they're waiting for a green light from us.

207

'It's a woman who runs the place and she was very cagey, on the defensive, and didn't really want to tell me anything at all. It's clear she thought it was something to do with the puppy being sick and having false papers. When I finally managed to convince her none of that was within my remit and I was only interested in the delivery driver, she eventually agreed to give me some information.

'She says that all she knows about him is that he's called Danny and he drives a white Sprinter. He does runs over to the continent and to Ireland and will pick up and deliver anything and everything, no questions asked.

'She always pays him cash in hand, so she has no other details, not an address or surname, no National Insurance number, of course, and just a mobile number to contact him when she needs him. I tried it. It goes straight to voicemail. The message just says, "This is Danny. Leave your name and number and I'll call you back." I didn't leave any message.'

'I should listen to his voice,' Jezza said. 'There's a chance I might recognise it.'

'You're not even supposed to be listening to this briefing, Jezza,' Ted told her sternly.

'Oh, come on, boss,' she protested. 'At some point you're going to have to get all the victims to listen to it to get an ID. I'm here. I've got a good ear for voices. I could do it right now for you. I could at least rule him out if it's not the right voice, save you a load of work.'

Ted hesitated, but he knew she was right. If Jezza said categorically that the voice was not their man, they would still need to double check it with the others, but it would save endless time if they weren't looking for a man who turned out to be nothing more than a van driver working on the black.

'Sal,' Ted said to him.

Sal got out his mobile, dialled the number and handed his phone to Jezza, who listened intently. They could all see by how pale she went that she recognised the voice. She nodded in confirmation.

'That's him. That's the man who attacked me.'

Maurice looked across at her, his expression concerned.

'You all right, bonny lass?'

She nodded wordlessly and went back to looking at the paperwork on her desk.

'Right, I need to let Pocket Billiards know we believe our man is called Danny, see if he can update his piece on the website, then in the paper when it comes out. See if that brings us any more leads. Have we had any more phone calls, just on the turn of phrase?'

'There was one man yesterday who was insistent he would only speak to you, boss,' Rob told him. 'I tried my best to persuade him, said you were off sick and I didn't know how long for, but he wouldn't talk to me. He said, and I quote, that he wanted the organ grinder and not the monkey.

'I did get him to leave a number, though, so you could call him when you were back. He wouldn't give me a name. He sounded nervous, but he said he definitely knows someone who uses that turn of phrase, frequently.'

Ted knew he needed to go and talk to the Ice Queen soon, to let her know he was back and that he would be leaving early for his doctor's appointment. He decided to follow up the phone call and speak to the local reporter first, then he might have a bit more to tell her.

'Ted! I was trying all day yesterday to get hold of you,' Pocket Billiards told him as soon as he answered Ted's call. 'What more can you tell me about Jenny Holden topping herself?'

Ted winced at his insensitivity, but tried to keep his tone neutral.

'Sorry about that, Alastair, I was off sick. And you know I can't possibly give you that sort of information. You'll get more from the coroner's office than I could give you. But you'll have to wait for the inquest to know exactly what happened.'

He continued, to cut across the reporter's grumbling, 'I have another snippet for you about our attacker, though, which I'm hoping you can put out there for us. It might lead to a breakthrough. I'm giving it to you exclusively again, and I won't forget your help with this.'

Once he had secured a grudging agreement, he next called the number Rob had given him. His call was answered with a brusque and somewhat suspicious, 'Hello?'

'This is Detective Inspector Darling. I believe you called in because you may have information about a man we're urgently trying to find.'

'Danny Boy,' came the reply.

Ted's ears pricked up. This sounded hopeful.

'What can you tell me about him?'

'He's a fucking nutter, for starters.'

'Can you be more specific?'

'They call him Danny Boy because he's from Derry. I'm not sure if Danny is his real name. He told me his second name was Quigley, but I was never sure what to believe, with him. I met him in a lay-by one time. We were both driving deliveries. I tried to start up a conversation. When you're on the road a lot, it gets lonely, it's nice to chat. But he's not easy to get talking to. He barely said two words the first time.

'We bumped into one another a few more times, though, and he gradually started to speak. I saw he had a Paras tattoo. I'm ex-Gunners, so that broke the ice a bit. We found we'd both been to Helmand Province.

'Look, if I tell you everything I know about him, I want to know there's no way it can get back to him. That it was me who said anything, I mean. He doesn't mess about.'

'Has he ever threatened you?' Ted asked.

The man snorted.

'There are different ways of threatening. The first time we exchanged more than a couple of words, he said he was just having a bite to eat, did I want to join him. He was sat in the back of the Sprinter, with the doors open. He had, like, some bread, cheese, stuff like that, spread out. I sat down, he cut me a lump of bread, and passed it to me on the end of his knife. He left the knife pointing at me a long while, even after I took the bread. I got the message.'

'Can you describe the knife?'

'Fairbairn-Sykes Commando, seven-inch black blade.'

'Does he live locally?'

'He mostly lives out of the back of his van. He told me he was born in Derry but that his family had to leave pretty sharpish at the height of the troubles, although he didn't say why, and I didn't press him. He's not the sort you make small talk with. Sometimes he told me stuff, not always. They came to Stockport and I think it's where he calls home, if he has one.'

Ted was making notes on his pad as the man was speaking. It confirmed his suspicions that this man was dangerous, certainly combat trained. If he'd been in the Parachute Regiment, he could well have seen service in some harsh places.

'What else do you know about his military service?'

'He told me he tried out for the SAS but was rejected after initial training as being too unstable and I can believe that. He's a scary bastard. All the more so because he just looks ordinary, like any other bloke, until you get up close.'

'Why do you think he's unstable?'

'I know blokes like to brag a bit sometimes. You know, women they've shagged, times they've got totally pissed, that sort of stuff.'

Ted didn't actually know, as they were not things he did or would talk about even if they were.

'He liked to talk a lot about shagging women, and he liked to give the impression it wasn't always when they were up for it, if you know what I mean. He made a thing about preferring it when they put up a bit of a fight.'

'And do you know anything about the deliveries he does?

What he transports, where he goes, anything like that?'

'Look, mate, I need to know this isn't going to get back to Danny Boy. I'm trying to earn a living with a bit of driving. I'm not saying it's all totally on the level, like, I don't always declare every hour I work, you know what I'm saying? But the shit Danny Boy gets up to? I'm not into any of that kind of stuff. That's why I'm telling you. Someone needs to stop him, the mad bastard.'

Ted didn't waste his time asking for the man's name. He knew he wasn't going to get it and he wasn't all that bothered. He didn't want to frighten the man off by insisting. It was Danny he was after.

'I can assure you that what you tell me is in confidence. If and when we apprehend Danny Boy, your involvement won't be mentioned to him.'

There was a pause then, 'Fair enough, mate. Danny will shift anything, but one thing he does a lot of is bringing in puppies, and fighting dogs. The pups come in from Europe. He said there's not much of a check at the ports at weekends, so he does it then. You can bring in five pups for each person in the van, he told me. So he picks up two illegals, on false papers, near to Calais somewhere. Then he can bring in fifteen puppies at a time. The illegals pay, the dog people pay, it's a nice little earner for Danny. And he told me he always tries to get the women illegals. I don't need to spell out for you why. He told me in a lot of graphic detail, and I really didn't need to know. Like I said, he's sick.

'One time, he had some puppies in the back of the van when we were talking. Funny little buggers. I don't know what you call them. The sort some woman sticks ribbons on and carries round in a handbag. One of them just kept skriking all the time, wouldn't shut up. Danny took it out of the cage and chucked it against the side of the van. Killed the little bleeder stone dead. I started avoiding him after that, the sick shit. It meant nothing to him. You could see in his eyes. They were just blank, like he was dead behind them. That's the part of him that looks scary. His eyes.'

Ted went over with him full details of description, known whereabouts and anything else the anonymous man could tell him. Then he thanked him and rang off, feeling equally as sick. It confirmed some of his worst fears about the man they were dealing with. He went back out into the main office.

'Finally, a possible ID. Daniel Quigley. Ex-Paras. Born in Derry, grew up here in Stockport. Drives a Sprinter, or did do. He may be driving something else by now, if it was his van which was burnt out. Shifts anything that needs delivering, particularly dogs and illegal immigrants.

'Mike, Army records, anything and everything they have on anyone with that name or a similar one. Ex-Paras. I want it with or without a warrant for it, their choice, but I want it yesterday. The rest of you, I'll draw up a list of places he's been known to appear and I want every one of them checked out. I'm going to talk to the Super and to Inspector Turner to suggest we make this a joint operation with Uniform, throw everything we have at finding him.

'Meantime, everyone, get on to your contacts, find out if anyone knows a Danny or Daniel Quigley. What our contact told me matches almost exactly what the victims have said for height, age, build, eyes. Especially the eyes. Apparently he has a Para tattoo on his right forearm. That's wings and a parachute, for those who don't know.

'Steve, full PNC check. Try all the spelling variations you can think of for Quigley until we get something definite from the military. Rob, if that was his Sprinter van which went up in flames, we need to know what he's driving now, so find out any van thefts on our patch or close by in the time since we found the Sprinter.

'Remember that this man is likely to be highly trained and dangerous. Don't anyone even think of approaching him alone. Jezza, you're not in on any of this, you pick up everything else that needs covering in the meantime.'

'Ah, Inspector, nice to see you back,' the Ice Queen greeted Ted when he went in and sat down as instructed. 'Are you better?'

'Considerably, ma'am, but I need to leave slightly early today for a doctor's appointment. Nothing serious, I just need a few pills to sort me out. But I will be restarting counselling sessions.'

Ted filled her in on the latest update on the case while she served coffee.

'I hope the case is not getting on top of you?' she asked. 'It's essential that you let me know if you need to take time off.'

Ted shook his head determinedly.

'It's fine now. I had a bit of a wobble. Now I'm back on track. We've got a name and a lot more information than we had before. I finally feel we're close to getting him in our sights. Once we nail him, then I might ask you for a bit of time off.'

'It's both one of your best and worst qualities that you take your cases so intensely personally,' she told him once again. 'Learning to stay detached is one of the hardest parts of our job, and it risks changing the person you are. Take all the help that's available to you, so that this case doesn't break you.'

Chapter Twenty-five

Kevin Turner's office was not far from that of the Ice Queen. As soon as Ted stepped out into the corridor, he could hear Kevin's raised voice coming from there, delivering what sounded like a monumental bollocking to one or more of his unfortunate officers.

The door opened to a bellow of, 'And if I hear about anything like this again from you two clowns, a bloody disciplinary will be the least of your worries!'

Two guilty-looking young constables slunk out of the office, standing aside and holding the door open for Ted to go in. He'd only just sat down when the door opened again behind him, after the briefest of knocks, and the Ice Queen came in. Ted and Kevin both snapped instantly to their feet, probably looking equally as guilty as the young officers. She had that effect on them both.

'Raised voices, Inspector Turner? Was it something I should know about?'

'No, ma'am, it's all sorted. Just young officers who take themselves for boy racers and like throwing their weight around. It won't happen again.'

'I'm pleased to hear it. But may I just remind you that there is a procedure to be followed in dealing with such matters? I don't want to be confronted by allegations of bullying by senior officers.'

She turned to leave, then paused and looked back at them.

'Gentlemen, please don't feel obliged to stand up every time

I come into the room. But thank you for the courtesy,' she added as she left the room.

'Bloody hell, Ted, all this sodding paperwork and disciplinaries. Why can't we just kick them up the arse, like in the good old days? How do they expect us to get any respect from the public when they don't show any? Allegations of bullying? Utter shit. But blimey, what did you make of that? Is the Ice Queen going soft?' Kevin said, busily rummaging in his top drawer.

'Aslan's breath has reached Narnia and started the thaw,' Ted smiled.

Kevin had found what he was looking for. He pulled out two small sachets of a preparation for indigestion, ripped the corners off both of them with his teeth, and greedily sucked out the contents. One hand instinctively went to his stomach as he did so, rubbing it gently.

'Er, aren't you supposed to take those one at a time?' Ted asked him.

'One does nothing for me. I might as well eat Smarties. I'll be mainlining them next. What is it with you and this Narnia stuff, anyway?'

'Didn't you ever read it to your girls? My dad and I read all the Chronicles of Narnia together when I was little.'

'My two were much more into Beauty and the Beast and that sort of stuff. Speaking of the girls - and if you breathe a word of this to anyone, you're a dead man - I'm going to be a granddad. Melissa's pregnant.'

'Congratulations, Kev, that's great news,' Ted leaned forward and shook his hand. 'Have you time for a quick pint after work? Wet the baby's head? I'd say lunchtime but I promised Maurice a pint for services above and beyond the call of duty. But first, please tell me you've seen someone about the state your guts are in?'

Kevin nodded, still gently massaging his stomach.

'The doc thinks it's an ulcer. Wants me to be seen in

hospital for one of those, what d'you call it? Where they shove a camera down your gob while you're awake? But I can't do it, Ted. I'm shitting myself at the prospect. Makes me gag, just thinking about it. I've told the wife it's just indigestion and it'll be fine.'

'What a pair of old crocks,' Ted smiled. 'I'm on pills for stress at the moment, but keep that between us, if you would. And seriously, you can't mess about with an ulcer. It might perforate. I think they can knock you out for it, if you tell them you're that worried.'

Kevin snorted.

'Twenty-two years of wedded bliss, because there's a lot about me the missus still doesn't know. Particularly what a big coward I am about stuff like this. But you, on stress-busters? I thought all the green tea and high kicking took care of that? We're getting bloody middle-aged, Ted, that's about the long and the short of it.'

Ted nodded in agreement, then went on to bring Kevin up to speed with the latest developments on the case. He also broached his suggestion that they pool their resources in terms of officers when it came to trying to track down the attacker, now they had a name to go on.

'He is dangerous, Kev, it needs to be stab vests all round, all the time,' he warned.

Another snort.

'Assuming we have enough to go round. Honest, Ted, the way they keep cutting back resources, they'll be issuing us with lolly sticks instead of batons next. And the dog section will probably get toy poodles instead of German Shepherds, because they cost less to feed.'

'I'll keep you posted, as soon as I have some definite locations to check. We're also trawling through what vans have been nicked recently, see if we can get some idea of what he's likely to be driving round in now. Always assuming the burnt-out Sprinter was his. Let's do that pint, later on.'

When he got back up to his office, Ted decided that he better send Trev a text, just to let him know he was fine but was going for a drink with Kevin after work. He knew his partner would be worried and didn't want to cause him any more anxiety than he already had.

A brief knock on his door was followed by Jezza's head appearing round the gap. She was still not used to seeing the boss in his new reading glasses but wisely made no further comment about them, seeing how self-conscious he looked as he pulled them hastily off.

'Have you got a minute, boss?'

'Of course, Jezza. Come in, sit down. Do you want some tea? How are you doing?'

'I'd be a lot better if people stopped asking me how I was doing,' she retorted, but she was smiling at him. 'Green tea would be perfect, thanks, boss.'

Ted had only just made himself a drink so it didn't take long to boil the kettle again and put a mugful in front of her.

'What can I do for you?'

She took a swallow of her tea before replying. She drank it straight, not laced with honey as Ted preferred it. He'd always had a sweet tooth.

'I went to see Olivia Radnor a couple of days ago,' she began. 'The crime writer. The one who found me. I wanted to thank her, so I took her round a bunch of flowers. She was very kind to me. I wanted to tell her in person how much I appreciated it.'

'Dances with Wolves?' Ted asked her, then, seeing her querying look, he laughed. 'That's what Rob calls her, because of those two great big beasts of hers.'

'Those dogs are impeccably behaved. She has them beautifully trained. I've met plenty of coppers with worse manners, believe me. Anyway, we had quite a chat. She was caring and considerate. She said if I needed to talk to someone, about what happened to me, she could recommend a friend of hers who specialises in such things. She said her name was Heather Cooper.'

Ted put his mug down and stared at her.

'Does she not know Ms Cooper has left town under something of a cloud? Does she not read the papers?'

'Apparently not. She told me that when she's in the middle of writing a new book, as she is at the moment, she avoids the papers and the radio, apart from listening to classical music. She said she doesn't have a television, and I certainly didn't see one. According to her, she likes to keep away from it all, to keep her mind clear and uncluttered for working on the book.

'She gave me a signed copy of one of her books. Crime fiction, right? Not my sort of thing at all, but I thought I'd give it a go. It was only a light read, didn't take me long. The thing is, boss, it was Jenny Holden's story. Not identical, of course. But the bare bones of it were all there. A woman who discovers, during a therapy session, that she was raped in the past by a man she knew and trusted.

'In the book, the woman goes to the police and tries to get them to take her seriously, but for reasons which aren't all that clear from the way it's written, the police decide on a massive cover-up instead. A lot of the police procedure is just total crap, but close enough to be credible to gullible readers who don't know any better. The woman goes on a sort of solo mission and solves it all herself, forcing the police to arrest the man, blah-blah-blah.

'What's really interesting, boss, is that all this was written and published before any of the stories about Jenny Holden and the Dodgy Doc made the papers. Well before. So it looks as if Ms Cooper was feeding her friend the Agatha Christie woman with ideas for her fiction. And we know now that some of what she was feeding her was probably fiction to begin with.'

'We don't know that for sure,' Ted reminded her. 'Jenny Holden had a lot of problems. I believe it's just possible that the idea could have come from her, not from the therapist. But we won't know anything for sure until the inquest. That might just throw up more information than we have at the moment.'

'I presume there will need to be some sort of police enquiry into the Dodgy Doc? So I wondered if I could be a part of that? It's not connected to the rapes, so there's no reason why I shouldn't work on it, is there?' she asked.

'I've read up on everything that was in the press already, and on the basis of that, I've just started reading the Cooper woman's Barbed Wire book. In particular, I read the chapter about her 'saving' young people from their mistaken ideas about their sexuality. And I read the interviews Pocket Billiards did with some of the young people.

'Boss, we have to go after this woman. She's dangerous, and there must be something illegal in it, surely? So can I work on that?'

Ted leaned back in his chair and looked at her thoughtfully. More than anything, he wanted to see Heather Cooper brought to justice, if it was humanly possible. The idea that she had been leaking sensationalist stories to form part of fiction written for titillation disgusted him beyond measure. But he was well and truly off the case. His hands were tied.

'Jezza, what I'm going to tell you now stays between you and me, within these four walls, please.'

She nodded her understanding, so he continued, 'I did go and see Ms Cooper, in connection with the Jenny Holden case, it's true. I took Maurice with me for back-up. She made the mistake of showing me her leaflets with her so-called treatment for sexuality issues. That was the first I knew about that. I'm not proud to say I nearly lost it in there. Maurice had to drag me out.

'For that reason, I cannot take any part at all in an investigation of any kind into her, although clearly there needs to be one, and there will be. I've also made some enquiries with the CPS and it seems that in terms of the claims about sexuality in her leaflets, nothing there breaches any laws. It's all been carefully worded.

'Because of my run-in with her, and her reaction to it, I am not allowed to pursue the issue any further myself. Therefore, I cannot put you onto the investigation, and I cannot give you any work hours to look into her.

'However, I have asked you not to take any part in the morning briefings into the rape cases. So, what if I were to ask you to get all of Ms Radnor's books, and slip me the bill? Then you could use my office during briefings to see how many of her fictions have any basis on the cases mentioned in the Barbed Wire book, during that time. I could then probably see that the information went to the right place.'

Jezza grinned broadly at him.

'Boss, you little rebel, are you actually playing it other than by the book?'

'Perish the thought, DC Vine,' Ted said with a wink, 'just covering all bases. And by the way, I really hope you will consider going and talking to Carol, whose card I gave you. I'm sure you'd find it helpful, and she is easy to talk to. She's a trained professional and nothing remotely like Ms Cooper. You just won't be able to have the last appointment on a Wednesday afternoon – that's mine.'

Ted walked and Maurice limped the short distance to The Grapes at lunchtime.

'Sorry about your feet, Maurice,' Ted said apologetically, as they sat down at a quiet corner table, Ted facing the door, Maurice sideways on to it. 'In fact, I'm sorry for my behaviour generally. I was a bit low so I behaved like an idiot.'

Ted took off his trench coat and pulled a box of tablets out of one of his pockets.

'You'll be pleased to see I'm now on medication, so there shouldn't be a repeat performance. And thanks for keeping it to yourself.'

'No worries, Ted,' Maurice replied, relaxed and informal

while it was just the two of them, away from the office. 'The job's a bitch at times, it can get to any of us. Probably affects you worse because you're a decent bloke. You care about stuff, and about people.'

'Pint, is it? And do you want something to eat?' Ted asked, standing up to escape his embarrassment.

'A half's fine. And have they got any salad?'

Seeing Ted's startled expression, he explained, 'All that yomping round the hills made me realise just how unfit I am. I put on a ton of weight when I quit smoking and started eating sticky buns instead, so now I'm trying to do something about it.'

Ted's mobile phone rang as he was waiting at the bar for their drinks and food. It was his good friend and former boss, Jim Baker.

'Afternoon, Darling.'

'Afternoon, Super.'

He and Ted could never resist the chance to exchange the old joke. It masked their strong mutual affection.

'I hope you and Trev are free Saturday week? I've finally popped the question, Bella's said yes and we're having a bit of an engagement party that evening. Of course, we'd both love it if the two of you could be there, to wish us well.'

'And we'd both be honoured to be there, Jim. You know that, for me, it will depend on the local scrotes and what they get up to. I have a feeling we have a karate tournament that weekend. We're both on the club team. But I'll get there somehow, for as long as I can, and I'm sure Trev will be there, too.'

Jim was keen to chat about the current case, but when Ted explained that he was armed with a half pint and a meal with Maurice's name on it, he said, a slightly wistful note in his voice, 'Fair enough, Ted, another time. Give my best to Maurice, and to all the team. I hope to see you Saturday week.'

He'd no sooner sat down at the table with their food and

drinks than his mobile went again. It was Trev, and he was not best pleased.

'What's this text about taking Kevin for a pint after work?' he demanded. 'Have you forgotten already that you've got a doctor's appointment this evening?'

Ted cringed. He had forgotten. Completely. He guessed it was because he had no faith in their GP and didn't really want to go.

'Er, I thought I could go to the appointment then meet up with Kevin afterwards,' he began, lamely.

'Don't bullshit me, Ted, it doesn't suit you and it won't work. You're rubbish at it,' Trev actually sounded angry with him. 'You either completely forgot about it or you were going to swerve going then tell me you'd forgotten. If I wasn't so busy at work, I'm come and take you myself.'

'Sorry,' Ted told him, genuinely apologetic. 'I honestly had forgotten, nothing more sinister than that. I will go, promise.'

Trev ended the call much more abruptly than usual. It looked like Ted would have more making up to do when they were both back home that evening.

'In the dog house?' Maurice asked sympathetically. 'Someone sleeping in the spare room tonight?'

'I completely forgot I had a doctor's appointment this evening, to get more pills. Trev was not amused. If it's anything like last time we went, for him, she'll give me two minutes of her time while she just scribbles out a repeat prescription,' he sighed. 'But I have promised Trev, and I'll make the same promise to you, Maurice. I'll get on top of it. No more night-time concerts on Kinder.'

'My feet are bloody glad to hear it, boss,' Maurice grunted in reply.

Chapter Twenty-six

Ted decided he better return home bearing peace tokens once more. He hated being at odds with his partner and he had genuinely forgotten all about his appointment, even if Trev hadn't believed him. Now that he'd been reminded, he would go, because he'd promised. He could easily put his drink with Kevin off to a different day.

He stopped on the way to buy a decent bottle of wine then, on a whim, nipped into a nearby florist and bought a single red rose in a cellophane sleeve. He'd inflicted one of his favourite films, *Blazing Saddles*, on Trev so often that he hoped he would remember the line and appreciate the joke.

It was a different doctor to the one he'd seen when he'd been with Trev for his appointment. They were both lucky enough to be in good health and hardly ever needed to visit the surgery. This time, the doctor was a man, a good bit older than the woman they had seen, and his manner was considerably less peremptory.

He did, at least, check Ted's blood pressure and his heart, then he carefully studied the prescription he had been given at the hospital. He asked a few questions and nodded in satisfaction when Ted mentioned he was attending counselling sessions.

'I don't envy you your job in these difficult times, Inspector,' he said, as he wrote out a prescription renewal. 'It looks as if we are currently covering all bases and your blood pressure is already looking a little less disconcerting. I hate to

224

trot out the old cliché but, keep taking the tablets. Above all, keep attending the counselling. If you ever have any more concerns, don't hesitate to come back.'

Trev's bike was already in the garage when Ted put his Renault away and went into the house. He headed for the kitchen, the bottle of wine held in front of him like a shield, the rose concealed behind his back.

'Sorry,' he said as soon as he saw Trev. 'I honestly had forgotten all about it. But I've been, just now. The doctor says I'm doing fine and I just need to keep taking the tablets. Here, have some wine. Is that the right one?'

Trev took the bottle, still looking a little cool and unforgiving, then studied the label.

'Wow. I thought we were economising? This is very nice indeed. Thank you.'

'We are, but I wanted you to know I'm really sorry, for everything,' Ted said sincerely, then produced the red rose from behind his back. It had exactly the desired effect.

Trev threw back his head and laughed out loud, his blue eyes suddenly sparkling with their familiar warmth.

'Oh, a wed wose. How womantic,' he lisped, the perfect delivery of the line from the film.

Ted knew then that it was going to be all right, so he moved in for the hug which followed.

'I'm sorry, too,' Trev told him. 'I was getting angry that you weren't taking your health seriously enough. We're run ragged at work at the moment. Whose bright idea was it to pull in all this extra work, I wonder? I just didn't need the extra stress from you. It's hard, this being a grown-up lark, isn't it?'

'Welcome to my world,' Ted grinned. 'Oh, are we free on Saturday week, in the evening? Jim and Bella's engagement party. We're invited.'

'Don't forget it's the karate tournament, but we should be able to do both. You are coming to that, aren't you? You know the team needs you. You're our secret weapon.'

'I'll be there for both of them, if I can. It will depend on work, as ever, but I'm looking forward to both in equal measure.'

After Ted had changed out of his work suit and they had eaten, they sat close together on the sofa, feet up, Trev's arm round Ted's shoulders, Ted's head resting against his partner's chest. There was something mindless on the television, the sound low, which neither of them was really watching. They were just enjoying the quiet, relaxed moment in each other's company.

For once, it was Trev's phone which shattered the silence.

'Shewee,' he said, taking the call and putting the phone to his ear. 'Hi, Shewee, everything all right?' He listened for a moment then smiled and raised a thumb towards Ted who was poised, anxiously, wondering what the news would be.

'Tell her I said hello. And ask her if she's in the pub,' Ted said with a grin.

Trev dutifully repeated the message then laughed as he relayed her response.

'She says she's doing her prep and she's mortally wounded at your insinuation.'

It was clearly going to be just a brother-sister chat, and a horsey one, at that, by the way Trev laughed and said, 'Oh God, yes, Foxy was always banging on the brakes at anything with water under it. Blue must have inherited the gene. I just used to have to give it some welly and hope for the best.'

Ted was enjoying relaxing, watching his partner chat to the kid sister he'd only recently discovered he had, clearly enjoying every minute of it. He decided that moments like these made up for the tough days of his work.

Then he remembered the young women whose lives had been damaged, possibly forever, by the attacker, including one of his own team, as well as the one who had lost her life, and he thought that probably nothing could.

Ted firmly sent Jezza packing into his own office during the briefing the following morning, armed with her collection of new books. He'd asked Kevin Turner to join them as they now had some locations to check out and needed to divide up what officers were available in the safest and most effective way.

'Just to make it absolutely clear to everyone, once again. This man is armed and extremely dangerous. Do not attempt to apprehend him unless you have back-up available. So for my team, that means leaving Uniform officers with Tasers, or spray at the very least, to handle him, if you do come up against him.'

'It may be water pistols and cap guns, if I can't lay hands on enough Tasers,' Kevin Turner muttered, half under his breath.

'Absolutely no heroics, from any of you. Is that perfectly clear?' Ted stressed.

There were nods and murmurs of assent then, under the strength of Maurice's glare at him, Ted laughed and said, 'All right, me too. No heroics, I promise. All of you stay in contact all the time. I want to know where you are at every moment of the shift. And let's have you all back in by four o'clock at the latest for a regroup and debrief, see where we're up to.

'Sergeant Hallam now has the last known address the Army had for Danny Boy, in Brinnington. It's well out of date but it's all we have from that direction at the moment, so that needs checking out first of all. I'll take that one. Mike, you're with me. Inspector Turner, can you give us a Taser-armed officer to check out that address, please, just in the unlikely event that it is his bolt-hole and he's gone there?'

Between them they covered a lot of miles and knocked on a lot of doors in what turned out to be a fruitless and frustrating few hours. There were new people at the Brinnington address who had never heard of anyone called Quigley, no-one who was ex-services, nor anyone called Danny. Ted and Mike questioned the occupants at length but believed their story. They were new to the area and genuinely didn't seem to know anyone.

The story was similar for all of them when they got back together later on. One or two had found people who claimed to know of a Danny Boy, but none had fitted the description of the man they were looking for.

Once again, Ted packed Jezza off to his office with her books before he addressed the team. He knew he needed to lift morale, after a disappointing day. They were so close to finding Danny Boy now, he felt sure. He just had to keep the team convinced of that and focused on the search.

He was just about to allocate new tasks when the phone rang. Rob took it and passed it over to him.

'A supermarket manager, boss. Reports of someone acting suspiciously in the car park. He says the man appears to have left the premises but he does have CCTV footage which may just show him.'

Ted took the call, asked for full details and location, then looked round at his team. 'I'll take this one. Maurice, do you fancy coming? At least you can watch the tapes while sitting down, so you can rest your feet.'

He tossed Maurice the keys to his car as he said, 'I'll catch you up in a minute. I'll just see what back-up Inspector Turner has available, just in case our man has not, in fact, left the premises.'

The answer from Kevin was not encouraging.

'Bugger all of very much available, Ted. We've just had a shout of an armed robbery under way in the town centre, with reports of a possible hostage situation and some talk of a terrorist attack. Just what we bloody need. I'll send what I can, as soon as I can. But you say our man may have left the premises?'

'Clearly we won't know until we get there, but that's the intel at the moment. We're mostly hoping to see something from the CCTV that will be of help. I'll radio in as soon as I have any update at all.'

The supermarket car park looked packed when they arrived. Ted couldn't immediately spot a parking space as he cruised up and down the first two aisles.

'Bloody post-Christmas sales, boss,' Maurice grumbled. 'People buying yet more tat, even though they've bled themselves dry in the run-up to Christmas. I think I saw somewhere that there was a special discount offer on today, which I suppose is what's brought the crowds out in force.

'Look, we could be going round in circles for ages. Why don't I get out here and go and find the manager? Then you can join me once you've found a parking space?'

'Good idea, Maurice. I won't be long.'

Maurice hopped out and Ted carried on to the end of the aisle. Suddenly, in his rear view mirror, he caught sight of Maurice breaking into a run and ducking between cars to get into the next aisle. He couldn't see what had prompted him to do so. But he could think of only one reason why Maurice would start to run, especially with his sore feet.

Ted speeded up to the end of the row, swung round and started to head back down the next one, the way Maurice had gone. He found himself confronted by an elderly driver, trying to get into a parking space and making a dog's breakfast of it. He was effectively blocking the flow of traffic as he fiddled and faffed about. In his impatience, Ted leaned on his car horn, which startled the other driver into stalling his car, making matters worse.

Seething, Ted leapt out of his car and started to run. Now he could hear loud-pitched screaming and saw a woman standing next to her car. Then he saw a man jump out from the passenger side and run into the passageway between the parked vehicles. He was wearing dark clothing, a black woollen hat on his head.

Ted hit the transmit button on his radio, barked out his call sign and location and said, 'I have eyes on our suspect. I need back-up, and I need it now.'

He saw the man stop and coolly, deliberately, assess the danger he faced. He looked first towards Ted, small, slight and running fast in his direction. Then he turned his head and saw Maurice, overweight, limping, and lumbering slowly towards him. He picked the line of least resistance, put his head down and charged straight at Maurice.

Ted saw his fist fly up and connect with Maurice's midriff. The speed and force with which the DC went down told Ted that it was not a mere punch which had felled him.

'Officer down!' Ted bellowed into his radio. 'DC Brown is injured. I need an ambulance, and where's that bloody back-up?'

He grabbed his warrant card in his free hand as he came level with the car where Maurice was lying, face down. He could see that a pool of blood was already starting to form under him.

'Police,' he said to the woman, who had now stopped screaming and grabbed an impressive-looking first aid kit from her car.

'I'm a nurse. I've got this. Go after him.'

Ted hesitated, bending down to Maurice.

'Is he …?'

'Not if I can help it,' the woman told him. 'Go.'

The man was fast and he had a head start. Ted was faster and driven by feelings of vengeance, even more so now that the attacker had hurt two of his team. He pelted down the car park, in the man's wake, and out into the main road. The man turned right, some distance ahead, but still in sight.

'I still have visual on our suspect. I'm in pursuit to see where he goes. DC Brown is receiving medical attention but his condition looks serious. Back-up urgently required.'

Kevin's voice replied to him.

'Bugger it, Ted, I'm trying to mobilise whatever units I can find. I'll get someone there as soon as I can.'

The Ice Queen's voice came over the radio next.

'Inspector, do not attempt to engage an armed suspect until back-up arrives. That is an order.'

Ted was running out of breath for the pursuit and the conversation. Just ahead of him, on the other side of the road, he saw a bus pull up at a stop and the suspect race across, dodging traffic, to jump on to it. It had already moved away by the time Ted found a way to cross over, through the busy stream of traffic.

'Shit!' he exclaimed. 'Suspect has just boarded a bus, heading in the direction of Stockport. I couldn't see the number. Get me some back-up, on the main road, as soon as possible. And we need that ambulance. I'm going back to see how Maurice is.'

As Ted jogged back up the approach road to the car park, he was nearly mown down by his own car, heading towards him at high speed. He saw two teenagers in the front, flicking middle fingers at him, as he jumped out of their way.

'And some bastard teenage toerags have just nicked my car,' he said into his radio, 'so can you put out an alert for it, please,' and gave the registration number.

When he got back to the scene, the nurse had carefully positioned Maurice onto his back, his chin lifted to help maintain a clear airway. He was unconscious and there looked now to be a lot of blood.

'How's he doing?' he asked anxiously, crouching down and taking hold of one of Maurice's hands.

'Slipping in and out of consciousness and losing a lot of blood,' the woman told him candidly. 'We need that ambulance, and fast. What's his name?'

'Maurice,' Ted told him. 'And I'm Ted. What can I do to help?'

'Hello, Ted, I'm Fiona. I've got a pad over the wound to try to stem the bleeding. Can you keep constant pressure on that while I check his airway again?'

Ted moved closer to take over from her. There was the usual crowd of gawpers standing round, but one of them stepped forward and offered help.

'Can you call the emergency services again and see if you can find out how long the ambulance will be? Ted asked him then, to Fiona, 'Should we cover him up at all?'

'Our main priority is to try to reduce that bleed as much as we can, until the ambulance arrives. They'll need to stabilise him before he can be moved. But a light covering would be helpful, if there's one handy.'

'Ambulance is on its way and should be here in five minutes. Is there anything else I can do? I could get a blanket from in store, if that would help?' the same man asked.

'Thank you for your help. Could you please ask everyone to move back, to give us some space, and some privacy?' Ted asked. 'And someone needs to inform the management of what's happened. The car park will need to be closed off at some point.'

'I am the management,' the man told them. 'At least, I'm the duty evening manager, just coming in to start work. I can see to that side of things for you. You're police officers? I'll go and get that blanket. I hope your colleague will be all right.'

'So do I,' Ted said through gritted teeth. 'Come on, Maurice, hang in there, bonny lad.'

Just then two cars came screeching into the car park and skidded to a halt nearby, carefully leaving room for an ambulance to get through. Jezza and Steve leapt out of her car, which she had recovered after Ted's advice. Mike Hallam and Rob jumped out of the second, all of them running over to where Maurice lay on the ground, still bleeding heavily, despite Ted's best efforts. Thankfully, at almost the same time, Ted finally heard the welcoming wail of sirens. Hopefully, the ambulance they were waiting for was on its way.

'Maurice! Maurice?' Jezza asked anxiously, crouching

down next to her friend and colleague, Steve close on her heels. 'Is he going to be all right, boss?'

'Everything's going to be all right, Jezza,' Ted said calmly, fervently hoping that it was.

Chapter Twenty-seven

It seemed to take the ambulance forever to negotiate its way through the crowded car park. Mike Hallam and Rob had quickly moved to direct it, then hurried anxiously back to Maurice's side. He had still not shown any signs of regaining full consciousness.

As the two paramedics got out of the ambulance and walked towards their casualty, they recognised the nurse who had been looking after him.

'Hello, Fi, not enough coming into A&E under their own steam? You're picking them up on the way? What have you got here for us?'

'Hi, guys, this is Maurice. He's a police officer, he's been stabbed and he's bleeding significantly. This is Ted, who's also a police officer and who's been keeping pressure on the wound for me while I've been monitoring him. He's been unresponsive much of the time.'

'If it helps, the weapon is likely to have been a seven-inch stiletto blade,' Ted told them, moving aside to allow them to take over and do their job.'

'Hello, Maurice, I'm Phil, and I'm just going to take a look at you,' one of them said, crouching down next to the inert form.

'Mike, we need witness statements from anyone who saw anything,' Ted stood up and briefed his sergeant. 'This is Fiona. It was her car the attacker tried to get into, and she's been helping keep Maurice alive since the attack. Perhaps you could go somewhere quiet to talk? Your car, maybe?

'Rob, can you ask around anyone here, see if there are any witnesses. Steve, you can help, but Jezza, you know what I'm going to say, don't you?'

'Don't worry, I'm going to hospital with Maurice anyway. He needs someone he knows to be there, when he wakes up.'

'Good, you can give me a lift. Some toerags have nicked my car.'

'Do you know who his next of kin is, Ted?' one of the paramedics asked him. 'Is there someone we should call for him? We're not going to be moving him just yet. We'll get him into the ambulance but we need to stabilise him before we go anywhere.'

Ted looked at Steve and Jezza, who probably knew him best.

'He's divorced, I'm not sure he has much contact with his ex-wife, does he?'

Unusually, Steve spoke up.

'Sir, I want to go with him too. Please.'

'It's fine, boss, Rob and I can manage here, if the three of you go. And it looks like the cavalry has arrived, finally,' Mike Hallam said, nodding at the blue lights of two police cars which were just pulling into the car park.

'Right,' Ted said decisively,' the three of us will go with him and keep you all posted. Jezza, you should wait in your car for now.'

She started to protest so he said, more firmly, 'In the car, please. Steve, get some witness details while you wait. Mike, you've got this one.

'I have just a hunch that Danny Boy may possibly try to slip out of the country for a while, especially if he sees through the media that this time he's stabbed a police officer. Mike, make sure we get his description circulated to all ports, just in case. And Rob, chase up details of stolen vans that he might be driving, circulate those, too.'

'I have to be at work very shortly,' the nurse told them. 'Could I possibly give a statement tomorrow, after I've finished my double night shift? I work on A&E, so I'll be following Maurice in.'

'If I could just take your contact details?' Ted asked, taking her gently by the arm and steering her away from the crowd of onlookers still gathered round. 'Also, I'm very sorry, but we're going to have to keep your car, for the time being. It's effectively a scene of crime and will need to be tested.'

'Oh, bugger, that's all I need,' she said. 'It's my boyfriend's car. Mine's in the garage having rather too many bits replaced. He's not going to be amused, and that's going to leave us both without transport.'

'I really am very sorry. Perhaps my officer could give you a lift to the hospital with us? I need a lift too, my car's been stolen, while I was going after the attacker. Can I just ask you, how did you manage to jump out of the car when an armed attacker got into it?'

Fiona gave a short laugh.

'The car looks the business, doesn't it? A really sporty number. Only it has a little peculiarity. The passenger door is dodgy and it gets stuck sometimes. The man tried to get in next to me as soon as I released the central locking, but the door snagged a moment. Working on A&E, you develop very quick reflexes for danger, so as he was climbing in, I was leaping out and screaming, which I suppose is what brought poor Maurice running. Then the door stuck again so the man had a struggle to get out quickly when he'd finally got in.'

The paramedics had transferred Maurice to the ambulance and one of them now put his head round the door and called across to the nurse.

'Fiona? We're ready to go now. See you there?'

Ted led her over to Jezza's car, collecting Steve on the way and handing over to Mike. He promised to let him know of any developments, and gave him the keys to Fiona's car.

Jezza had to stick frustratingly to the speed limits, with the boss in the passenger seat, although it was clear that she was itching to go faster on their way to the hospital.

The ambulance got there ahead of them and by the time Jezza had found a parking space, a long walk from A&E, Maurice was out of the ambulance and being seen to. Fiona proved a valuable ally as she was able to get information for them without too much of a problem.

'They're taking him straight to theatre,' she told the three of them. 'It looks as if the knife may have ruptured his spleen. He's lost a lot of blood, and is bleeding internally from the spleen and probably from one or more other sites. They won't know the full extent of the damage until they get him on the table.

'I know this is easy to say, but please try not to worry. He's in the best possible place. They will take good care of him. Perhaps one of you could give his details to reception, then I'll show you a quiet place where you can wait for news. I should warn you that it might be a long wait. They need to do their job.'

Steve and Jezza sat down close together, Jezza in her familiar slouching posture. Her legs were stuck out in front of her, her arms folded protectively across her chest. Next to her, Steve sat bolt upright, looking acutely uncomfortable but poised for action. Ted sat on the end of the row of chairs next to them, fervently wishing he could think of something useful to say to reassure them, other than meaningless platitudes.

They sat in silence for some time, anxiously waiting for news, any news. Then Jezza's mobile phone shattered the stillness. She answered the call, listened, then said, 'Put him on, please. Let me speak to him.'

Then, keeping her tone as calm and reasonable as she could, 'Tommy? Tom? Listen to me, please. I'm at the hospital with Maurice because he's been hurt. I can't come home just yet, I have to stay with him to make sure that he's going to be all right.

'No, Steve can't come either because he wants to be here too. Tommy, please listen and try to understand. I need you to understand. I can't come just yet, Tom. I can't. But you won't be on your own. It's Julie with you this evening, isn't it, and you like Julie. I'm going to ask her to stay with you a bit longer, just until I can get home. Please, Tom. I need your help with this. Can you do that for me? And for Maurice?'

She listened a bit more, then said patiently, 'No, Tom, you can't talk to Maurice now because he's very poorly. But listen, I'll be home as soon as I possibly can, and I promise to tell you everything then. Can you please put Julie back on the phone for me now? Good boy, Tommy, thank you.'

It was never easy for Jezza, dealing with an autistic younger brother who lived with her since the death of both of their parents in a car accident. The slightest change in his normal routine could send him into meltdown. Both Maurice and Steve had become vital helpers and stabilising factors in his life, often helping to look after him when Jezza had to work. Luckily the paid child-minder was going to be able to stay on a bit longer, to cover Jezza's unexpected late arrival home. Jezza just hoped that, whatever the news was going to be, they would get it soon.

All three were surprised when the Ice Queen came striding along the corridor towards them. They were all too tense to even think of standing up, though Steve did move to sit on the other side of Jezza, to allow her to sit next to Ted. She had clearly come straight from work and was still in uniform.

'Any news yet?' she asked anxiously as she sat down.

Ted shook his head, feeling too weary for any kind of formalities.

'He's still in theatre. They think he may have a damaged spleen. He's lost a lot of blood. Luckily the attacker's intended target was a nurse, who helped to keep him alive until the ambulance arrived.'

The Ice Queen picked up her bag, took out her wallet and got out a banknote, which she handed to Jezza.

'DC Vine, would you please go and get us all some sort of a hot drink? Perhaps you could both go, to share the carrying?'

It was clearly an instruction for Jezza and Steve to make themselves scarce while she talked to Ted. They both got to their feet, Jezza pocketing the note.

'What do you want, boss?'

'Get me a hot chocolate,' Ted told her. 'It's Maurice's cure for everything. It's what he would suggest.'

'Ma'am?'

'That sounds perfect, I'll have one, too.'

As the two of them walked away down the corridor, she turned to Ted.

'You and I will need to get together first thing in the morning. I'll need your full report on everything that happened. But I think, whatever the outcome, that can wait until tomorrow. What I do need to know from you now, though, is, did DC Brown ignore instructions and procedure and attempt to engage the attacker, without back-up in place?'

'Absolutely not,' Ted said emphatically. 'We were led to believe the suspect had left the premises. We were going in to look at CCTV tapes. The attacker was, in fact, running away when we arrived. He just ran straight into Maurice and stabbed him. And with respect, there was no back-up to be had. We were on our own there.'

The Ice Queen sighed.

'I know, and I'm sorry. And to make matters worse, the call which took all units out was largely a waste of time and valuable resources. No hostages, no terrorism, just a couple of young teens, trying to get a bit of money from a newsagent. One unit could have dealt effectively with the whole thing. Why do people do that, waste our time like that? Then they complain when we don't have enough available units to send to genuine cases.'

At that moment, Ted's mobile rang. He excused himself to take the call.

'Sergeant Wheeler, at the station, sir. Bad news about your car, I'm afraid. A couple of our lads were keeping an eye out and spotted it, on a patch of waste ground, but it had already been torched. Because they knew it was your car, they got the fire brigade out as soon as they could, but I'm afraid it was beyond saving. Sorry, sir.'

Ted thanked him and rang off with a groan. It was lucky he'd kept his coat on for the short drive from the station to the supermarket. The heater on the little Renault would not have made much of an impression over the distance. It did at least mean he had his tablets in the pocket, and the Fisherman's Friend lozenges he liked to suck in times of stress. His briefcase was safely back at the office, so he had only lost the car.

The worst of it was, he knew he was not going to be able to claim anything on his insurance. He'd been negligent in leaving the car open and the keys still in the ignition. Despite the emergency situation, he wouldn't be able to make a claim. Two thousand quid down the drain and he was once again without wheels.

'Bad news?' the Ice Queen asked him, looking astutely at his expression.

'That was the station. My car got nicked while I was following the suspect. They've found it, burnt out, and I'm not going to be able to claim. I left it open, with the keys in,' he sighed.

'I'm very sorry to hear that,' she said, and sounded as if she meant it.

Steve and Jezza reappeared with their drinks. Ted got his pills out of his pocket and took them. He needed all the help he could get to stay calm and deal with whatever the news was.

'Has anyone informed DC Brown's next of kin? He's not married, is he?' the Ice Queen asked.

'Not on good terms with the ex-wife, although he still sees his daughters regularly,' Jezza told her. 'Me and Steve are probably as close as he has to family, apart from the twins.'

They sipped their drinks in silence. Ted noticed that everyone had opted for hot chocolate, a token of acknowledgement to a valued colleague and friend, fighting for his life.

'How long's he been in theatre now?' the Ice Queen asked.

Ted checked his watch. 'Just over an hour. It seems like forever. They did warn us it might take some time.'

Ted finished his drink and found a quiet corner so he could phone Trev.

'Hi, it's me,' he began, as he always did, despite Trev assuring him countless times that he had a ringtone to recognise each incoming caller, as well as the name being displayed on screen. He quickly filled Trev in on what had happened to Maurice.

'I've no idea how long I'll be. We're still waiting on any news. The Ice Queen is here, too, showing support.'

'Do you want me to come? Maybe bring you something to eat, and some green tea?' Trev offered.

'That's kind, thanks, but no. I couldn't eat anything. Oh, and my car was nicked and torched. I'll tell you more about that when I see you.'

'Let me know when you're ready to leave and I'll come and pick you up.'

'Don't worry, I'll catch a lift back, or I might even walk. Depending on what the news is like, I might want to walk a bit. I'd better get back. We must surely hear something soon.'

Ted went back to join the others and they sat in the same taut, brittle silence, looking up hopefully any time a member of the medical staff came near.

After what seemed like an eternity, a woman came walking towards them, pulling her scrub hat off and shaking free her springy, short, auburn curls.

'You're here for Maurice Brown? Are you next of kin? I'm Ms Taylor, his surgeon. I've been operating on him.'

Three warrant cards appeared in three hands as they all stood up as one. The Ice Queen, in full uniform, had no need to identify herself. She spoke on behalf of all of them.

'DC Brown is a colleague and is also now the subject of a police investigation. Can you please give us an update on his condition?'

Out of the corner of his eye, Ted could see that Jezza and Steve had their hands locked together, white knuckled with tension. He was astonished when the Ice Queen took hold of his hand and squeezed it gently, waiting for the news. He was not sure if she was trying to reassure him or seeking his comfort for herself. After a brief hesitation, he squeezed hers back in response.

'Well, he gave us quite a worrying few moments in there. We had to remove his spleen, which was damaged beyond repair, and see to other sites of bleeding. But I'm happy to be able to tell you that he is going to be fine. We've got him sedated for now so you won't be able to see him until tomorrow.

'Depending on his progress, he will be in hospital for a week or so, then will need to rest and recuperate. But you should hopefully be able to have him back within two months.'

Ted was not sure who actually initiated the group hug. He was just amazed to find the four of them locked in a brief embrace of total relief. Maurice was going to be all right, and that was all that mattered at the moment.

Chapter Twenty-eight

Ted declined lifts from both Jezza and the Ice Queen. He wanted to walk back, to help clear his head and hopefully leave behind him some of the images of the day. It wouldn't take him long to get home on foot. He sent a quick text to Trev as he set off, to let him know when he'd be there.

He felt the sort of extreme fatigue that follows a prolonged period of stress. His adrenaline levels had been through the roof for the past three hours or so. Now he felt totally exhausted. The relief at knowing Maurice was going to be all right had left him feeling weak and wobbly. A brisk walk in the chilly night air was just what he needed.

He had barely left the hospital premises before his mobile phone rang and the caller display showed him that it was the local reporter.

'Yes, Alastair, what can I do for you?' he asked, trying to keep the irritation out of his voice.

'Is it true that a copper's been stabbed this evening? One of your lot?' Pocket Billiards asked, without preamble.

'You know I can't tell you anything about that.'

'But just off the record, Ted? Can you at least confirm that it happened?'

'On or off the record, there's nothing I can tell you at this stage,' Ted repeated patiently. 'There will be an official statement issued, if there's anything for you. The best I can possibly do is to promise to let you have it before anyone else gets it.'

The journalist was still grumbling when Ted ended the call. He understood he was only doing his job, but making a sensational piece out of the near death of an officer was not something he liked to think about.

His walk home took him past the end of the quiet road where Kenny Norman's sister lived. As he reached the junction, a police car was just pulling up to give way to traffic. Recognising the two officers in the car, Ted nodded to them and the constable in the passenger seat let his window down to greet him.

'Evening, sir. Are you on foot? Can we give you a lift somewhere?'

'It's fine, thanks, I need the walk to clear my head. I'm just on my way back from the hospital.'

'Yes, we heard about Maurice. How's he doing?'

'Hopefully going to be all right. He's had a long operation but he seems to be out of danger now. What brings you round here?'

'We were called out to a sudden death, sir. According to the ambulance crew, though, it looks like natural causes. An elderly lady, collapsed in her back garden. Her neighbour saw her lying there and dialled 999. She's been taken away now. We've just been getting a statement from the neighbour.

'She said she spotted her as she was closing the back bedroom curtains. She was lying in the garden. The neighbour thinks she'd been feeding the birds when she collapsed. It seems she had a bad heart. She was on medication for it. The paramedics said it was probably a heart attack.'

Ted looked down the road as he asked, 'What was the name?'

'A Miss Norman, sir. She lived on her own, according to the neighbour. Are you sure we can't drop you off somewhere?'

Ted thanked them but refused again. Now more than ever he felt in need of a walk in the cool night air. Hearing of the woman's death affected him more than he expected as he continued on his way home. He kept thinking of the sight of three lonely Christmas cards sitting on her mantelpiece. He just hoped her death had been quick and that she had not suffered.

As soon as he heard his key in the door, Trev appeared in the hallway and, without a word, wrapped his arms around his partner and simply held him. It was just what Ted needed, after the day he had had. It was moments like this which made him realise just how lucky he was with his relationship.

'So, Maurice is going to be all right?' Trev asked, steering Ted towards the kitchen, where they both sat down at the table, immediately invaded by six purring cats.

'Hopefully, although he clearly has a long road to recovery ahead of him. I thought he was a goner at one point, I must say. And I just found out by chance, on the walk home, that someone else I was talking to recently has died. Not one for the team, it looks like natural causes. But sad all the same. An elderly lady living on her own, who'd been through more in her life than she should have.'

'Do you want food? There's some shepherd's pie. I can heat it up for you? I've not eaten much, I thought I'd wait until you got back, keep you company.'

He got up and busied himself, preparing their food.

'Tell me about the car.'

Ted sighed.

'I was parking when I saw Maurice go down. I just jumped out and ran. Didn't lock the car, didn't even close the doors. So I'm not going to be able to claim a penny from the insurance. I'll have to phone the garage tomorrow and see if they can find me something else cheap and cheerful.'

'We'll get through it. Like you said, we'll just have to tighten our belts a bit more. No more expensive wine and red roses. Now eat something, or economy won't be the only reason you'll need to tighten your belt.'

Both Ted and the Ice Queen were in early the following

morning for their debriefing on the events of the evening before. Even though it was a Saturday, all the team members were in voluntarily, all anxious to make progress on what had now become an even more intensely personal case.

'Any news on DC Brown this morning?' she asked first, as she set her coffee machine in motion.

'I phoned first thing but they wouldn't tell me very much, as usual,' Ted replied, not bothering with formalities.

Having held her hand and shared a hug the night before, he decided he could take the liberty, with just the two of them in her office.

'All they would tell me was that he's passed a comfortable night, which sounds unlikely, and that it's still an assault case, not a murder. I'll try and get in to see him later on, find out how he's doing.'

'Do please pass on my best wishes to him. It was a terrible business. I'm going to need your report on the incident as soon as humanly possible, if not before,' she said, trying to make a light-hearted remark to ease the tension.

Ted wondered fleetingly if she was still feeling the effects of the rare moment they had shared the night before.

'As you can imagine, I'm going to have to make a report to the next level. I need to make absolutely certain there were no breaches of procedure which need addressing, before I do so.'

'Perhaps you can ask why we were so short on available units that Maurice and I were on our own there, despite repeatedly calling for back-up.'

She sighed as she served the coffee.

'I do raise it, repeatedly, and the response is always the same. Budgetary constraints. We have to make do with what we have, and continue to work miracles.'

'I had the local press on, too, last night, wanting a statement. I promised to let Pocket Billiards know first, as soon as we had anything.'

'I'll have a word with the Press Office first thing and get

something out as soon as possible.'

'We also need to consider what we're going to do next. This man is highly dangerous and so far, we're not having much luck catching him. We do have his mobile phone number, though. At least, just a pay as you go one, so we can't trace it to him. We know he drives for hire, so what if we set up a meeting with him, supposedly to put some work his way?'

'A sting operation? That would have to be cleared at the highest level and it's not something which can be mounted in a hurry. The paperwork alone is not quick.'

'But we have to do something, before he goes on to kill again,' Ted said earnestly. 'I saw him in action yesterday. He's cold and calculating, clearly highly trained, and prepared to stop at nothing. We've now got a murder, an attempted murder and four rapes down to him on our patch alone. Surely it's time to take drastic measures?'

'Give me a written proposal and I will certainly take it forward,' she told him. 'With my full backing, as long as it stacks up on paper. So now that I need two reports from you as soon as possible, I'd better allow you to go and get on with them.'

All of the team members were eager for news of Maurice, as soon as Ted appeared to join them for the morning briefing. Jezza had also tried phoning for information but had been told little more than Ted. He told them what he did know and promised to go and visit Maurice later in the day, as soon as he was told he was up to a visit.

Once he'd sent Jezza off to his office, armed with her books, he also shared with them the idea of trying to lure Danny in with the promise of some work.

'We'll have to jump through hoops to get it approved from on high, and he is very wary, so he might not fall for it anyway. But we have to try something. We can't just sit around waiting for his next victim.

'Speaking of victims, Virgil, how's Nathan doing? We

mustn't forget he's collateral damage in all of this. How's he getting on, and how are the fish?'

'Nat's back in the flat, limping about on crutches, so I'm still calling in whenever I can, to give him a hand. And to see the fish. I've become fond of those little guys. I gave them all names. I must be getting as broody as the missus,' Virgil grinned.

'Right, Mike, can I leave you to take over? I have reports to prepare for the Super. Can you sort out witness statements from yesterday and let everyone see copies, then we can regroup later and see what we've got.

'Any news of a likely vehicle, Rob? And any reports of sightings at ports, if he has tried to leave the country?'

'There's a couple of stolen vans unaccounted for. I'll let everyone have details, although the plates will almost certainly have been changed by now, boss,' Rob told him. 'No port sightings, but that was always a long shot, as we've no idea what vehicle he's driving now and the description could fit almost anyone.'

'That's another thing to check. Where does he go to do things like change van plates? Ask around. Rob, can you try ringing that other ex-soldier again, the one I talked to. Ask him if he might have any idea where Danny Boy would go for something like that. See if you can convince him to talk to you. Tell him I'm tied up.

'And remember, all of you, stab vests on if you're going anywhere near where Danny might be. Maurice wasn't expecting to come face to face with him, or he would have been wearing his.'

'How's the research going?' Ted asked Jezza as he went back into his own office.

'It's certainly reinforcing my thoughts that I don't like crime fiction,' she replied. 'What a load of old rubbish, and looking at her ratings, Olivia Radnor is supposedly one of the better writers of the genre. But there's a definite pattern here. Almost every case the Cooper woman refers to in her Barbed Wire book appears in some form or another in Radnor's fiction. Altered a bit sometimes, but always recognisable, if you read the two side by side, as I'm doing.

'Boss, what if Jenny Holden was not alone? What if some of the other case studies here also had False Memory Syndrome? There must be something that can be done about her. We can't just let this go.'

'Write your report, Jezza,' Ted told her gently. 'I've said I'll pass it on to the right quarters and I will. I can't do any more than that. Now I need my office back, please. I have reports of my own to write, then I want to try to see Maurice. And before you ask, no, you can't come. I'd better go on my own this time, find out if he's up to visitors.'

Jezza gathered up her books and headed for the door.

'Give him a big, fat, soppy kiss from me,' she grinned at him over her shoulder.

Ted phoned the hospital again at lunchtime and was told that Maurice could have visitors, no more than two at a time and only briefly. They must be prepared to leave if he showed any signs of getting overtired.

Ted found him in a quiet side room off the main ward and was surprised, when he went quietly in, to find Maurice's ex-wife sitting at his bedside.

'Sorry, Barbara, I didn't know you were here,' Ted said, hesitating.

'Come in, Ted,' she told him, indicating a spare chair. 'It's fine, he'll want to see you.'

Partners of Ted's team members all called him by his first name at the social occasions, which were usually the only times their paths crossed.

'I'm still down as his next of kin, so the hospital called me.'

'How's he doing?' Ted asked quietly, sitting down.

Maurice appeared to be sleeping, so he didn't want to wake him. He clearly needed to rest after major surgery.

'Sleeping, most of the time, although he's woken up a few times and we've spoken a bit. He always was a lazy great lump,' she said, but there was a touch of affection in her tone. 'Can you tell me how it happened? I don't know very much, only that he was stabbed, working on a case.'

'You've probably read about the serial sex attacks, in the paper,' Ted began. 'Maurice and I were on a shout. We were going to the supermarket in connection with a possible sighting of our suspect. We had no reason to believe that he was still on the premises, we were just going to look at CCTV footage which might have shown him.

'I was having trouble parking so Maurice got out to walk to the store. He heard a woman screaming and ran to find out what was happening. He was just unlucky enough to run straight into the attacker, trying to leave the scene.'

'Stupid, stupid man,' she said, but there was no trace of bitterness in her voice. 'That's Maurice all over, a sucker for anyone who's hurt or upset. The big soft fool.'

'You sound as if you still care for him?'

'He's the father of my children, and I love him for that. I'm still very fond of him. Part of me still loves him. I just couldn't live with him. He's like a bloody big kid, he never grew up. That's why he's so brilliant with the twins. He's not a parent, he's just another child. It's why I couldn't stay with him. It was like having three small kids in the house, when the twins were little. I was the only grown-up, and that was hard. That and seeing him go off to work every day and not knowing if and when something like this might happen to him.'

'I think I must have died and be floating around in heaven somewhere. I'm hallucinating about my ex-wife saying nice things about me,' Maurice growled softly, opening sleepy eyes to look from his boss to his ex-wife and back.

'How are you feeling, Maurice?' Ted asked him. 'Jezza sends you a big soppy kiss, but I hope I'm not expected to pass it on personally. You gave us all a bit of a fright last night.'

'I've felt better, boss,' Maurice said ruefully, wincing at the effort of speaking. 'Did you get him?'

'Sorry, Maurice, but no. He did his usual trick of hopping on a bus and I was on foot. My car got nicked while you were busy scaring everyone. I had no way to follow him and there was no immediate back-up available.'

Maurice smiled then grimaced again.

'Don't make me laugh, boss, it hurts too much. Losing a suspect and losing your car at the same time is a bit careless,' then he continued earnestly, 'Boss, it's true, what the victims said. His eyes. He's dead behind the eyes. I remember thinking that, while he was stabbing me.'

'You stupid man!' Barbara said harshly. 'Putting yourself at risk like that. What about the twins? Did you think of them and how they would be affected if you got killed playing the hero?'

She was choking back tears, though whether of anger or relief, Ted couldn't tell. She started to pound her fist against one of Maurice's arms which lay on top of the covers. It was perilously close to where the suspended drip went into one of his veins.

Ted got up quickly and gently took hold of her arms, pulling her against him to restrain and comfort her.

'Barbara, I don't think you should be hitting him when he's just had major surgery,' he said gently. 'You've had a fright. He gave us all a bit of a scare, but it's going to be all right. He'll be fine.'

He let her turn to him and put her head against his shoulder as she started to sob. He kept his arms lightly around her shoulders in silent comfort.

At that moment, the door burst open and Maurice's twin girls erupted into the small space, launching themselves towards the bed with squeals of, 'Daddy!' They were closely followed by Barbara's new husband, who raised his eyebrows at seeing his wife in the embrace of some short bloke he didn't know.

'Girls, gently,' Barbara admonished them, pulling guiltily away from Ted. 'Daddy's just had a big operation. You mustn't jump on him.'

Maurice's face broke into a beaming smile of pleasure as he lifted his unencumbered arm towards his beloved daughters.

'Hello, my princesses. This is the best possible medicine I could have. Just be careful of these tubes. And don't forget to say hello to my boss.'

'Hello, Mr Darling,' they said dutifully in unison, giggling, as always, at his name.

'Mark,' Maurice nodded curtly to his replacement.

'Maurice,' came the equally brusque reply, then the man turned to Ted, who suddenly felt acutely uncomfortable. 'Can I have my wife back now, Mr Darling?'

Ted opened his mouth to explain, but was interrupted by the door opening again and a nurse coming in, looking severely disapproving.

'Far too many people in here at once,' she said sternly. 'Mr Brown must get his rest. Only two at a time, and only for short periods.'

'The girls only count as one,' Maurice told her with an attempt at a grin, although he was clearly tiring and in a lot of pain.

'I'll go now, Maurice, but I'll be back some time tomorrow. And I know Steve and Jezza want to visit, as soon as you're up to it.'

'Thanks for coming, Ted, I really appreciate it. Oh, and boss? Make sure you get him.'

Chapter Twenty-nine

The Super and Kevin Turner joined Ted and his team for the morning briefing on the following Monday. Ted had submitted his proposal to try to draw Danny Boy out with the offer of driving, and he wanted to air his ideas.

'The logical place to use for the set-up is the kennels, the one he already does driving work for,' Ted began. 'It's one place he might not be quite so suspicious of visiting, as he's been there before. But, it throws up as many problems as benefits.

'Following his visit there, Sal's spoken to the RSPCA, in the form of Rob's fiancée, and they're anxious to get in there and carry out at least an assessment and possibly a seizure of animals on the premises as soon as possible. Now, they can't go in without a Uniform branch presence and a search warrant, neither of which should be a problem.'

'But as murder, rape and attempted murder trump animal welfare issues every time, I'd be happy to hold back on making my officers available until after we've dealt with Danny Boy,' Kevin Turner put in.

Ted nodded.

'The tricky thing is, we'd need to try to persuade the owner to contact Danny to get him to come for a pick-up or whatever the deal is. And she's probably not going to cooperate with us without a very good motive.

'Now, talking to Sally, Rob's fiancée, it sounds as if the woman is going to be closed down and have all the dogs seized, whatever else happens. We can't tip her off to that, it needs to happen, by the sounds of it. If we can get her to cooperate with us, the best we can do for her is to see if Trading Standards can be persuaded not to take any further action on the dodgy pups she's already sold.

'If we can get her to call Danny, then we can set things up to be waiting for him. And ma'am, I want armed response officers there. So far he's only used a knife that we know of, but we know he's ex-military and therefore firearms trained and I don't want to risk any further casualties.'

The Ice Queen nodded.

'Noted, Inspector.'

'Mike, is there anything at all in Danny's records to suggest mental health issues? Any suggestion of PTSD? It would help to know exactly what we're dealing with.'

'Boss, they only sent the bare bones. There's not a great deal there, although he has served in some difficult areas, including Northern Ireland, Sierra Leone, Kosovo, Iraq and Afghanistan. He was a career soldier, did twenty-two years after basic training. Came out four years ago.'

'Can you chase them up again and see if there's anything else at all they can tell us?'

'With respect to you, Sergeant Hallam, would you like me to make the phone call?' the Ice Queen put in. 'Not that I'm suggesting for a moment that you're not up to the task, but knowing how the Army loves rank, perhaps mine might be of some use in loosening tongues?'

'It's not like we're all on the same side or anything,' Kevin Turner grunted darkly.

'Thank you, ma'am, glad of any help I can get with this one,' Mike said thankfully.

'As soon as I have something for you, I will get it emailed to you directly so that you can share it with the team.'

'What I'm proposing now is that Sal and I go to see this woman, as she's already met Sal so there's a contact established,' Ted continued. 'We'll try to persuade her to call Danny to arrange for him to come for a supposed pick-up. I'm assuming she just leaves him a message and he calls back, probably from a different phone. So one of us will need to stay with her until the arrangements are made. Unless she manages to contact him immediately.

'We need to give ourselves at least twenty-four hours notice to prepare. I'm assuming that's enough, ma'am? I want firearms in place, and as many Uniform units as Inspector Turner can make available, with plenty of Tasers. We don't want to have to shoot him unless it's unavoidable. I'd personally favour immobilising him so he stands trial, if we can do it without risk to anyone else.'

'All noted, Inspector,' the Ice Queen said as she rose to go, gesturing to everyone present that there was no need to stand. 'Keep me posted with what arrangements you have made, if you can indeed make any, and leave the staffing level issues to me.'

Kevin Turner followed Ted to his office after the briefing. Jezza was already gathering up her books as they came in. She nodded briefly to the Uniform inspector then asked eagerly, 'Are you going after him then, boss?'

'The reason you're banished in here is that you're not involved in this case. All I will say is that I promised you we'd get him, and I intend to keep that promise.'

Kevin took the seat Jezza had just vacated while Ted put the kettle on.

'How's she doing, Ted? I can't even begin to think what it must be like for her. I know how I'd feel, if that happened to one of my daughters.'

'She's a tough nut, is our Jezza. I've tried to persuade her not to bottle it all up, to go and see someone. The business with Maurice has upset her, too. They're close friends, those two, and young Steve. Green tea for your ulcer, or gut-rotting coffee?'

Kevin made a face.

'My guts give me enough trouble already, without chucking your mystic potions into them.'

'You're going to have to get it seen to, Kev, you can't just ignore it.'

'Are you going to Jim's engagement do? The missus and I are invited,' he said, clumsily changing the subject and accepting the mug of coffee which Ted put in front of him.

'Hopefully, depending on Danny Boy. I need to sort a car out, too. With luck, my garage can find me another cheap little runabout.'

'Yes, I heard about that. It was bad luck. Why don't you get yourself something decent?'

Ted shook his head.

'I've just helped Trev out, buying into the bike business. Anyway, I'm not interested in cars, just as a way to get about. For fun, I prefer the bike, with Trev.'

Kevin drained his coffee mug in a few big gulps and stood up.

'Well, let me know if you both want a lift. I'll be driving, which gives me a good reason not to drink, so the wife doesn't get suspicious. Pouring alcohol down my throat is the last thing I feel like doing at the moment.'

Ted took a moment to phone his garage, to see if they could find him another car, quickly and cheaply, and explained why he was once more without wheels.

'Oh, dear, Inspector, you're not having a lot of luck with your cars at the moment, are you? I haven't much available in that price bracket, certainly not in Renault. It would help if you'd consider another make, then I might be able to do something for you.'

'I like Renault. The seats are comfortable,' Ted said stubbornly.

It was about the sum total of his interest in cars.

The man laughed.

'Well, look, you're a good customer, and I always like to help the police when I can. Let me ring round a few contacts and see if anyone else has anything which would do you. I'll try and get hold of something today then we can give it a good service for you, have it ready for you after work tomorrow. How's that?'

Ted thanked him profusely, then rang off and went in search of Sal. They needed to go and see if they could get anywhere with the dog dealer. She was their best hope of making contact with Danny and bringing him to a place of their choosing so they could hopefully, finally, make an arrest.

The address was down a rutted track off a quiet road, water-filled potholes everywhere. Sal pulled his car up outside a ramshackle gate and both men got out. The whole place had a run-down air and there was an all-pervading smell of dog urine and faeces. A cacophony of high-pitched barking greeted them.

Ted looking around him.

'I can see why you thought this might be an RSPCA matter, Sal, and that's without even seeing any of the dogs.'

'I don't know a lot about dogs, boss, but even I can see these are not the right sort of conditions to keep them in. It smells as if they never get cleaned out, for one thing.'

'Are there any loose dogs about?' Ted asked him, peering warily over the gate. 'The biting kind, I mean. I know about cats but I'm not very good with dogs.'

'I didn't see any, boss, they all seemed to be locked in tiny cages and pens. There was just some ancient farting and snoring thing curled up on a cushion in what passes for an office, where I talked to the owner.'

As if knowing she was being talked about, a woman stuck her head out of the door of an old Portakabin and peered at them suspiciously.

'What d'you want?' she called out, her tone not particularly friendly.

'Mrs Marston? It's DC Ahmed, I spoke to you before. This

is Detective Inspector Darling. We wondered if we could just have another word with you? It's about Danny.'

Both men took out their warrant cards and held them up. She ducked back inside the office and reappeared a moment later, pulling on an ancient waxed jacket, her feet thrust into old Wellington boots which looked a size too large. She came over to the gate and scrutinised the cards the men were still holding up for her attention.

'Darling, eh?' she asked, looking from the cards to Ted. 'Can't have been easy, growing up with a moniker like that.'

She turned her attention back to Sal as she asked, 'What do you want this time?'

'May we come in, Mrs Marston? It's not all that warm, standing out here,' Ted said reasonably.

Without a word, she swung the rusty gate open on its sagging hinges to let them in, then stumped off back to the office, calling over her shoulder as she went, 'Shut the gate after you.'

The smell inside the cabin was overpowering. Either the woman had the most appalling case of flatulence or it was coming from the indeterminate ball of fur curled up, snoring, on a chair in the corner. An ancient portable gas fire didn't smell too healthy, but even its fumes were barely disguising the noxious smells. Ted wondered if the woman had simply become so accustomed to the stench that she no longer noticed it, although he found that hard to believe.

She sat back down at a table strewn with paperwork, with a surprisingly new-looking laptop computer amongst the chaos. She didn't invite them to sit down and, looking at the stains on the various available chairs, neither of them felt much like doing so.

'What do you want this time?' she asked again, although her eyes were on the computer screen, checking her emails, as she spoke.

'Mrs Marston, we urgently need to set up a meeting with

the man Danny who, I understand, does deliveries for you sometimes. Now, you kindly gave DC Ahmed his mobile number, but he is likely to be very suspicious of anyone he doesn't know. I need to ask you if you would be prepared to phone him and ask him to come here? Police officers would then be on hand, on your premises, with your permission, to arrest him when he arrives.'

She turned away from the computer screen, her dark eyes suddenly interested. She was, Ted guessed, in her mid to late fifties and looked, like the whole of the place, a stranger to hygiene.

'What's in it for me if I help you?'

'There can be no financial reward, Mrs Marston, if that is what you're asking me. I would simply say that you could consider it a civic duty. We have reason to believe that Danny may be a dangerous individual, someone we are most anxious to take into custody for questioning. I can assure you that you would be protected. In fact, we would need you to leave the premises at the time of the meeting.'

'I'm not leaving the dogs,' she said immediately. 'Who knows what would happen to them with a load of flat-footed coppers trampling round the place. Anyway, Danny would expect to see me here.'

'Mrs Marston, we would need to have armed officers on the premises, so for that reason, we would normally clear the area of civilians. I cannot stress enough that we believe this man may be dangerous, and is most probably armed. Do you live on site? Is there somewhere safe you could be, somewhere away from this building, and from the entrance.'

'I've got a mobile home, round behind the kennels. I'll go there, but no further. All right, if I agree to do it, when do you want him here?'

'We would need some time to prepare, so not before tomorrow at the earliest,' Ted told her.

'And none of the dogs would be harmed? You wouldn't be

bringing police dogs in?'

'No police dogs would be involved in the operation, and we would do our utmost to protect the safety of anyone on the premises, including your dogs,' Ted said guardedly.

Without replying, the woman started to rummage around amongst the paperwork until she found a mobile phone. She made a call and put it to her ear.

'Danny? Pat Marston here, love. Got a few puppies to be shifted from my place down to London, as soon as you can. A decent rate for you, while it's a bit of a rush job. Call me back as soon as you can, love.'

She looked from Ted to Sal.

'He sometimes calls back fairly quickly, it just depends where he is and what he's up to.'

'Have you known him long?' Ted asked.

'I don't know him, not really. He's just done some driving for me, on and off, over the past couple of years. He's usually pretty reliable.'

The mobile phone on her desk rang. She looked at the screen, mouthed 'Danny' and took the call.

'Hello, love, thanks for getting back to me quickly. When are you free?'

She looked at Ted as she said, 'Not before the day after tomorrow?'

Ted nodded. That would give them more time to prepare.

'All right, love, that's fine. There's just a half dozen pups to go down to the usual drop-off. Can you be here by ten, then I'll have all the paperwork ready for you? Thanks, love.'

She ended the call, then looked at Ted again.

'This better all be on the level. I don't want to lose a reliable driver if you lot have bungled things as usual. And you'll have to pay for any damage you cause.'

'Mrs Marston, did Danny ever arrive with fewer puppies on the van than you were expecting?' Ted asked her.

She looked at him suspiciously.

'Once,' she said grudgingly. 'He said one had been seized at the port because there was a mix-up with the paperwork. I didn't follow it up. It would probably have cost me more than I paid for the pup to sort it all out.'

'Once we get our operation out of the way the day after tomorrow, I should be in a position to tell you a little bit more about the man who has been transporting puppies for you. Including the story behind that missing pup. Thank you for your help. I'll be in touch.'

Ted felt contaminated when he got back into the car. Not just from the smell and the squalor of the place but from the thought of how the whole operation was run. He'd heard terms like puppy farming but hadn't really had any concept of what went on in the dog world. He felt sickened by what he had learned so far. He was looking forward to giving the RSPCA the green light to go in, the minute they had Danny in custody.

Back at the station, Mike Hallam had an update for them.

'Boss, the Super came up with the goods. Army records emailed me some more detail on Danny, that wasn't on the original files they sent over. He divorced his first wife when she ran off with another soldier from the same regiment as him, while he was serving overseas. He married again, a much younger woman. She was killed on active service, just around the time that Danny left the forces. No children from either marriage.'

'So if the tours of duty he's done didn't leave him disturbed, it's just possible that that tipped him over the edge? That makes him even more dangerous than I feared,' Ted replied. 'He has nothing left to live for.'

Chapter Thirty

Ted was accompanied by the Superintendent and Kevin Turner the following morning for a thorough recce of the dog dealer's site. They were joined by a firearms inspector, Paul Jenkins. Ted and the Ice Queen knew him, both of them having served in firearms previously.

One of the reasons the Ice Queen commanded respect was that, unlike a lot of the modern generation of senior officers, whose role was more politics than policing, she had done her share in the front line.

The four of them arrived in her car, wearing dark coats over their uniforms, Ted in his hated suit and tie, with his raincoat over the top. Hopefully, if Danny was watching the place for any reason, they might just pass for visiting Environmental Health inspectors.

'We're going to need a way to block off the end of the lane if and when he arrives, to stop him getting away if he rumbles us. And that's not going to be easy. There's no cover at all for waiting vehicles. If we have them holed up too far away, they won't be able to get there quickly enough if he smells a rat,' Inspector Jenkins said. 'And if he's as savvy as you say, Ted, he'll be on the look-out for the slightest thing.

'There is a bit of cover along that lane, so I could possibly put someone in there with a stinger, as back-up. We need a sure way of stopping him reaching the road and turning it into a car chase, with all the dangers that would entail. Plus the risk of losing him, if there's no authorisation to exceed the speed limit in pursuit.

'I imagine he'll be something of an expert in urban warfare, including assessing for ambush, from some of the places he's served. Not least from his days in Northern Ireland. And the same goes for getting my officers in here, out of sight. There's not a lot of cover, if he's watching us from a distance.'

'From the look of this place, it wouldn't seem out of the ordinary to bring in something like a pest control van, with your firearms officers and some of mine in it,' Kevin Turner said thoughtfully.

'What about dog food delivery?' the Ice Queen suggested. 'I imagine a place like this buys in bulk, assuming they actually feed the poor dogs? That might possibly be an even better cover. Or perhaps they use other delivery drivers for moving dogs around?'

'The owner will certainly be able to fill us in on that,' Ted said, as the four of them got out of the car and made their way towards the gate. As before, Pat Marston appeared from the cabin as she saw them approaching.

'How much can we trust her?' the Ice Queen asked quietly.

'Probably not a lot,' Ted told her frankly. 'Worryingly, though, at the moment, she is our best chance.'

He approached the gate and said, 'Mrs Marston, these are my colleagues, Superintendent Caldwell and Inspectors Turner and Jenkins. Is there somewhere we could talk, please? Rather than standing around outside in the cold, looking suspicious?'

The look she was giving the four of them was definitely one of suspicion.

'We won't all fit in the cabin. I suppose you'd better come round to the mobile home,' she said grudgingly.

Ted fervently hoped that her living accommodation might smell better than her workspace. They picked their way carefully through mud, past ramshackle outbuildings, where dogs and puppies were crammed into dark, confined pens and what looked like old pigsties. The noise of the dogs and the stench of their excrement made him want to gag. When they got to the mobile home and followed the woman inside, there was the same smell, just to a lesser intensity.

She led them to a small kitchen area at one end of the caravan. Every visible surface was dirty and grease-encrusted and their feet stuck to the filthy lino as they crossed it.

'There aren't enough stools for everyone to sit down. You'll have to fight over them,' the woman told them. 'I suppose I could make you a cup of tea, if you're going to be long?'

The chorus of refusals was instant and unanimous. None of them fancied drinking out of anything in that squalor.

The Ice Queen assumed charge.

'Mrs Marston, thank you for allowing us to use your premises. I understand that this man Danny is due here tomorrow morning at ten. Is he usually punctual?'

'Always on the button, sometimes a bit early. Ex-Army, he tells me, and it shows in his timekeeping.'

'In that case, I want to have all our officers in place before eight o'clock, so we won't be caught unawares. I'm sorry if that is an inconvenience to you. We will need you to remain in here, until the operation is concluded. An officer will stay with you to ensure your safety. If there is anything which needs doing to your dogs, it will need to be before eight o'clock, I'm afraid.'

'I can give the little buggers extra food tonight,' she said. 'That way it won't matter if I'm a bit later than usual with their brekky.'

From the way she said it, Ted had a feeling that it wouldn't be the first time the dogs in her care had missed a meal. Although it was not within his own remit, he hoped someone would take action soon to get the place sorted out.

'Has Danny been in contact with you since your phone call yesterday, while DI Darling was here?' the Ice Queen asked.

The woman shook her head.

'No, but I wouldn't have expected him to. He knows the

routine. When I call him for a delivery, he just turns up at the time I tell him to and does the job. That's why I use him.'

'I cannot stress enough that it is absolutely essential you don't talk to him at all, from now on. If for any reason he should try to contact you, please do not take his call. You should not discuss anything about the operation with anyone for whatever reason.'

She went on to explain in broad terms how the operation would unfold, then asked the woman about what sort of a van could be parked at the premises, without looking too suspicious.

'There is a van comes round, a young chap, who sells dog food, wellies, overalls, that sort of stuff out of the back of it. It's not knock-off, it's on the level, but his prices are good. I buy stuff from him. Winter socks, for one.'

The van, she told them, was a plain white Transit, with no logos. Good news for the operation. They had plenty available which would fit the bill. It meant they could transport officers to the scene without arousing suspicion. It could then be parked not far away, ready to block the lane end when Danny showed up.

The smell in the confined space suddenly intensified noticeably. Ted realised he might have done the old dog an injustice, blaming it for the atmosphere in the cabin. He wondered if the woman was a drinker, which was causing her digestive problems, as well as possibly explaining the state the place was in. There must be a reason why she lived in the conditions she did.

They now had the information which they had come for and were keen to get away. The Ice Queen thanked the woman again for her cooperation and led the way back to her car. None of the four officers offered to shake her hand before leaving. Once they were all inside and on their way, she said, 'Inspector Turner, what is the situation with the RSPCA and their inspection visit on that vile place?'

'Ma'am, they're waiting to hear from me on the outcome of tomorrow's operation. Clearly, I didn't want them going in first and spoiling the one chance we have to date of bringing Danny Boy to us.'

'Ask them to be on stand-by to go in, the minute we have completed our operations. I want that abomination closed down as soon as possible. If I can do anything at all to expedite matters, in terms of sorting out warrants or anything, do please let me know.

'I think we should now all adjourn to my office for some decent coffee, which might hopefully go some way to getting those disgusting smells out of our nostrils. In fact, why don't I stop somewhere on the way back and buy us all some utterly iniquitous sticky buns to go with it? I think we all deserve something.'

Ted had thought he was beyond surprises with the changes he was seeing lately in his boss. As hard as this case was proving, it was certainly doing a great deal to improve relations between them.

Over the promised coffee and cakes, they thrashed out the final details of the forthcoming operation.

'What's your instinct on this one? Will our man show up?' the Ice Queen asked Ted.

'You know I'm not into any kind of psychological profiling, nor am I equipped to take even a stab at it,' Ted began. 'But I do have a feeling that Danny doesn't care whether he's caught or not. All the witnesses, including Maurice now, say that he's dead behind the eyes.

'There is a strong possibility he's had enough. Not only does he not care, he might actually welcome the end, when it comes. Now I've seen more of his record, and thank you for getting that for us, ma'am, I wonder if there's not some degree of guilt in what he's feeling. He did all those tours in countries with high death and injury rates and came out unscathed. Yet his young wife was killed.

'Something like that must be very hard to live with. I can see how it could drive someone over the edge. Especially if they've been hovering pretty close to it already. It may be that he doesn't care when and how it ends, just that it does.'

'He wants his Butch Cassidy moment, you mean?' Paul Jenkins asked him. 'Going down in a blaze of glory and a hail of bullets?'

'I don't want your officers opening fire unless there is absolutely no other option,' the Ice Queen warned him. 'I would personally favour taking him alive, if we can do so, without risk to any officer. I, too, think that the public would like to see him brought to trial. But I must stress to all of you, and please impress it on all of your officers, there must be no heroics. If the operation goes to plan and he turns up unaware of the reception committee, we take him by the quickest and least dangerous means at our disposal.

'Make sure everyone is fully equipped for all eventualities, and all equipment is checked and up to operational standards. This could be it, gentlemen. We could finally be close to getting this man off the streets and behind bars, where he belongs.'

Ted relented and let Jezza stay in the main office while he briefed his team on the plan for the following day's operation. He suspected she would have gone head to head with him if he'd tried to order her out, so he opted for the line of least resistance. He squared it with himself by the thought that it wasn't to do with the enquiry itself, but its hopeful outcome. He also thought it would be good for her morale, as she couldn't be in at the end, to at least hear how it was planned to go.

'Mike, you, Rob, Virgil and Sal are with me on this one. Stab vests on. Jezza, you're holding the fort and Steve, you're helping her.'

He saw the young officer's disappointed expression and said, 'Don't worry, there'll be other opportunities, in the future. And you can guarantee there will be plenty of other crime going on at the same time which needs sorting. I'm counting on the two of you to be on top of anything that comes this way while we're out.'

'We need to be on site and in position before eight o'clock, so I suggest we RV here at seven. There's not much room for vehicles so we all need to go in one. I'm picking up a new car this evening, but I've no idea what it is or how big it is until I see it, so it would be better if one of you four drives. Then whoever takes us in needs to park the car up somewhere well away and come back on foot, taking care not to be seen or to run into our suspect.

'I'm hoping the operation won't take long. Theoretically, Danny will arrive at ten o'clock. Once his van is down the lane, an unmarked van, which will have brought in firearms and other officers, will be used to block his exit route if he does get wind of an ambush.

'As soon as he gets out of his van, Mike, you and I, with a couple of Uniform officers, will approach him and attempt to arrest him. We will be covered at all times by Firearms officers, but the hope is we'll be able to bring him in. We'll have Tasers ready if he produces the knife, and Firearms are on stand-by just in case he has a gun on him.

'Rob, Sally will probably tell you, but we're hoping to let the RSPCA go in as soon as we have cleared and secured the site, with Uniform officers. The Super was quite keen that the place was wound up as soon as possible, having seen it for herself.

'So with any luck, we could have Danny in custody by midday tomorrow, and that filthy flea-pit of a dog place could be closed down and all the animals removed to somewhere a lot nicer for them by close of play. Keep your fingers crossed.'

Jezza followed him into his office after he'd finished briefing the team.

'Boss, I wanted to ask if it was all right if I go a bit early tonight? Only I've got an appointment. With that Carol you suggested.'

'I'm delighted to hear it and of course you can leave early,' Ted told her, inviting her to take a seat. 'She really is very good. Easy to talk to. Well, I have to admit, I spent the first few sessions staring at the carpet and not saying much, but that's just me. I'm rubbish at talking about feelings. It's a very nice carpet though,' he said with a grin. 'Tea?'

Although it was not all that long since his coffee and cakes, Ted could always find room for a mug of tea, and he wanted to hear how Jezza was getting on with her investigations.

'I'd like to call in and see Maurice on the way, too, if that's all right, boss?'

'That's fine,' Ted said, brewing up. 'Give him my best wishes, but no soppy kisses, all right? Tell him I'll try to get in later this evening but it will depend on whether or not I manage to get a new car which actually goes, and is ready for me to collect. If it's good news on the Danny front tomorrow, I'll definitely go in to see him, to tell him myself.'

Ted phoned his garage later on, to save himself a wasted trip if the car wasn't ready for him.

'I've found you a nice little Scenic hatch, Inspector. Mileage isn't too high and it's in good clean condition for the age. A couple of quid change out of two grand, which was the best I could do for you. It's got central locking, too – perhaps remember to use it, this time,' the man laughed. 'She'll be all cleaned up and ready for you if you want to call round between half five and six.'

Ted knew it was going to take a long time before he was allowed to forget how he'd been robbed of a car he'd only had for a few days.

It was dark, cold and raining as Ted set out to collect his new car. It wasn't all that far to walk, so he pulled up the collar of his trench coat, put his head down, and marched briskly on his way.

There weren't many pedestrians about. The wet weather was keeping most of them in, apart from a few bedraggled souls waiting patiently at the bus stops he passed.

As he trudged along down the hill towards the town centre, through the rain, he saw a man walking towards him, carrying a bag of shopping. The two of them did the customary side-stepping dance of two people trying to avoid bumping into one another.

They both made to nod in acknowledgement to each other. Just at that moment, recognition hit both of them at the same time. At the exact moment that the knife appeared in Danny's hand.

Chapter Thirty-one

For a brief instant, neither man moved. Each was assessing the other, instincts taking over, as a highly trained killer weighed up a potential adversary. Ted knew he urgently needed back-up but had no means of summoning any. The slightest movement on his part towards his phone would certainly provoke an instant and deadly attack.

He carefully and deliberately lowered his gaze towards Danny's chest area, avoiding eye contact. There was just a slight chance that Danny would take the opportunity to make a break for it. If he didn't, Ted averting his eyes meant he would not betray any sign that he was about to go on the offensive.

Danny had already seen, on their previous encounter, that Ted was fit and ready to wade in, but he had no way of knowing his capabilities. Ted had four martial arts to call on. He was fervently hoping his Krav Maga knife defence training would be up to handling a killer of such capabilities. Even then, he was not sure how it would go. His precision was excellent, but Danny was utterly ruthless.

Ted was using his peripheral vision to scan for anyone nearby. He desperately needed to call for help if anyone was in earshot. He also wanted to ensure that no passers-by were endangered, if it was within his power. He especially wanted to make certain that anyone who might be walking past was not grabbed as a hostage by a man who would certainly have no hesitation in killing them, if he had to.

A lot of opponents made the mistake of dismissing Ted as a

threat because of his small stature. He was incredibly quick and a technical master of his chosen arts. He knew several disarming techniques but also understood the risks in attempting to disarm a trained attacker. Disarming was always a last resort tactic, but Ted feared he would have no choice. He was also restrained by the knowledge that, as a police officer, he was only allowed to use proportionate force to detain even an armed criminal. He suspected that limit might be stretched in his frantic attempts to get the knife away from a combat-trained soldier.

Even with his eyes slightly averted, he read Danny's body language and leapt into action a split second before his opponent sprang towards him with the knife. Ted tried a jolting strike to Danny's knife hand, followed by a lightning-fast kick to his groin. Both moves were avoided so effortlessly that Ted knew he had to quickly reassess his opponent's skills.

The words of Ted's Krav Maga instructor were ringing in his head as he looked for his next move.

'Control the weapon that is trying to kill you by grabbing the hand with the weapon in it. You may well get cut by the knife, but that's better than getting a stab wound to your body.'

He switched all his focus to Danny's knife hand and went for that. Somehow he had to get the lethal blade away from him and out of harm's way, before he could do anything else.

'Be a fighter, and keep fighting until you finish the problem,' the voice in his head echoed.

He had a grip on Danny's wrist now with his left hand and he threw all his strength and impetus against him to knock him back against the wall of the building behind them. His shorter height gave him an advantage. It put his shoulder in a good position to shove it against Danny's solar plexus, slightly winding him. Then he brought his head up, hard, under his chin, knocking his head back against the wall, while he desperately tried to get a second hand to the knife grip.

Danny grunted slightly, but his hold on the knife barely

slackened. With all the strength he could summon, Ted slammed the knife-hand against the wall with his left hand, several times in rapid succession. At the same moment, his right hand came up to try to land hammerfists that he hoped might just stop Danny in his tracks, giving him the leeway to control the knife hand with both of his.

Just then, Ted heard running footsteps behind him and a voice shouting, 'Stop that, now, or I'm calling the police!'

Ted felt relief wash over him. At last, someone to call back-up. If he could just hang on to Danny a bit longer and keep the knife from doing any damage, he might yet get a successful arrest out of this.

'Call them. I am the police,' he panted gratefully.

'This is bloody police brutality, then. I'm filming this, mate!'

To his dismay, Ted realised that in the darkness, with the black-bladed knife, whoever the man was behind them, all he could see was a man who had identified himself as a policeman attempting to punch and kick another man.

'Move back and call 999 now,' Ted bellowed. 'This man is armed and dangerous.'

With his attention momentarily distracted, his grip slackened just enough to allow Danny more freedom of movement. He pulled his knife hand down at speed. Ted felt the blade slice through his skin, his flesh, then felt blood spurting as it bit into an artery.

Now Ted was in serious trouble and he knew it. Two-handed, he was just about a match for Danny. With one hand out of action and bleeding badly, he was struggling hard to keep the knife from doing any further damage. His normal course of action would have been to try to get the knife away from his attacker, let him go and call for back-up to pursue him. But the last thing Ted wanted to do was to let someone as dangerous as Danny get away, whatever the cost to himself.

At least the sight of all the spurting blood seemed to have

galvanised the unknown man into action. Ted heard him exclaim, 'Oh, bloody hell,' then he was shouting into his phone, 'Police! Quick! And an ambulance. There's a man with a knife, and a policeman who's badly hurt,' then he gabbled out the location.

Ted now found he couldn't use his left hand at all. He could neither make a fist nor grip with it. He was surprised at how little it hurt, then realised it probably meant that the nerves were damaged. All he could do now with that side was to use his left forearm to block attacks, and yet another slashing manoeuvre was already heading his way. He tried to bring a foot up to launch a kick and again felt the sting of the blade as Danny moved forward and it swiped his thigh.

Bleeding as he was, Ted felt his strength leaving him at an alarming rate, but he used what force remained in his left arm to sweep Danny's knife hand as far away from himself as he could. It left him a brief opening which he was quick to exploit. His right foot shot up yet again, as fast and as hard as he could manage. It caught Danny in a brief off-guard moment, right in the groin.

Ted had the satisfaction of hearing the breath rush out of his attacker as he staggered back a few paces, towards the wall. Ted was just moving in when he heard a car squeal to a halt behind him and the doors open.

He couldn't remember when he had last been as relieved as he was to hear a familiar voice shout, 'Taser officer! Drop the weapon. Now.'

Ted's knees were buckling under him. He knew he needed to move to give PC Susan Heap a clear shot with the Taser. At the same time he was certain that the minute he backed off, Danny was going to use the last of the fight left in him to come forward on the offensive for one last desperate attempt.

'Drop the weapon, now,' Susan repeated, then, 'Taser, taser, taser! Sir, move it. Please.'

Now that Ted was up close and staring Danny in the eyes,

he could see that the victims had been right. His eyes were cold and calculating. He was dead behind them. He was not afraid of being hurt. He clearly didn't care if he lived or died. The most dangerous opponent of all.

'Taser! Sir, move. Now!'

Timing was now critical. Ted needed to distance himself, and fast, to give Susan the clear shot she needed. But he knew that the moment he dropped his blocking arm, Danny was going to have one last attempt at him with the deadly knife. If either he or Susan got their timing wrong, he could be staring death in the face. Ted needed to put all his trust in the officer behind him.

He made a feint to the left then, as Danny lashed out viciously to that side with the wicked stiletto blade, Ted flung himself to the right in a judo fall, then rolled to his feet. He was just in time to see the Taser barbs hit Danny squarely and knock him off his feet.

Ted whirled and went for the knife, kicking it back against the wall, well out of reach of Danny, should he somehow recover from the jolt of electricity fast enough to try to grab it.

At the same moment, PC Jack Hargreaves sprang forward to get the handcuffs on the fallen man.

Another patrol car slid to a halt behind the first one and two more officers joined the scene, another identifying himself as a Taser officer and giving a warning.

'Watch him, he's highly dangerous,' Ted panted, then, to Danny, 'Daniel Quigley, I'm arresting you for the murder of Maureen O'Hara, the attempted murder of Maurice Brown and the rapes of Kathy Finn, Helen Lawrence, Jayne Wright and Jessica Vine. You do not have to say anything. But, it may harm your defence if you do not mention when questioned something which you later rely on in court. Anything you do say may be given in evidence.'

He turned to Susan Heap. '

That'll do for now. Make sure he's seen by a doctor as soon

as possible. I'll sort out the rest when I get into the station. I'll need a lift, though.'

The two officers from the second car were already helping Danny to his feet and leading him, handcuffed, to their car.

'Oh, no sir, no way,' Susan said firmly. 'There's an ambulance on its way for you. The only place you're going is hospital. Jack, grab me the first aid kit, please, the Inspector is bleeding all over everywhere. Sir, I think you better come and sit in the car before you fall down.'

When Ted hesitated, looking mutinous, she continued, 'Sir, I'll arrest you for obstruction if I have to. I've seen at first-hand what your Trevor's like when he gets mad and I don't want him angry with me because I didn't look after you properly. You must know yourself that you have an arterial bleed which needs urgent medical attention. You're lucky we got here so quickly. We were only on Petersgate when the call came through.'

As if noticing the extent of his injury for the first time, Ted looked at his hand, his expression almost puzzled. Reluctantly, he allowed himself to be led over to the car, where he perched on the back seat, his feet out of the open rear door. Susan quickly pulled on gloves and set to work with the first aid kit, getting pressure onto the spurting artery, raising Ted's hand up high to help staunch the bleeding.

'I'm supposed to be picking up a new car. I need to phone the garage.'

'Jack can do that for you, sir, if you tell him which one. I need you to stay still for me now, so I can get this bleeding under control. You're losing a lot of blood. Your leg's bleeding too, but it doesn't look as serious.'

Ted looked ruefully at the ruined leg of his trousers, now flapping open and soaked in blood.

'Trev's going to kill me when he sees the state of my work suit,' was the first thing he thought of.

A man appeared next to the car. In his thirties, smartly dressed, not at all as Ted had pictured him from his voice, and his attitude. He was looking mortified.

'I'm so sorry, mate. I honestly thought you were beating up some innocent bloke. I suppose it was me interfering that made you lose concentration and get injured. I'm really sorry. But I did film some of the attack, if you need it for any reason?'

'It's fine, really, don't worry,' Ted assured him. 'I had my own job to do, I should have focused on that ...'

Suddenly Ted felt himself incredibly light-headed and had a horrible feeling he may be about to pass out. Swiftly, Susan intervened.

'If you can just go and give your details to my colleague, sir, and perhaps show him the footage you took,' then, to Ted, 'Come on, sir, stay with me, the ambulance is just on its way. I can see the lights now. Look, just lie back on the seat, let me get your legs up. That'll help. Hang on in there.'

Ted was beyond resisting. The world was spinning around him and he felt as if he was being sucked into a vortex. He wasn't sure if he had lost consciousness for a moment, but the next thing he was aware of was a man in green bending over him.

'Hello again, Ted. Remember me? Phil? Me and my mate picked up your Maurice the other day. We're just going to slide you out onto a trolley and get you into the ambulance, so we can take a proper look at you.'

Susan Heap stayed next to his side until he got to the ambulance. Ted was feeling decidedly woozy by now but still anxious to keep charge of his case.

'I need to talk to Mike Hallam, bring him up to speed.'

'Jack and me can do that, sir. I'll do it straight away. You need to get yourself seen to. You've lost a lot of blood. I'll get one of your team to contact your Trevor, too, get them to tell him to go straight to the hospital.'

'Please tell them not to worry him. Tell him it's nothing, just a scratch. I'm going to be fine.'

As the paramedics closed the doors behind them, once Ted

was safely loaded, Susan turned away, muttering to herself, 'If that's fine, I'd hate to see you when you've been seriously hurt.'

Ted wasn't aware of much on the short journey to the hospital, which was made with lights and sirens going. He was starting to get confused, feeling agitated, convinced there was something he should be doing. The paramedic travelling with him in the back kept patiently trying to reassure him and above all, to get him to keep still.

'I need to talk to my team. I need to find out what happened about Danny,' Ted kept insisting.

'No, Ted, you just need to keep still for me until we can get you seen to. We'll be there in a tick, then you can get someone to make a phone call for you.'

The ambulance pulled up outside the A&E department and the two paramedics unloaded Ted's trolley to wheel him inside. A nurse came to meet them and, even in his confused state, Ted knew her face was familiar.

'Brought you an old friend, Fiona. This is Ted Darling, forty-one. Knife wound to the left hand and wrist, with significant arterial bleeding and some loss of sensation. GCS was 15 at the scene but it's been dipping a bit to 13 on the way. He's been getting a bit confused and agitated. There's also a slash wound to his right thigh which appears not to be as serious, so we've concentrated on trying to stop the bleeding from the hand and just put a dressing on the leg.'

'Hello, again, Ted. Straight into cubicle five, please.'

'Ted? This is Fiona. You may remember her? We all met up on the car park the other day. We'll leave you with her now. You're in safe hands. You take care of yourself, and try not to worry. Just relax and let them take care of you.'

'I need to phone my team to find out what happened,' Ted told the nurse insistently, trying to sit up. 'And I'm supposed to be picking up my new car.'

'Can you keep still for me, Ted, please? I'm just going to get someone to take a look at you, but for the moment you just need to keep calm and not move about. Is there someone I can call for you?'

'I think the officers attending were seeing to that. I'm not sure.' Ted was looking and sounding confused again. He was finding it hard to concentrate.

'Well, try not to worry about anything. Was it the same man as before?'

Before Ted could reply, the cubicle curtains parted and a doctor came in. The nurse made the introductions, though Ted was getting beyond taking in much of anything, then she briefly outlined the details. The doctor's examination was swift but thorough.

'We're going to need to take you into surgery as soon as possible, Mr Darling, to get control of this bleeding. There's also some nerve and tendon damage, which is going to need repair. We can hopefully sort everything out at the same time. Try not to worry, it's all relatively straightforward,' he said, then left the cubicle.

Fiona could see from Ted's face that he was worried. He looked anxious, confused and rather vulnerable.

She patted him gently on his good arm and repeated, 'Really, try not to worry. We'll take good care of you.'

The curtains opened again and Trev strode in, dressed in his motorcycle leathers, filling the small space with his presence, as he always did.

'Hey, you,' he said softly as he moved straight to the bedside, with just a brief but courteous greeting to the nurse. Even in times of crisis, Trev's impeccable manners seldom deserted him.

'It's going to be fine. I'm here now.'

Watching the two exchange a hug of great tenderness, Fiona thought to herself, 'It really is true what they say. Why are all the nice ones always either married or gay?'

Chapter Thirty-two

Ted opened his eyes and blinked a few times, trying to focus and to work out where he was. Trev saw that he was stirring awake and moved closer to the bed, bending to kiss him lightly on the forehead.

'Hello, sleepy, are you fully back with us this time? You tried to wake up about half an hour ago but you weren't making much sense. I'll let someone know you're properly awake now.'

He leaned over to press the call button at the same moment that Ted struggled to sit up and said, 'I need to go and interview Danny.'

'No chance,' Trev laughed. 'In case you haven't noticed yet, they've got your arm strung up to the ceiling. It's to stop post-op swelling, they told me. They had you on the table quite a while, stitching you all back together. You're as good as new now, but you're going to have some impressive scars.'

Ted's eyes were taking in more now and he saw that Trev was right. His heavily bandaged left hand was suspended in some sort of sling. There was a drip on a stand running into a cannula in his right hand. He could go nowhere, trussed up as he was, even though he desperately wanted to.

There was a light tap on the door and a nurse came in.

'Hello, Mr Darling, how are you feeling now?' she asked, moving over to him to make her checks.

Ted still wasn't sure how he was feeling but, after consideration, he said, 'Very thirsty.'

'You can have a few sips of water, but don't go mad. It

might make you feel a bit sick but that's perfectly normal, it's just the anaesthetic. Do you know where you are now?'

She helped him to take a few mouthfuls from a beaker of water. His mouth and throat felt like sandpaper and the liquid was an enormous relief.

'Stepping Hill, I imagine? But when can I go home?'

She laughed at his optimism.

'Not just yet, I'm afraid. You've only just woken up after a fairly major operation. You're in a recovery room at the moment. We'll leave you here tonight so you can hopefully get a good night's sleep, then we'll be moving you onto the ward in the morning.

'You've had some pain relief, which will also be making you feel a bit groggy, but don't be afraid to ask if you need more. Don't be a martyr. I'll leave you for now.'

She looked at Trevor and added, 'I would suggest you just stay another ten minutes, then leave him to rest. You can give him another small drink before you leave, but not too much.'

'What time is it?' Ted asked as she left, leaning back on his pillow and feeling utterly exhausted.

'Past midnight. They had to do quite a bit of embroidery on your nerves, so it took a while. But hey, you got the bad guy.'

'I need to talk to Mike Hallam,' Ted insisted.

'And you will,' Trev assured him. 'Just not now. He and Jezza were in earlier but I sent them away. No sense all of us sitting around waiting for you to wake up. I've been texting them updates. Jezza sends her love.

'Right, now I know you're safely back in the land of the living, I'm going to go home and leave you to get some sleep. I'll come back as soon as I can tomorrow, but I have to go into work first. My brilliant idea of taking on extra work didn't allow for you doing something like this. I'll bring in whatever you might need when I come back.'

'I'll be home tomorrow, I'm sure. Just bring me some

clothes to go home in. My work suit may be a bit of a write-off. Oh, and can you make sure the garage knows to hang on to the car for me? I'm going to need that for going back to work.'

Trev shook his head in mock despair.

'Are your handcuffs in your coat pocket? If so I'm going to attach you to this bed so you have to stay there until the doctor says you're fit for discharge.'

Ted slept more deeply and for longer than he expected to. He barely stirred as he and his bed were wheeled out of the recovery room and parked at one end of a ward early the next morning. He did wake up for a cup of tea at some point, although it was not his preferred green tea. At least it was liquid.

His doctor came round during the morning to check on him and assess his progress, but it was not the news Ted was wanting to hear.

'We need to keep you in for at least a couple of days yet, Mr Darling. I need to be sure that any swelling is under control, and that there is no risk of infection. I'm afraid you'll just have to bear with us for now.'

Ted must have dozed off again because he awoke with a start at the sound of a familiar voice saying, 'Now then, boss, what have you been up to?'

He looked up to see Maurice Brown, sitting in a wheelchair, smiling at him. The chair was being pushed by another familiar face, a man who greeted him with, 'Hello, Mr Darling. How are you feeling now?'

'Hello, Oliver,' he greeted the hospital porter he had met through an earlier case. 'I'm all right, thanks. Thank you for bringing Maurice to see me.'

'You're welcome, Mr Darling. You've always been very kind to me. Right, Maurice, I'll go on my break now. I'll be back in fifteen minutes,' Oliver Burdon told them and went happily on his way.

'Jezza told me what happened,' Maurice explained. 'I'm

only down the far end of the ward but I can't get about very well by myself yet. I bribed Oliver with the price of a coffee and a cake to wheel me up here.'

'Let me guess. A white chocolate chip cookie?' Ted asked, remembering the man's preference for white chocolate. 'Can you get hold of Mike Hallam to come in and see me, Maurice? I'll go crazy if I don't know what's happening with the case and I don't know where my mobile is to call him myself.'

'You need to take it easy, boss,' Maurice cautioned him. 'A big operation knocks the stuffing out of you more than you realise. I'm still as weak as a kitten, but they say I can probably go home in a couple of days. At least I've got young Steve to fetch and carry for me.

'I'll text the sarge for you if you like, but Danny's in custody, where he can't do any more harm. You'd be better off just resting a bit, get yourself fit again.'

'Mike will need to get my statement, though. Wounding me is another charge we can stick on Danny, to make sure he gets as long as possible behind bars.'

'Boss. Ted. Look, you've done your bit. Now just let Sarge and the team take over. I'm no medical expert, but you don't look to me like someone who's about ready to leap back into action and lead a case,' Maurice told him patiently.

He must have kept his promise though, as Mike Hallam appeared just after lunch for afternoon visiting time.

'I'm under strict instructions not to stay too long and not, under any circumstances, to tire you out, boss,' Mike told him as he sat down.

'From the nursing staff?' Ted asked.

Mike laughed.

'No, from Maurice and from Trev, which is much scarier. How are you doing?'

'I'm fine, really,' Ted said dismissively. 'I just want to know how the case is going, and give you a statement. What's Danny saying?'

'Not denying anything. The duty solicitor is trying to persuade him to stay quiet but like you said, it's as if he just wants it all to be over. We'll put him up in front of the bench tomorrow when we've finished questioning him, and get a remand in custody. I can't see his defence even wasting time trying to oppose bail.

'We've got plenty to hold him on for now, boss, so why don't I wait until you're out to get your statement? You look tired out. Have a rest, while you can. Everyone sends their best wishes. Jezza sends her love and even the Ice Queen asked me to pass on her regards.'

Ted realised just how weak and tired he was when he didn't even bother to pull his sergeant up on calling their senior officer by her nickname, which he would normally have done.

'What's happening with the dog place?' he asked, anxious to hear more positive results.

'That's all sorted too, boss,' Mike reassured him. 'Almost all the dogs have been seized and taken to a nicer place. They did let her keep a couple, including some ancient farting thing, according to Rob's fiancé, but the RSPCA will be monitoring her closely in future.'

Ted spent an intensely frustrating two days and two more nights in hospital before he was told he could go home. Only visits from Trev, his mother, his team members and other friends stopped him from climbing the walls. He was totally unused to periods of inactivity, or to the feelings of complete helplessness which being strung up like a turkey brought him.

He spent a lot of time dozing, interspersed by welcome, but brief, visits. On one occasion he opened his eyes to the growling voice of his great friend DCI Jim Baker saying, 'Bloody typical, Ted. If you didn't want to come to my engagement party, you only had to say so. No need for all of this.'

Professor Bizzie Nelson also came up from her post-mortem suite in the bowels of the hospital, to sit and chat with him for twenty minutes or so.

'Apart from the hand, Edwin, how are you doing? The genuine version, please, not the sort of flannel you may reserve for young Trevor or your team. How are you doing emotionally?'

'We should have got him earlier, Bizzie,' Ted told her. 'Certainly before he went on to attack Jezza, and Maurice.'

'Only you can know what more you could have done. Try to stay detached, look at how you handled the affair then ask yourself honestly – was there anything else you could have done, with the information at your disposal.'

'I should have done something more, Bizzie,' he said stubbornly. 'I don't know what, but I should have.'

Trev had arranged to go and pick up Ted's new car for him so that, when he was told he could go home, Trev could come in during his lunch-hour to pick him up and take him back.

'I can't stay, unfortunately, and Annie's working this afternoon, too, so I need to be able to trust you, without a babysitter,' he told him sternly. 'No going out anywhere, no doing anything. Just rest and relax a bit. I know you're going to phone Mike the minute I'm out of the door, but just keep it brief, all right?'

Ted kissed him and said, 'Thanks for caring. But you know I can't just sit here twiddling my thumbs all the time. Especially as I only have one working thumb to twiddle, at the moment.'

'I mean it, Ted. Seriously. Give yourself some time to heal. I'll be back as soon as I can. Oh, and Shewee sends her love. I managed to convince her she couldn't use you as an excuse for skiving off school and racing up here.'

He probably hadn't even reached the top of the short cul-de-sac they lived in before Ted was on the phone, asking for an update.

'Boss, it's fine, we're on top of it. Danny's in custody, we're all over the paperwork. Everything is under control. Just put your feet up for a bit, while you have the chance.'

He rang off, leaving Ted feeling redundant and unsure what to do with himself. He was just about to switch on daytime television, in desperation, when the doorbell rang. This time he wouldn't even have minded if it had been Jehovah's Witnesses, he was so much in need of some sort of distraction.

Instead, he found the Ice Queen on his doorstep, brandishing a paper bag from a cake shop.

'I come bearing sticky buns,' she told him with a smile, so unlike her formal work demeanour. 'I thought you might be in need of sustenance after a couple of days of hospital food. Shall I make tea to go with them? Just point me to where everything is.'

Ted smiled back as he indicated the way through to the kitchen.

'I think I can manage to make tea, even with one hand out of action. Do you mind sitting in the kitchen? I have to warn you, you will be assaulted by cats with absolutely no manners.'

She sat down at the table and asked, 'Is that some sort of initiation test? If your cats approve, I can't be quite as glacial as my nickname would suggest?'

True to his warning, six felines suddenly appeared, interested in checking out the new arrival. Senior cat, Queen, jumped straight on to the table to sniff at the visitor, then sat down and began to wash herself.

'You passed the test,' Ted told her, awkwardly picking the cat up with his one functioning arm and putting her back on the floor, then switching the kettle on.

'How are you feeling now? I imagine it's painful, but I understand the prognosis is good?'

'I might have some slight reduction in use, according to the surgeon, and some scarring, but it should be just about as good as new. I have to exercise it, to help the healing. I'm signed off for the week, but I should be back in next Monday. Green tea all right?'

She nodded, then said, 'There will have to be an enquiry into what happened, of course. I expect you realise that. It's just a formality, but as ever, we need to look at what lessons can be learned, how procedure may need to be overhauled.'

'Procedure?' Ted echoed bitterly, putting her mug of tea in front of her slightly more forcefully than he meant so that some of it slopped onto the table and he had to mop it up.

'I walked straight into an armed and dangerous man who then came at me with a knife. What was I supposed to do? Reason with him? Run away?'

'Ted, as I've told you, repeatedly. I'm not your enemy. I don't make the rules, I just try to apply them as fairly as I can. As I said, it's just a formality. There is no question of apportioning blame. It's just about trying to apply best practice, to see what lessons can be learned. Cake?'

Ted shook his head as he sat down opposite her. Eating was the last thing he felt like doing.

'You know what? Forget me coming back on Monday. The team are managing fine without me. They don't need me. I think I'd like to ask for a couple of weeks leave, starting from when my medical certificate runs out. I feel I need to get away for a bit. Do some serious thinking.'

'I see.' She took a sip of her tea. 'Ted, you are an excellent officer, one I hold in the highest regard. The reason your team is managing so well is that you have trained and led them to become an outstanding unit.

'Young DC Vine came to see me, with a dossier she has been working on about Heather Cooper. I was most impressed with her work. You helped that young officer achieve her potential where many others before you had failed. There is an investigation ongoing, by other officers within the division, into the activities of Ms Cooper and I have passed the file on to them.

'You have the potential to go further in your own career,

should you chose to do so, and it would be with my full backing. I am happy to agree to your extended leave, but I fervently hope that the thinking you intend to do does not involve considering a career change. There will always be a place for you in any team for which I am responsible. I hope you will remember that.'

After she'd left, Ted made another phone call. Then, to the best of his ability with his limitations, he put a meal together ready for when Trev got home. The Ice Queen had left both the sticky buns behind, as their conversation seemed to have robbed her of her appetite, too. They would make a dessert for them without Ted having to do anything.

Ted was waiting in the hallway when he heard Trev's motorbike arrive, and opened the door for him, greeting him with a hug and a kiss.

'How was work?' he asked. 'I made us a bit of supper. It's not much, but the Ice Queen called and left sticky buns for afters.'

Trev looked at him shrewdly.

'That's nice. But what is it you really want to tell me?' he asked, as they went through to the kitchen and sat down.

'Would you mind if I went away for a bit? Just a week or two? Instead of going straight back to work? I just need a bit of a break, time to get my head together. I phoned Jack Gregson. You know he's been on at me to visit him, ever since he left.'

Jack Gregson had been Ted's sergeant before Mike Hallam. He had to leave the force after a totally unexpected diagnosis of Parkinson's disease. His marriage had not survived the strains of his job, and he had now gone to stay in Wales with one of his daughters, who lived alone.

'I'll have to go on the train, of course. I won't be up to driving by then. I promise to text you every day, but I can't guarantee we can always talk. The reception there is dodgy sometimes. I'll miss you. I just need some time to clear my head.'

'I'll miss you too, of course. But if this is something you need to do, then it's fine with me.' He was studying Ted intently, his vivid blue eyes troubled. 'Ted, you are coming back, aren't you?'

'I will always come back. To you.'

The End

Lightning Source UK Ltd.
Milton Keynes UK
UKHW041824061019
351114UK00001B/160/P

9 782901 773054